CONTRACTOR

Contracting Sometimes Requires Special Training & Technology

Stan Bain

ISBN: 979-8-8693-5588-1

They were beautiful this time in the morning, but Jim was lost in thought. He sat on his dock. Jim and Jane built their retirement home on a bluff overlooking the lake outside Helena, Montana. The path, lined with various plants, led to the dock. Jim still to the office several times a month to keep his thumb in the business. Jill proved to be a great manager, and the Company was doing well.

Jim got up to walk back to the house. Another cup of coffee was needed when Jane walked out on the deck.

"Hi, hon. Are you here in deep thought? Worrying about something?"

"Oh, I'm just enjoying the view," Jim said. "I was thinking about how lucky we are. We have a nice house in a great place, and the business is going great, so what is there to worry about?" They held hands and walked towards the house when Sally and Bill walked out onto the deck. "Well, we're all packed and ready to head back to school," Sally said. Both of Jane's kids were in college.

"Okay, you drive carefully, and let us know when you get there. You know there are crazy drivers on the road," Jane said.

"We will, mom. We will see you next month ok, Dad." The kids waved and headed out.

Jim thought it was nice to be called dad. The kids had accepted him some time ago and treated him as their real dad. They had developed a great relationship.

Jane handed him another coffee as they walked out on the deck. Jim sat down in a lounge chair, looking at the lake. The sun was up and was reflecting off the lake. He sat back, enjoying his coffee and the view.

Jane walked over to approach him and said, "Here is the morning paper."

Jim enjoyed his morning paper. His only way of keeping up with the world's activities. He seldom watched TV. There was too much negative stuff in his view. Jim, reading through the paper, turned the page. He noticed an article regarding the rescue of high-ranking government officials in South America.

'A highly trained special unit made the recovery,' so the paper said. The team is unknown but was employed by the government for the mission. The mission lasted several days in a dense jungle. According to the article, the terrorist group holding government officials was eliminated. The team of five had parachuted at night. The leader of the team was only known by the name of Scorpio. The government officials are now home and safe.

"Anything interesting in the paper this morning?" Jane inquired.

"Pretty much the same stuff." Jim didn't want Jane to know he was following the team via the paper. The team has been active, Jim thought. About once or more a month, there had been a blurb in the paper about a rescue or assassination. But this was the first time a name was in an article. He thought about maybe stopping by the base someday.

The phone rang, and Jim picked it up. "Hello."

"Hey buddy, you having a bad day?"

"No, who is this?"

"This is John; you remember... I saved your ass in Afghanistan.

"Oh, sorry, buddy, what's going on?"

"Well, you didn't make the trip last time, you know, the hike? Well, this year, the guys are going to Mexico. We plan to check out the Mayan Ruins for a week and do a hike. How about it? Can you squeeze time in for your buddies, or are you going on another bullshit mission?"

Yeah, Jim gave out a chuckle. "No, I mean, yeah, that may be fun. And no, I'm not signing up for any missions." He sipped the remainder of his muddy Turkish in one big gulp. "It'll be great to see you guys. I'll talk to my wife about it."

"Wife? Jim, you fall on your head? What is this wife stuff?"

"I know… I know John, but she is the best thing that has happened to me. So, tell me about this hike!"

"It is a couple of weeks off. We fly into Mexico City, we have a ride to a trailhead, and we spend a week hiking and investigating two Mayan Ruins. I have made arrangements for the gear and supplies we need. So, you only have to bring your ass. So, check with the boss. We hope your love will let you come along. It would be great to reminisce about our time in Afghanistan."

"Okay, John, I will get back to you later today So why did you guys choose this destination?" He looked at the door that Jane had just walked through. "Hold on a second." Jim went inside and poured himself some more supply soluble. "Yeah, hi..."

"Are you with someone?" John was curious.

"No, it's just me and Jane. Why?"

"Never mind, you asked me why did we choose the ruins."

With the sip of coffee altering the phonemes, Jim responded, "Ye… wha abo ith?" He cleared his throat once the coffee had slid down his pharynx, "Mea culpa." Jim apologized and continued: "Why did…?"

"Got you the first time. Well, we thought the ruins would be impressive, and the trail we chose would take us to four different ruins. There are a couple of good campsites along the way and a couple of lakes. We plan on fishing for a day or two. We have a guide for most of the trip.”

“Sounds fun, John. I’ll get back to you soon.”

Jane walked in just as Jim was finishing his conversation with John. “The team going to Mexico?”

“No, that was John. One of the guys I spent another lifetime with while in Afghanistan. They're going on another hike to visit ruins in Mexico. It will be about a week-long hike.”

“You going? I think it would be good for you to spend some guy time with your buddies.”

“I don’t know. I just haven’t had the energy lately, but maybe this is what I need to return to the groove. It is only for a week. I guess it would be good,” Jim said, as his mind still processed ‘the recovery of hostages and the name in print: Scorpio.

Several Days Later…

Jim had been doing yard work installing a sprinkler system. Jane walked up. “Looking good. You are all packed for your trip tomorrow. If you get a chance, you could bring back a bottle of vanilla. I love their stuff.”

“Sure, I could do that. Yeah, I think I’m ready to go. My plane leaves at 7:00 a.m. I don’t know the whole plan yet other than the three ruins I told you about. John said there are a couple of places to go fishing."

The following morning, Jane took Jim to the airport. On the way there she gave him a present.

"Oh, what's this?" He opened the box, "a compass."

"Yeah, you said the compass you had would stick sometimes, and I didn't want you to get lost."

"I won't get lost. This is a nice compass, thank you."

Jane pulled up to the Delta departure door. "Have a safe trip and enjoy yourself. I love you, take care." They kissed goodbye.

Scorpio was in his usual position, feet up on the desk with a Cuban stogie. The Ireland mission went off without a hitch, and he was in contact with Sergeant Ryan of the Ireland police. Ryan had invited the team back just for a visit. Ryan wanted to know more about their training and how they planned their missions. There was a short skydive mission into Brazil, which Barber, Zula, and Cosmo handled with only being gone a couple of days. Overall, he felt the team was in good shape, and the new gear arrived to replace some of their old stuff.

Jasper walked in, "It looks like you are enjoying that. Something I couldn't do was smoke. I was not too fond of the taste or the smell. But those Cuban things don't smell that bad."

"No, I don't smoke anything but these," taking a big draw and letting the smoke out slowly. "Sometimes I chew on it and not smoke it, just a bad habit."

"So, what's up? Got the gear all cleaned up and the new gear ship-shape?"

"Yeah, Cosmo is healing okay from the bad landing," Jasper said. "What about the proposed mission? Don't we have enough information? Someone on our team has to infiltrate this group from what it looks like. We already dealt with them because of the CIA. Go back to Brazil and get embedded into a group of 300 thugs. Doesn't it sound like something a smart guy would do? I sure don't, and nothing the Senator has provided has made it inviting."

"I know what you are saying. I think we all feel the same way. I was thinking about calling the Boss. He is a good planner and could look at this more objectively. But you are right. I don't feel comfortable about being around 300 thugs."

"I agree with you, Scorpio. I missed the Boss during our planning phases. He always had a different way of looking at things that made more sense. You think he is willing to come to the base for a few days and help us look at this mission?"

"I bet he would. Once the Senator gives us more data, maybe I'll give him a call. Also, how is Angelique doing on her prep for her interview next week on citizenship?" Scorpio questioned. "Also, I noticed Angelique isn't using the name Francisca anymore. What gives with that?"

"Well, from what I understand," Cosmo explains, "When the terrorists killed Angelique's family, Mama Bear changed her name to Francisca and hid her among the terrorists. She was safe as long as she didn't use the name Angelique. The terrorists didn't know the girl they were still looking for was under their noses."

"That was clever," Scorpio said. "Then why now use Angelique? Aren't the terrorists still looking for her?"

"Probably, but they still think she is hiding in South America among friends. She wanted to use her real name, Angelique, now that she will become an American citizen," Cosmo explained. "She is smart and knows more about our country and government than most congressmen. I know that's not saying much. But she is better informed and knowledgeable than most people. Yes, she is ready. Have you noticed that she and Joker seem to be close?"

"I have noticed that, Jasper. I'm okay with that. Angelique is young and beautiful, and Joker has never had a girlfriend that I know of."

"You know, I'm happy for both of them. Be nice if it works out for them. That would make history if we had a husband and wife on our team."

"Good to hear that she is ready for the interview. I will be going with her to Vegas for the citizenship interview. I hope we can celebrate when she becomes an American. We'll all go R&R to a nice place. I'm so glad she is with us. I love the tracking system she came up with. I talked with TJ yesterday about them getting that system. They have been after us for two years, so I'm arranging a meeting with Angelique, TJ, and probably with the CIA Director. I told them their payment would be favors when needed."

"Never know when we'll need that; probably if we get in the middle of 300 dirtbags," Jasper said, sipping a beer. "I wonder if the CIA is involved in the Senator's proposal?"

"Good question. I think that's something I'll ask the Senator next time. Also, do not change the subject. What is this about a hooker and a nun?"

"Oh, something we would bring up during our afternoon meeting, okay? The hooker goes by Madam Elizabeth, her professional name, but she likes to be called Lizzy. The nun is Sister Karen. They have teamed up. I'm not sure, but I think the CIA is involved somehow. But yeah, I think Joker has a lot of information on them. I have a feeling Joker is going to propose they be part of our team for a mission. I think because they can get in and out of the terrorist camp and have many contacts throughout South America."

"Okay, I need to make a few calls before our meeting. Ah, Joker and Bingo, get back from the hideout yet?"

"No, but I know they plan to return in time for our meeting this afternoon. Bingo had some information on getting updates on some of our equipment. We're short on parachutes. They weren't included in our last delivery, and we don't bring many of those back."

Bingo walked in, "The hideout is in good shape. So, anything exciting going on?"

"No, not yet," Scorpio answered. "Oh, where is Joker? Leave him at the hideout?"

"No, we ran into Angelique. She was on a walk. Joker decided to walk with her."

"Okay, the only thing we need to do is make a list of new gear we'd like to have. Maybe you two can take a shot at that."

Angelique stopped, "I sure love the desert."

"I know what you mean," Joker said. "Let's walk up to the overlook, just up the hill a short distance. You will get a great view."

It didn't take long, and they were sitting on a rock at the overlook. Angelique was taken by the view. "This is beautiful. What do you think, Joker?"

"One thing I like about my job is the travel. There are many beautiful things to see. Be nice to take a couple of months off and travel. I have a list of places I want to visit before I die. I want to spend some time visiting the islands in the Pacific. Do some diving."

"That would be fun." Angelique looked at Joker and then crawled into his arms. They kissed. "You know I love you, Joker."

"Yes, and I love you." He laid Angelique down next to him, looking into each other's eyes. Their lips met. Joker's hand slid under her blouse; she never wore a bra. He felt her breast.

"Joker," Angelique said in a soft voice while unbuttoning her blouse.

Joker's heart was pounding. He had never felt like this before; it was his first time with a woman.

"I love you. I have not felt this way about anyone before, Angelique. I never want to lose you and want you to be happy, always."

"Joker, I love you too. I feel the same way. I want my future to be part of yours."

Joker held Angelique, kissed her, and then her breast. They continued to make love.

Jane was getting worried. It had been almost two weeks since Jim called her, letting her know they were leaving in the morning for the hike and would call when he could. She called information and asked for the number of the U.S. Embassy in Mexico. She dialed the number.

"Hello, U.S. Embassy. How may I help?" A young person said.

"Yes, I need some information. My husband and friends flew to Mexico City about two weeks ago to hike the ruins." Jane gave the person the hike information.

"Just a moment." A couple of minutes, another person answered. "Ma'am, I'm with the Embassy investigation unit. The information I just received tells me your group was in an area where several drug lords are active. We sent out a bulletin restricting that area. However, that went out the day your group was in that area, so I suspect they didn't see the warning. When was the last time you heard from this group?"

"About two weeks ago, the day they started the hike. They had planned on only being gone a week."

"Sorry, ma'am, the only thing we can do is contact the Mexican government and see if they could check out the area for any information. Give it a few days, and I'll get back to you if we find anything."

"Okay, I guess I don't have any choice. Thank you, I will be looking forward to your call," Jane hung up. I wonder if the number to the base is in Jim's phone book. She went through his desk, finally found what she was looking for, and turned pages until she found the number Dragon Men LLC and the word base written next to it. She picked up Jim's phone and dialed the number. After a couple of rings, "Hello, Boss."

Jane thought for a second; this must be Scorpio. "Is this Scorpio?"

There was a pause, "Yes… Who is this?"

"This is Jane, Jim's wife… I mean, Boss."

"Oh, yes, sorry, I was surprised. What can I do for you?" Scorpio asked.

"Jim, I mean Boss and his buddies who he served with, went on a hike to see the ruins in Mexico. That was a couple of weeks ago. They had planned on being gone a week. I called the U.S. Embassy, but the only thing they could tell me was that there were drug lords in the area, and all they could do was ask the Mexican government to look into it. I thought of you. Boss talks about you and the team all the time."

"I'm glad you called. I'll get on it. Let me make a few calls and get back to you shortly. Oh, do you know which ruins they were going to hike to?"

"Sorry, the only thing I knew was there were three of them, and they talked about fishing near one. They were to have a guide for part of the trip," Jane said.

"Well, that does narrow the area down some. I will get back to you soon."

"Okay, thank you."

"Cosmo, call the team together. Need to talk." Within a few minutes, the team was in the meeting room. "Ok, guys, the Boss is in trouble. He and his marine buddies took a hike in this area," pointing to a map. "At least, I think this area, based on Jane's description. Boss and his buddies were visiting the ruins in the area. They have been gone for two weeks. They were only to be gone a week. According to the U.S. Embassy, several drug lords were working in the area. Cosmo, call Mama Bear and see if she has anyone in the area. The rest of you call any contacts we have; get some new satellite data and any ground information we can gather. Then let's get back together in a couple of hours."

Everyone went to their office to do what they did best … gather intel. They made calls and looked at new imagery, including classified data. A couple of hours later, the team started to gather in the conference room.

Scorpio asked, "Cosmo, what have you found out?"

"I talked to Mama Bear. Her contact in that area had contacted Mama several days ago about Americans being held captive by a drug lord. This contact was to provide more information later today."

"Hope that will be where they are."

"Yes, also, Jasper has excellent imagery of that area. We must wait on Mama Bear and see what information she will have," Cosmo said.

"Cosmo, Mama Bear is on line 2," Star said.

"Got it, thanks, Star, that was good timing," Cosmo said. "Hello, Mama Bear. Have good news?"

"I don't know if it is all good news, except if it is the Boss and his buddies. I don't know what the drug lord has planned for them. My contact who deals with this group will find out more and get back to me again, maybe in a few days. I do have the coordinates of their location." She read off the coordinates. "Maybe you can pull up high-resolution imagery. I'll get back to you when I have other information." Bear rang off.

Cosmo walked over to the computer, signed in, and put in an address that came up as a classified site asking for a code. Cosmo typed in his code. A few seconds later, it asked for a project password. Cosmo typed that into the system. It processed the information and asked for a user code, which he typed in. Shortly afterward, it asked for his thumbnail. Cosmo reached over to the scanner, put his hand on the scanner, and pushed the scan button. He knew he would go through several security levels because of the system's security. Several levels of security had to be satisfied. The network asked for the coordinates, which he typed in. In seconds high, resolution classified imagery came up on the screen. Cosmo enlarged the imagery. He then studied the image and couldn't believe the detail. He found the location of the coordinates.

There were two small huts or maybe cabins. Cosmo counted nine guys standing around. Humm. I wonder how many are in the huts. He ordered three more images at different times from the day the Boss may have been captured. It didn't take long for the thumbnails of the images to show up. He clicked on them to enlarge them to full size and then sent all the images to the printer. Twenty minutes later, he had all the images on the table. Cosmo started taking notes on what he was finding regarding each image. A couple of hours later, he sat back in the chair. Scorpio entered the room, followed by several team members.

"Find anything we can use?" Scorpio inquired.

"Yes, lots. Here is what I know for sure. The target site has two huts or small cabins, and they are about 175 feet square each. Comparing the images and looking at their hats, it appears we have eleven thugs. Look at the first image. This image must have been taken minutes after they captured the Boss and his buddies. Look here," Cosmo was pointing, "I count seven guys. Those seven are wearing different hats, like baseball hats. You notice they are standing in a group with eight others pointing weapons at them."

"These are amazing pictures," Star said.

"Yes," Scorpio said. "How did you come up with eleven thugs?"

"By comparing the images, knowing the time of day, and giving me the sun angle, I can compute the height of the individuals from their shadows."

"Really?" Scorpio questioned Cosmo.

"Yes, I taught photogrammetry in college for eight years."

"What is photogrammetry?" Star asked.

"Well, *it is the art, science, and technology of obtaining reliable information about physical objects and the environment through processes of recording, measuring, and interpreting photographic images and patterns.*"

"Are you kidding me?" Star wanted to know.

"No, Cosmo is right. I took a class in Forestry School. I was going to be a forester," Bingo said. "You can get all the information, even make topography maps."

"Okay, Cosmo. Then how did you come up with eleven guys?" Scorpio asked.

"From the measurements I made and comparing the images, I found eleven unique targets. That's not counting the group of seven, which I'm sure is the Boss and his buddies."

"Cosmo, you're right about the seven. According to Jane, his wife, Boss, was with six of his buddies. There's your seven."

"So, how positive are you on the eleven targets?" Scorpio asked.

"I give it about 90% sure. Only because there may have been people in the huts that never were outside when the imagery was taken."

"Okay, I have the Global on the way. He will be here this evening, and we will leave for Mexico City in the morning. Now we need to get a plan together," Scorpio said.

"Here is my thought," Bingo said. "Looking at the data and from what Mama Bear told me. Mama will meet us at the airport and can get us to the site during nighttime hours. Depending on where all the bad guys are, we may be able to get close to the huts or cabins, whatever they are. Then, use the pin cameras and find where our people are. Then come up with a plan. We probably can take everyone out at the same time outside.”

“Well, it looks like it will be one of those jobs, meaning plan as we go. Okay, let's get all the gear together and be ready to load when the aircraft arrives. We’ll get a good night's sleep and head out in the morning,” Scorpio said.

Scorpio walked into his office and dialed a number. It rang twice. “Hello Jane, this is Scorpio.”

“Hi, Scorpio. You hear anything,” Jane asked in a concerned voice.

“Yes, Jane. Jim and his buddies accidentally walked into a camp of several thugs, drug runners. We have found their camp through satellite data. We plan to be on the ground on that site tomorrow night. So far, we think Jim and his buddies are alive and being held in a hut.”

“My God,” Jane said. “I wish you luck. I know you and the team will do your best. Thank you, Scorpio.” She started to cry.

“It will be okay, and we will do our best, Jane. I’ll call or have Jim call you when we complete the mission. Later…”

It was early morning, and the team was walking from the team house toward the Global. The team's gear was already loaded on the aircraft and ready to go. The team walks on board. The pilot was already on board, going through a preflight check.

Scorpio popped his head in the flight deck, "how are we doing?" He asked the pilot.

"We are about ready, and we should be airborne in about fifteen minutes. I have clearance in Mexico City. It will probably take us about four hours. I just talked to Mama Bear. She said she would pick you up at the corporate hangar. It will probably be about midnight by the time she gets you guys to the target area."

Scorpio gave the pilot a thumbs up. Then, I walked back and took a seat. The Global was starting to taxi for takeoff. Before long, the Global was airborne, and the pilot turned to a heading of 136 degrees for the first leg towards Mexico City. The team relaxed, sometimes dozing off, for the next four hours. They knew they weren't going to get much sleep for the next couple of days.

Scorpio and Cosmo studied the new imagery they picked up just before leaving the base. Cosmo said, "It doesn't look like there has been any change."

"No, I don't see any changes either," Scorpio confirmed. He could hear the engines slow down and feel the aircraft begin descending into Mexico City. Looking at his watch, he said, "We made good time."

Fifteen minutes later, the wheels touched down. A couple of minutes later, they pulled up near the corporate hangars. Mama Bear was standing next to a van. When Scorpio opened the door, the pilot shut the engines down, and the stairs went down. "Hi, Mama," Scorpio waved at her.

"Good to see you, Scorpio. You ready for a long walk?" she said in an inquisitive voice.

"Is it liking our other walks?" Scorpio asked, walking down the stairs.

"Oh, no, we won't have dangerous things crawling around. It is a little easier hike. I'm familiar with the area but haven't been there for several years."

The team walked down the stairs, saying hi to Mama Bear. After all the greetings, they loaded their gear in the van, and Mama Bear headed out of the airport grounds in a northeast direction.

"Mama, could you brief us on how we will reach the target site?" Scorpio asked.

"Sure, we have about a ninety-mile drive to a farm where we can hide in the barn until ready. The hike is about eleven miles, about three hours. We should be there between 12:00 and 1:00 a.m."

"Looks like we have good cover around their camp, looking at the satellite image," Bingo said.

The drive took them through several small towns, finally reaching a small farm. Mama drove up the driveway, past the house, towards the barn. At the barn, the double doors were already open. She drove in and got out, walking over to the doors and closing them.

"What about the people that own the farm? Are they tied in with you?" Scorpio was addressing Mama Bear.

"Yeah, you can say that. He is my first husband."

"Huh? I hope you are on good terms with him!" Scorpio remarked.

"I guess we are. His wife is now one of my best friends. We have done a lot of favors for each other for several years. You're safe here."

"Get your gear together, fellows. We need to be on the trail in a few minutes," Scorpio said.

It was a pleasant walk compared to other hikes. It was easygoing. After about three hours, Mama Bear stopped. She raised her arm. Everyone kneeled, and then the team moved up close to Bear. "Okay, we're doing great, ahead of schedule. We have about a half-mile to go. We will come up on their East side, near the huts. Be close to midnight. So, if you want to check your night vision and commo gear, now is the time."

Everyone took a moment, then approved and endorsed by raising their thumbs. Mama Bear continued towards the camp. A few minutes later, she slowed down, taking a cautious approach. Finally, she stopped and kneeled. "Okay, they sure have a big fire going. I only see three guards. Do you hear that noise? It is from crickets and other creatures. Nice to have some background noise."

"Cosmo, use the thermal scanner and see if you pick up anyone in the trees," Scorpio said.

"No one, but there are three perches in the trees, but no one is on them. I see the three guards Mama sees, but I have four others between the huts. There must be cots there. They appear to be sleeping. Overall, they don't seem too worried about anything."

"Bingo, take the first hut, use the wand camera, and see what you have. Star, you do the same on the other hut. We will stay as we are until you find out what is in the huts," Scorpio said.

Both Bingo and Star crawl up to the huts. It took fifteen minutes. The undergrowth was up against the huts, making crawling near them easy. They both used wand cameras.

Bingo reported first, "Scorpio, I have three guys. Two are asleep, and one is by a table and appears to be monitoring a radio. There are no windows, and one door looks like a blanket as a door."

Shortly after Bingo, Star said, "I have eight. Seven appear tied to cots, and one is sitting in a chair. He must be the guard, and it looks like he may be asleep. The ones bound to the cots must be our guys. The hut is like Bingo's."

"Here is the plan," Scorpio said. "Barber, you join Bingo and Zula; you crawl over to Star's location, and when I give the word to go, you take out the ones sleeping between the huts, then enter the huts and take out the scum bags. Jasper, Cosmo, and Joker crawl to the left and position themselves to take the three guards. When you're set, let me know. Once I give you the word to go, take them out and position yourself to support the huts' effort. Mama Bear and I will provide backup where there is a problem. Everyone understands the plan."

Everyone was on the same page. "Okay, Jasper, Cosmo, and Joker get into position." About ten minutes later, Joker said, "Scorpio, we are in place and ready!"

"Bingo, are you four ready?" Scorpio asked.

"Yes, we're set," Bingo replied.

Scorpio looked over to Mama Bear, "you ready?"

Mama Bear smiled. "Yes," she winked while pulling out her bowie knife. "Let's do it."

"Okay, gentlemen, 3, 2, 1, go!" Scorpio said over the commo in a whisper.

The jungle noise was increased due to the faint noise from the silencers. The three guards were laid out without knowing what had happened. The sleeping guards just moved slightly. The guard stood up from the table with the radio mic in his hand, about to say something, when Bingo put him down with a single shot. Barber took care of the other two, completing the mission in less than a minute. Star and Bingo untied the boss and his buddies.

"Hi, Boss," Star said, "you'd do anything to get involved in a mission," He was chuckling.

"God, sure, good to see you guys. How did you find us?"

"Mama Bear, mostly, and satellite data," Star said.

"Hi, Boss," Scorpio said. "Good to see you."

"Good to see you too, Scorpio." Jim turned to his buddies. "These are my guys; do as they say, and we will leave here alive."

"You got it, Jim," one of his buddies said.

"Anyone needs medical attention?" Bingo wanted to know.

Everyone was okay, just a few bruises. "Okay," Mama Bear said, "to be on the safe side, I think we need to get out of here!"

Within minutes, Mama Bear had everyone heading down the trail. The sun was rising, and it didn't take long to get back to the little farm and barn. Just before arriving, Scorpio asked Mama Bear,

"What about transportation? The van we came in won't do the job."

"Not to worry, Captain Sixto should be waiting with a large passenger van. He will take you all to the airport." They were near the farm when Mama Bear said, "Get down."

"What's up, Mama?" Scorpio said.

"Captain Sixto is in the barn, but a Mexican police car is there. I don't see anyone. They must be in the barn."

"Okay, I don't know why. We didn't notify the Mexican government, so no one should know anything about this raid," Scorpio said. "Boss, you and your buddies stay here. I'll have the team check this out. Cosmo, Bingo, Star, and Joker take the right side, and Jasper, Barber, and Zula follow me to the left side. Keep in contact."

A few minutes later, they were alongside the barn. Scorpio said, "Hold on while I take a peek." Scorpio moved slowly to the open double barn door and peeked around the corner with his weapon raised. Captain Sixto was talking to two Mexican Federales. "Hold on. I'm going to walk in and see what happens." Scorpio put his weapon away and walked in. "Hi, Captain. We have a problem."

"Hi, Scorpio. I want you to meet Lieutenant Antonio and Sergeant Francisco. These two are my fishing and drinking buddies when I'm in Mexico."

"Oh, that's good. Nice to meet you both," Scorpio said, shaking hands.

"Where is the rest of the crew?" Captain Sixto asked.

"They're outside. We weren't sure what was going on; we didn't know if we were going to have a shootout or not."

"Oh no, senior, no shootout. We're here to escort my buddy Sixto to the airport."

"That will be the first time," Scorpio said. "Okay, guys, you can all come in. It is safe. We have a police escort to the airport."

Everyone walked in cautiously. "What is this about a police escort?" Jasper asked.

"That's right." Everyone took their gear and loaded it up in the large passenger van. "Boss!" Scorpio said. "I told Jane I would have you call her when we got you in a safe place."

"You talked to Jane?" Jim looked puzzled.

"Yes, she called me and asked for help finding you. She was worried because she hadn't heard from you. She was afraid something had happened."

"Oh gosh, I'm going to have to get a part-time job to pay you guys."

"Na, this one is on the house. We're just glad it worked out okay. By the way, how in the hell did you get mixed up with those guys?"

"We found a shortcut on the map and wound up walking into their camp unannounced. They were surprised, and so were we. We didn't have a clue who they were. But we found out that they were running drugs. Not sure what they planned for us, but I'm sure it wasn't in our favor."

"Here, Boss," Scorpio said, handing the satellite phone to him. "Give Jane a call."

Jim dialed the number. It rang once.

"Hello, Scorpio. Any word?" Jane asked in a hurried voice.

"Hi, Hon, we're okay. Scorpio did a great job of getting us out. We are at a farmhouse, getting ready to head to the airport. I should be home sometime tomorrow."

"Oh, now I can breathe. I didn't know who to call. I tried the embassy in Mexico City, but they didn't have any information. They did have a bulletin for hikers to use caution due to drug traffic."

"We never saw a bulletin and didn't check with the embassy. However, it's over, and I will gladly get home. Love you; see you tomorrow."

"Love you too; see you tomorrow," Jane said. Boss handed the phone back to Scorpio.

"Let's get loaded up. Time to go home," Scorpio said. "Nice to meet you, Lieutenant Antonio and Sargent Francisco. Thanks for the escort to the airport; that's appreciated. This is the first time we ever had a police escort."

"You are welcome," the lieutenant said. "Nice to meet some of Captain Sixto's friends. He never tells us what he does. Probably a good thing."

The drive to the airport was fun, with no stopping for traffic, red lights, or stop signs. Entering the airport, they headed over to the Global aircraft. They stopped at the bottom of the stairs leading up to the airplane. The pilot came down the stairs and said, "Hey, Scorpio, I knew someday you guys would be escorted out of a country. How much trouble did you get us into?"

"No trouble," Scorpio said. "This is Lieutenant Antonio and Sargent Francisco, some of my friends."

"This is a first," Pilot said. "Usually, we leave with someone chasing us. Nice to meet you guys." Looking at **Scorpio**, "I have clearance, so when you are ready, we can head home."

Jim was in his den, relaxing and recovering from the Mexico trip. He was looking through a boat catalog. He and Jane figured that you need to have a boat if you live on a lake. Jim got up from his desk and walked to the large window overlooking the lake when the phone rang. I recognize the number, he thought. "Hello."

"Hi Boss, I hope I'm not interrupting you."

"Hi, Scorpio. This is a surprise. No, you are not interrupting me. Just looking at a catalog on boats."

"Boats! You know the old saying, 'You own a boat; you have a hole in the lake you threw money into."

"Yeah, Scorpio, I think everyone has been telling me that. Anyway, what do I owe the honor of you calling me? Oh, one of these days, I'd like the team to stay with us for a few days. Do a little waterskiing and drink."

"That sounds great. Just let us know when. But I'm sorry; I didn't want to bother you. We have been busy for the last couple of years. But I have a mission. We may have several future missions and must change how we view and plan them. Boss, would you like to join us in a planning session regarding future missions? We have several things going on. We may have a hooker and a nun on the team."

"A WHAT?"

"Yeah, Boss, you heard me right," Scorpio said, chuckling. "But I think your input would be welcome. Besides, we're missing your common-sense approach in our planning."

There was a long pause. Jim thought… Part of me says no thanks, but the more significant amount tells me I need that involvement. "So, Scorpio…., I would love to join you."

"I'm glad. I know the team would like to see you again. I know Angelique talks about you all the time."

"How is she doing?"

"She is getting ready for her interview for citizenship in a few days. I know she'd love to see you. Oh, yeah, she is in love."

"Really, who is the lucky guy?"

"Joker. And it is not puppy love. It is serious shit.?"

"Well, I'm happy for both. Angelique deserves the best. Joker seems to be a great guy. I don't know much about his past."

"I know what you mean. I think Joker is a good match. I'm just concerned that Joker won't be focused when on a mission, doing his job, and not be thinking about Angelique."

"Yeah, understand. Maybe when I'm there, I'll talk to them."

"Boss, I think that would be a great idea."

"Okay, Scorpio, let me know a date to come to the base, and I'll talk it over with Jane and go from there. Is that okay with you?"

"Sounds great, Boss. Maybe bring Jane with you? I'll send you a couple of dates, probably soon. Talk to you later."

Jim walked out of the den onto the deck. He fixed himself a bourbon from a small bar he had built into the corner of the deck. Jim took a sip. He saw Jane sitting under the umbrella, reading a novel. He took his drink, walked over, and sat next to Jane.

"Hi, hon." Jane put her book down. "Sure, it is another beautiful day. This is the best thing we have done: building this place."

"Well, the second-best thing," Jim said.

"Oh, what is the first thing?"

Jim looked at Jane. He smiled. "When we got married!"

Jane smiled, "I stand corrected."

Jim took another sip from his drink and sat back in his chair, looking out over the lake. It was calm, and the mountains reflected like the lake was a mirror. He was thinking about his call from Scorpio.

Jane reached over and put her hand on his arm. "You are in deep thought about something. I have seen that look before. Is it about the team?"

"Yeah, I just had a call from Scorpio. We had a nice talk. They have been busy and have a couple of new members. They deal with world changes and requests they don't think they want to be part of. Scorpio asked if I'd like to join the base for a mission planning session. They'd like my input on future missions and capabilities."

"You think about that. I'm for it and think it would be good for you. I wouldn't want you to go on a mission."

"I would like to go, and I'd like you to go with me and meet this crazy bunch. Scorpio said he would send the dates."

<hr>

"Okay, let's get started," Scorpio stated. "I believe we should take some time to consider our missions and the management of upcoming missions. It seems that we are being asked to perform tasks that we have never performed, such as escorting tours in unstable locations and retrieving deceased victims. I want everyone to be considering this and other pertinent issues. Please give it some thought during the next few weeks. I invited the Boss to come along. His pragmatic approach will, I believe, be advantageous in that encounter. Any inquiries? "Scorpio, we have an unusual idea," Joker said, "maybe more like a request. Two additional team members."

Scorpio butted in. "Yeah, I heard, a hooker and a nun. Is this one of your jokes? You cannot be serious?"

"I'm serious," Joker said. "They teamed up. These two ladies work together, traveling throughout Brazil, helping families locate their missing loved ones."

"Wow," Scorpio said, "You want us to believe this combination, a hooker and a nun, are freelancing and helping families?"

"Yup, it was Mama Bears' idea, and according to her, it works well. The only problem at times is they are unable to get people relocated."

"You mean rescued?"

"Well…. I guess that would be more accurate. Bear thought they could use our support and be part of the team."

"Oh, Boy! Well… let's put that on the list. Be interested in what the Boss will think. A hooker and a nun. Joker, how did that happen?"

"Not sure," Joker said. "Mama Bear mentioned it to me several months ago when we were there during a mission. I chuckled about it but never thought about it until last week when Mama Bear called about that subject. I understand these two ladies do come from different ends of the spectrum. But they teamed up to save innocent Brazilian people from terrorist torments, murders, child trafficking, and other issues. They'd like to be working with us to rescue their people."

"Sounds like a task too big for us to do anything about now. But we can talk about it when the Boss is here." Scorpio was looking at his notes. "Oh, Bingo, you have information on equipment needs?" About then, the phone rings.

Cosmo got up to answer it. He picked it up and said, "Hello, Senator, this is Cosmo."

"Hi, Cosmo," she said. "You guys ready for another mission?"

"Sure, hang on, and I'll turn you over to Scorpio." Handing the phone to Scorpio, "Senator has a mission."

"Hi, Senator, so what's up? Cosmo said something about a mission."

"The State Department dispatched personnel to this briefing regarding the rainforest burning in Brazil. Their meeting was in the Brazilian jungle. They got together In Manaus. The length of the stay was three-day meeting. They failed to appear on the third day. They have not checked out or haven't met dispatched personnel to this briefing regarding the rainforest burning fire. They were set to leave their hotel, and their luggage is still in the rooms. Before that, it had been eight days. The State Department received a telegram through a private company claiming that a local terrorist group was holding them captive. Our people informants on the ground said probably tell us that they are most likely being held somewhere around the Negro River. This is not very useful, considering that it covers hundreds of square miles." Cosmo turned to the fax machine.

"Oh, just wait a moment..." Cosmo was digging out imagery and our data on Manaus, Brazil. "It looks like we may be going back there," Scorpio said.

"Okay, I'm back. "Senator said, "I just received information from someone that works for Mama Bear. This group is about forty-five miles up the Negro River from Manaus. There is a small camp and about thirty to forty thugs. They are demanding five million, or they will kill the captives. No other information."

"Okay, Senator, we will make contact with Mama Bear and see what we can work out. I'll get back to you, hopefully by tomorrow."

"Thanks, Scorpio. Talk to you tomorrow," Senator, **replacing** the receiver.

"Cosmo, see if you can get in touch with Mama Bear. We need to talk with her. Also, put everyone on alert so they don't take off somewhere. Call our pilot, tell him we're on alert, and we'll need the Global. We will get back to him on a schedule."

"Okay, Scorpio, I'm on it." Three hours later, Cosmo walked into Scorpio's office. "We got lucky; Mama Bear is online two."

"Thanks," Scorpio said. "Hi, Mama Bear. How did we get so lucky? You are usually in the bush, and it takes days to catch you."

"It's been a while since I was in the bush. So, are you calling about the State Department folks?"

"Yes, Mama Bear, we don't have much information."

"Right now, I have two State Department employees and thirty-seven thugs. It is close to the camp, as we call it; The Round Butte. I've traveled there a few times. I will email the coordinates to you. Situated in a roughly ten-acre open space with dense woodland surrounding it, the little cottage has just three ways and out. I can email you a sketch of the location of the guard post from my visit, which occurred around three months ago. However, I don't believe anything has changed. A few smaller openings nearby. If I remember, apertures in the vicinity. The Negro River is roughly two miles distant if I recall correctly. I'll email you some photos I shot on our most recent visit."

"And you were there, how…?" She sounded on the fence, her tone guarded.

"I bring in supplies, mostly food. That's my payment for having access to the area."

"Okay, I look forward to getting any information you have. Also, would you and Captain Sixto be available to help again?"

"No problem. But if we mix it up with the terrorists, they all must be removed. I can't afford to leave anyone behind. The last thing I need is them knowing that I was involved."

"Understand, we wouldn't want to leave anyone to follow us. Is this camp near their main force?"

"The main camp is about thirty miles further towards the mountains."

"Once I go over the data you are sending and have questions or scheduling a rescue, would you be around to contact me over the next couple of weeks?" Scorpio asked.

"Scorpio, I have nothing scheduled that I can't change. I am looking forward to working with your group again. Oh, say, how is Angelique doing?"

"Mama Bear, she is doing great. We're so happy she is part of our team. And we are on track for her to become an American citizen."

"That's wonderful. Are you going to have a party for Angelique? I'd sure like to be there."

"Sounds like a great idea. I'll let you know."

"Okay, I'll be talking with you soon. Also, you should have all the information and pictures in your e-mail by now. Later." Mama Bear replaced the receiver.

"Cosmo, check out our e-mail and download the data from Mama Bear. Make copies and have everyone study the data; we will meet on it after everyone has a chance to study it. Also, the Boss said he could make it and will be here Thursday afternoon."

"That's great. Seeing the Boss and getting his input on this mission will be good."

Jim was sitting on the deck overlooking the lake. He was reviewing the information Scorpio sent him, taking a few minutes before he and Jane catch a flight to Las Vegas. Jane walked out, "I'm ready to go anytime you are."

"Okay, I'll grab the bags. Our flight is about an hour and a half from now. That will put us in Las Vegas around noon. Be at the base about three or so."

"Sounds good. I'm excited to meet your team."

"I'm looking forward to it also."

They loaded up. The drive to the airport was about 20 minutes, and generally, it didn't take but a few minutes to get through security and board the airplane. It wasn't long before they checked in and were on their way to the gate. They were pre-boarded when they arrived at the gate. Flying first class, they were able to walk on board. Getting settled, Jim asked Jane. "Would you like a Bloody Mary?"

"That sounds great."

Jim waved at the flight attendant and ordered two Bloody Mary's.

They sat back, enjoying their drinks while the flight attendants finished boarding. Shortly, the flight attendant collected the glasses and did the safety check and announcements. The flight to Salt Lake and then to Las Vegas was about three hours. The plane touched down at 12:27 p.m. on schedule. It didn't take long to get through the baggage claim and on the road. Jim pulled off Highway 95 West on a graveled road about an hour later.

"Gee, what happened to the road? It wasn't bad until we went around the last corner. Like no one maintains this road," Jane said.

Jim chuckled, "This part is a private road, and we spend lots of money maintaining this road to be this way."

"Ah… Okay… Why? No one in their right mind would want to drive this road. It looks like the road was used for a bombing raid," Jane remarked.

"That's right. That is why it was built like this: to keep people from wanting to drive it. You noticed we haven't hit the potholes?"

"Yeah, and you are driving on the wrong side of the road."

"An average car or any truck or pickup would hit every hole. If you drive a small car with a short wheelbase and drive on the left side with the left wheels right on the edge of the road, you miss every hole. Outstanding engineering," Jim was smiling.

"I was wondering why we got such a small car."

"My design is to discourage people from finding the base. This road goes on for another 10 miles. You noticed a couple of turnarounds, encouraging people to think maybe it's time to turn around. In all the years we have had this base, there have been no reports from the guards that anyone has ever shown up that didn't belong there."

"How clever," Jane said. "I knew you were smart but didn't think you were a genius." She reached over, tapped Jim on the arm, and smiled.

A few minutes later, they made a left turn, and another 100 yards, there was a gate and a guardhouse. A young guy came out, smartly dressed in a uniform. Jim rolled his window down.

"Good afternoon, sir. Can I help you?" The guard said.

"Good afternoon, Scorpio sure got you guys some smart-looking uniforms."

"Yes, sir, he sure did. You must be the Boss. I was told to expect you."

"Yes, you're right."

"Go ahead, sir. Nice to meet you. Scorpio talks about you a lot. The whole team thinks a lot of you and your support." The guard opened the gate and waved Jim through.

Jim drove through and looked at Jane. "I sure have them fooled."

"No, I don't think so." She smiled.

Scorpio and the crew were standing at the bar. Cosmo asked, "When was the Boss going to be here?"

"I'm here," Jim said, walking into the conference room.

The team walked over, and they shook his hand like he had been gone for years. Finally, they stopped long enough for Jim to say, "Guys, this is my wife, Jane." Jim introduces each one to Jane. "Oh, where is Angelique?"

"Sorry, Boss, I was nose-deep in a computer program." She said, walking over and giving Jim a big hug. Then she turned and said, "You must be Jane," hugging her. "I'm so glad you came, Jane. I'm sure it will be nice to talk to another woman. These guys get boring after a while. You know what I mean?"

"Yes, Angelique, I agree with you. It will be nice to talk to you also. I heard about your background and experience from the Boss, which I consider very interesting. Looking forward to our visit. What kind of a program are you working on?"

"Let me show you while the guys talk." She led Jane into the computer room.

"Well, Scorpio, I'm glad to be here. So, what's this about a hooker and a nun? Is that for real, and what are they up to?"

Scorpio signaled to Bingo, "Would you like to take this subject?"

"Boss, yeah, they're real. I understand from Mama Bear that these two have been working together for years. How they got together is anyone's guess. But over the years, they have helped dozens of Brazilians escape from thugs and corruption and find a better way of life. Sometimes, they're too late, and innocent people die. At times, according to Mama Bear, they could have saved more lives if they had our assistance. So that is the nut in the shell. They need our help. This is the big question: how do we do that? I don't have the answer," Bingo said as he sipped his beer.

Everyone was quiet until Scorpio said, "On that note, we may have a mission back to Brazil to rescue some State Department folks."

"I see that in the information you sent me," Boss said. "So, have you come up with any ideas?"

"I think it will be one of those missions where most of the plan will be developed with boots on the ground. We do know we have thirty-seven targets. Our three new guys, Star, Barber, and Zula, are receiving training offsite with Mama Bear and Captain Sixto.

That will give us ten guns. You will meet the new guys in a couple of days.”

“What is their primary expertise?” Boss asked.

“They are ex-marine snipers. Zula was a medic, and Star and Barber were explosives experts, mostly with C-4-type stuff. All are experts with long guns and pistols. They are going through satellite communications and imagery interpretation training.”

“What is your basic plan as of now?” Boss questioned.

Jasper got up and went to the whiteboard, picking up a marker. “Well, Boss. We take the Global to Manaus. There, we will meet Mama Bear and Captain Sixto. We go up the Negro River, about 45 miles.” Jasper draws a map. “We go to this point.” Pointing to a location on satellite imagery. “There, we camouflage the boat. Mama Bear will guide us to this point.” Again, pointing to the imagery. “At this point, we plan on being at around midnight. According to the Mama Bear sketch, seven guards are on the tree platforms. Those are marked with a small square on the drawing. We think the captives are in the cabin. According to the drawing, most of the other thugs are in these four tents. I assume there are guards in the cabin.”

“You have enough shooters to take the guards out on the platforms. Looking at the drawing, the platforms are far enough away that a guard won’t fall on a tent,” Boss said. “But I do understand the need to finalize the mission on site. There is no other way."

"We're hoping the platforms are big enough that the guards don't fall off. In case they do, I'm sure the noise of them hitting the ground may wake someone up. So, we need to be in a position to be by the tents in short order when the guards are killed. We need to enter all the tents at the same time." Bingo finished his beer. "Then we move to the cabin, put a pin camera through the wall or under the door, whichever is easier. It depends on what we find to determine how we finish the job."

"That's the basic plan, but that could all change when we get there. Any questions?" Scorpio asked.

"What about putting tripwires when we go in? Just in case we miss someone that sneaks out. They would likely run down a trail and try to get through thick cover. We'd need to remember where they are when we head out." Jasper noted.

"So, Scorpio, when do you plan on the mission?" Boss asked.

"We are waiting on Mama Bear to call back. Her contact was going to give her an update. But by tomorrow, we need to have our gear ready. Call the pilot and have him stand by here. We need to be ready."

"Sounds like a plan," Jasper said. "So, what about our hooker and nun? Thoughts on that?"

No one said anything. Finally, the Boss said, "Maybe Mama Bear could get us in contact with them and get more details on what they are asking for and get a better idea of how they operate."

"Yeah, that works for me," Scorpio said. "The chef said dinner is ready. Also, Boss, we have room three for you and Jane."

"Okay, thanks. I better check on the girls. They may have sold this place by now!" Jim entered the computer room and saw both having a good time visiting and drinking wine. "How are you two doing? The chef said dinner is ready."

"We're doing fine," Angelique said. "I'm sure enjoying visiting with Jane."

"Yeah, it has been great," Jane said. "Where do we freshen up?"

"I'll show you," Angelique said. They got up, leaving Jim sitting there.

Well, I guess I know where I stand, he chuckled. He was happy they hit it off.

Everyone enjoyed the chef's buffet of oriental foods and drinks afterward. Jim and Jane headed to their room. As they were getting to their room, Jane said, "Angelique sure is smart. She sure had a hard life. She told me several times how she respects you and how you saved her life. You have a friend for life."

"Yeah, I know. We are lucky to have her as part of the team. I wish we could find her cousin and give her some family ties. Scorpio said she is getting close to becoming an American citizen."

"How long does that take?"

"You have to know all about the government the constitution, and have worked in this country for about five years."

"I think she has been on the business payroll for at least four years, so she's just about got it done. Is there anything else she needs to do?"

"Not sure, but the CIA is helping, and the Senator is also working on it."

"Scorpio, sorry for the interruption," Jasper said. "But Mama Bear is on line 1."

"Okay, thanks, Jasper." Scorpio was picking up the phone in his office. "Hi, Mama Bear. What do you have for us?"

"Hi, Scorpio. Just confirming thirty-seven targets. The sketch I sent you is pretty accurate. According to the latest information, they rotate the guards in the cabin every twelve hours, three guards, usually between about 7:00 a.m. and 7:00 p.m. A small generator lights the camp—no night vision capability. Most carry

AK-47s or AR-15s, and all carry sidearms, the .45s. Anything else I can help you with?"

"Yeah, where in the camp is the generator located?"

"It's on the north side, on the edge of the camp. It has a small lean-to over it."

"That's good information to have. What about a schedule? Any thoughts about that?"

"We can go anytime. But I would not wait long as a relief group comes in and replaces the group at the end of the month. That gives you about two weeks. But the group also gets pretty relaxed towards the end of their assignment."

"We're ready. We could go when you are ready."

"Okay, four days from today, you land at Manaus at midday?"

Scorpio thought for a minute. "Okay, let's do it. See you in four days."

"I'll let Captain Sixto know to get ready. See you in four days." Mama Bear disconnected the phone.

"Jasper," Scorpio said, "have everyone join us in the conference room."

"Okay, also, the pilot is here. Want him to join us too?"

"Yes." A few minutes later, everyone was in the conference room. Scorpio said, "We leave for Brazil in four days. We will meet Mama Bear at the Manaus airport next Tuesday around noon. Also, there is a generator on the north side, which they use to light up the place at night. They do not have night vision. I thought if we can fix it, let's say, run out of gas, they will be blind for a couple of minutes when the lights go out. We can see them. They can't see us. By the time they figured out what happened, we should have most taken out. What do you all think of that idea?"

They all agreed. Bingo said, "We can refine our plan when on site. Maybe change some now that we can blind them for a few minutes."

"Boss, what are your thoughts?" Scorpio inquired.

"Having lights turned out will give you a significant advantage. I think Bingo is right. That will provide you with the opportunity to have a better plan. The only thing that may create some confusion is the lights going out. The problem I see is that they may wake up or alert the cabin guards and kill the hostages."

"Yeah, I see what you mean," Scorpio said. "According to the sketch, the cabin is next to the vegetation. We could put a pin camera through the back wall and see what we have. Assuming the door will be unlocked. We may have one person focus on the cabin while the rest take care of the others." Pausing to finish his coffee. "Once we get on site, we need to do a little recon, then make our final plan, get people in place, and get it done."

"Sounds like we have a plan," Cosmo said. "When do Star, Barber, and Zula return from training?"

"They should be back tonight. We will all get together and review what we have in the morning. Bingo, is all the gear ready to go?"

"Almost. I must change the commo gear batteries and then pack them. Everything else is ready."

"Does anyone have any more questions?" Scorpio asked.

Angelique raised her hand, "I know I'll not be part of this mission, but Boss, is there a way I can keep Jane for a couple of days?"

"Huh, what you got going?" Boss asked.

"Jane is good at organization, tracking equipment, maintenance plans, etc. She has been helping me get that stuff together. We have the greatest team, but they are lousy at keeping track of our gear and maintenance. Jane has a method she has used before that keeps track and shows up in the report when things need replacing. I bet we spend a ton of money because we are not organized equipment-wise!"

"Yeah, she is good at that. She saved my company lots of money because of her business knowledge. We have nothing pressing that we need to be back home anytime soon. We can stay a few days and help you out."

"That's great."

Joker walked in, "Hi, Boss. Scorpio said you'd like to talk to me?"

"Yes, and Angelique. Let's go into the office." They followed Boss into the office.

"Boss, are we in trouble?" Angelique asked.

"No," they sat at a small table. "It's a rumor that you two are in love. It was explained to me as serious shit!"

They laughed, "Well, it is not a rumor," Angelique said. "It is true."

"Yeah, as you said," Joker commented. "It is serious shit."

They both laughed again.

"I don't poke my nose into other people's business, especially when loving someone. First, I'm happy for you both. Secondly, it is the team's business. This is the first time this situation has come up, and I'm unsure what your plans are. That is your business."

"We're not sure about our plans yet," Joker said.

"My concern," Boss said. "Well, Angelique will probably not be on a mission. But Joker, every time you go out on a mission, you may not return."

"Yes, Boss, we both understand and have discussed that."

"That's good, but you have to be 100% focused on a mission when you go out on a mission. You can't be thinking about Angelique or anything else. If you hesitate for one second, it could cost you your life or someone on the team."

"Boss, we both understand that," Angelique said. "I told Joker I would love for him to always think about me. But he can't do that when on a mission. I want him to come back alive."

Scorpio, Jasper, and the rest of the team came in. "Sorry to interrupt you, Boss. But if you're talking about these two love birds, we'd like to express our opinion," Scorpio said.

"Okay. Yes, we're discussing the risk Joker may be putting on a mission."

"Boss, Angelique, and Joker," Scorpio said. "We all have been discussing this and the risk it may put on the team. We all decided to accept the risk."

A long pause. "Okay," Boss said—another pause. "I will accept that for now. However, Joker is done during a mission if Joker hesitates even though it doesn't create a problem. Scorpio, I'll leave the call up to you."

"Yes, Sir." Scorpio, looking at Joker. "You okay with that?"

"Yes, I agree."

"Okay, the other thing," Boss said, looking at Angelique. "If you two get married, you better invite us to the celebration."

"Boss, I'll invite you, and you will give me away."

"That is a deal."

A light rain fell over the base most of the evening. The welcome sight augured well. The desert neared full bloom as the vegetation came alive with brilliant colors. The team was getting the aircraft loaded. It was 1:00 a.m. Scorpio said to Jasper, "Are we about ready? Need to be airborne in a few minutes to be on schedule."

"Yes, got everything on board. I need the guys to get on board."

The boss walked out to the Global 8000 with the team. "Good luck, guys. I think you will have a good mission. There is no one better than you guys for this type of work. See you when you get back." Boss shook their hands, walked back partway, and turned to watch the Global take off. About then, Jane and Angelique joined him and waved at the team as the Global lifted off the runway. The wheels went up, and the plane banked southerly. "Well, how are you two doing on your project?"

"Doing okay, probably get back to it after a nap and breakfast," Angelique said.

"A nap sounds good to me," Boss replied.

They were walking back to the team house when Angelique said, "Boss, thank you again for all you do. I miss my folks and never got over seeing them killed. I always had this void in my life. I know I'm not saying the right words."

"Angelique, I do understand how you feel. Missing your folks is a normal thing."

"I know, Boss. I love you, and you and Jane... Well, you are my family."

"We are proud of you. The whole team is proud of you. You have done amazing things that have helped the team out."

"That's one thing of many why this team is special. Everyone... well, it is like having a big family. Everyone cares for the other."

"Yes, Angelique. That is true."

They continued walking into the team house. Jim had his arms around them.

Scorpio was wakened by turbulence as the Global descended into Eduardo Gomes International Airport, Manaus, Brazil. He looked at his watch. It is 12:17 p.m., he told himself, and we are on schedule. He looked around; everyone was waking up.

The pilot came on the intercom. "Gentlemen, we will land in about 10 minutes and park by the corporate hangar at the north end."

A few minutes later, the Global 8000 was taxiing to the corporate hangar. It stopped, and the engines shut down. Scorpio walked over to the door and opened it.

"Okay, guys, grab the gear." Scorpio walked down the stairs. There to meet him was Mate. "Good to see you again, Mate, Captain. Ready for a couple of long days ahead of us?"

"Sure am," Mate said. "Good to see you too. We are all set. You can load your gear up in that van over there," she pointed. "Mama Bear is already on board the boat. The boat is parked at the Downtown Port."

"Okay, let's get going."

It seemed like a long ride to the Port. The traffic through town was heavy. Mate turned into the Downtown Port Marina and headed to a small dock where Captain Sixto had parked the boat. Mate drove up alongside and stopped. Mama Bear and the Captain were standing there.

Scorpio exited the van. "Hi, Mama and Captain. Good to see you both."

"Good to see you both again," Captain Sixto said. "Once your gear is on board, we will head upriver. We should be at the disembarkation spot just after dark and near the camp around midnight. We should be pretty much on schedule."

"That sounds great, Captain," Scorpio said. "What kind of walk are we looking at, Mama?"

"It's not bad. Once ashore, it will probably take us a couple of hours to get to a small opening near the camp. It is open enough to survey the camp and finalize your plan," Mama Bear said.

The trip up the Negro River was relaxing. Scorpio said, looking towards the shore, "The birds and wildlife along the river are interesting. Amazing, all the different types get along so well. A good example of how the world could be if it weren't for man screwing it up."

"Good thing they don't have political parties," Bingo said. Everyone laughed.

"We'll use this time to check out the equipment. Repack in smaller backpacks for the hike," Scorpio said.

Captain was cruising midstream and getting close to the disembarking location. Then, he slowed down and moved along the shoreline. The sun had gone down and got dark quickly. The captain used night vision, looking for a spot to tie up. He pulled up in a small cove near a large tree. Mate grabbed the gaff hook, pulled the boat up next to a tree, and tied it to it.

"Okay," Mama Bear said. "If you are ready, let's go. We are doing good as scheduled."

The walk through the heavy brush was challenging. At times, visibility was less than 10 feet.

"Mama," Jasper asked. "How do you know where we are at? Even with night vision, the vegetation is so thick that I can only see a few feet ahead!"

"Well... Jasper, I guess it is just experienced over the years. Oh, have you noticed the vegetation is different occasionally, and sometimes we hit a small opening?"

"I noticed that. Those are your checkpoints?"

"Right on, Jasper. I made notes of the imagery, bearings, and distance to each checkpoint. So far, it has been right on. We should be near their camp, maybe twenty to thirty minutes."

Finally, they entered a small opening after a few minutes and saw lights nearby. Mama Bear waved them over to the far side of the opening. Mama Bear said, "Okay, this is a good view of the camp. Scorpio, how do you want to do this?"

Scorpio was scanning the area. "Looks better than I figured. Make sure you all have your silencers attached. Jasper," a pause, "how long will it take you to get behind the cabin, put a pin camera in, and give us a report?"

"I think twenty minutes should do it."

"Cosmo, can you get over to the generator, check it out, and let me know what we can do with it?" Scorpio asked.

"Sure," Cosmo replied.

"Okay, you two take off, and we'll plan the rest of the mission after your reports," Scorpio ordered. "The rest of us study the area and the guard platforms, see who is sleeping and who is not."

It was fifteen minutes later, and Cosmo reported. "The generator is running off a 5-gallon can. But I can turn the valve off, and it will probably run a few minutes before it shuts down."

"Okay, can you stand there and stay out of sight?" Scorpio questioned.

"Yeah, I'm good."

A couple of minutes later, Jasper said. "We have two people tied to chairs, and appears one guard, and it looks like he is asleep. Also, the door is slightly open."

"Okay, we have four guard platforms, but it looks like only two are used. Two large tents, assuming that is where most of the thugs are. It seems like everyone is pretty relaxed and surely doesn't expect anything. You'd think they would be more alert after our last visit." Scorpio paused, taking a drink of water. "So here is the plan. I'll have Cosmo turn the valve off the generator when everyone is in place. I'm sure just before the generator shuts down, it will spit and sputter a couple of times before quitting. That may wake them up, so be on your toes once the lights are off. Jasper, head into the cabin and do your thing. Cosmo, you can take the platform guard to your left from your location. Bingo takes the other guard's platform. Joker, you and Star take the tent to the north, and Barber and Zula take the tent to the south. Put a couple of grenades in the tent, then clean the house after exploding. Captain, Bear, and I will place ourselves to take out anyone who tries to escape. Any questions?"

No one had questions. They move closer to the edge of the clearing. "Okay, Cosmo, turn the valve off." Cosmo moves to the generator and turns the gas off.

"Stand down, stand down," Scorpio said. "We have two guards coming out of the south tent. Everyone stays in place, out of sight. Stand by… It looks like the two decided to have a smoke. Everyone stays still."

Cosmo turned the valve back on the generator.

A few minutes later, Cosmo said, "I think I can take both out in short order."

"I think we better let them have their smoke," Scorpio says. "Let's stay with the plan."

About 10 minutes later, the two guards finished their visit and cigarette and returned to the tent. "The guards are back in the tent.

Barber and Zula, your tent will have awake people." Scorpio said, "You want to have grenades in their tent as quickly as possible when the lights go out." Scorpio paused… "Okay, Cosmo, proceed as planned."

Cosmo reached over and turned the valve back off.

It seemed like forever before the generator slowed and then shut off. When the lights went off, both guards on the platform fell at about the same time. Grenades went off at the same time when Jasper entered the cabin. The guard was getting out of his chair when Jasper took him out. The others entered the tent, and there were a couple of shots. Then, all was quiet.

"Everyone okay?" Scorpio asks. There was a pause. Then, everyone checked in. Scorpio smiled, "Just the way we like it, fast and done. Jasper, how are the two State guys?"

Jasper said, "They are okay, a little surprised, but doing good."

"We better get going," Mama Bear said, "the noise from the explosion could alert others in the area."

"Yeah, you are right. Let's go, guys," Scorpio said. "You State guys, sorry we don't have night vision for you. Grab onto someone and hang on. The trail back is pretty much cleared.

The walk back to the boat was faster than going in. Getting to the boat, Mate had the engine warming up. Everyone piled in. Captain

Sixto backed up and headed downstream. Scorpio sat back. I can't believe how well this mission went. Or maybe we're getting so good at this stuff that it is a no-brainer. He looked over at the State guys. "You all doing, okay? Do you need anything?"

"No, Sir, we are just happy to be alive. Who are you guys, military?"

"Sorry, I can't disclose anything about us. You only need to know that we are your ticket home. Once we get to Manaus, we will fly you out to the States."

"Thank you. I didn't think I would see my family again. How can we ever repay you?"

"That's easy," Scorpio said. "Just say thank you."

"THANK YOU!"

"Sit back and get some rest. We will spend several hours on the river. It should be daybreak in an hour or two; some snacks and water are in the cooler. I think there is beer in there. Help yourself," Cosmo said.

"Where are we going to in the States?" One of them asked.

"Not sure," Scorpio said. "We will find that out once we're airborne. We will probably go through Dallas, Texas customs, then on to wherever your boss tells us. But for now, relax."

Boss watched Angelique and Jane work together; he thought they made a good team. They were laughing about something.

"Okay, what are you girls laughing about?"

"Oh, I told Jane about TJ at the CIA when we discussed the tracking software. His expression. You know, Boss. I'm sure you got a kick out of it!"

"Oh, Angelique, I was going to ask you, when will you install the software on the CIA system?"

"Not sure, but probably when the team gets back. Scorpio wanted to escort me there."

The office phone rings. Boss reached for the phone. "Hello."

"Hi, Boss, Scorpio here. Just let you know we have the State Department guys. They are doing well. We are still on the river and should return to Manaus in about three to four hours. All targets down, and we're all okay."

"That's good news, Scorpio. You guys are getting so good at this you will probably want a raise someday!"

"No, Boss, just more jobs. There are enough scum bags around to keep us busy for a long time."

"Okay, not sure if we will be here when you return, but good job."

"Well, I hope you will be. Buy you a drink when I get back."

"A-okay. See you tomorrow, maybe."

"Later, Boss, thank you." He got off the line.

Jim dialed the number for the Senator. It rang a couple of times.

"Hi Jim, I bet you have good news. Hey, how come you're calling from the base?" Senator asks.

"Well, it is because I'm at the base. Scorpio asked me to be part of the planning for the Brazil mission. Anyway, the task is completed, and they are heading back. They should be back at the base tomorrow sometime. But Scorpio wasn't sure where to drop your State Department people off?"

"Oh, good question. I don't know. Let me call you back in a couple of minutes." She hangs the phone.

About fifteen minutes later, the phone rings.

Jim picks up the phone. "Hi, Senator, so what did you find out?"

"The State Department will have people picking them up when you go through customs in Dallas."

"Sorry, Senator, we cannot do that. That will bring too much attention to the team. I recommend, after customs, we taxi the plane to the corporate hangar and meet your people there. Less attention on the transfer of the State folks and the team."

"Yeah, you're right. I'll let the State folks know. I'll text you a number to call them when you arrive in Dallas." Senator ended the phone conversation.

Captain Sixto throttled back the engines. "Guys, be alert. We have a boat ahead of us. I recognize it. I had an issue with these guys before. Mate, have your M-79 ready."

"What's going on, Captain?" Scorpio asked.

"Not sure. We will continue as usual. I hope they will move on toward shore and not bother us. If not, we will have to mix it up with them." Captain turned the boat slightly to Port. "I'm surprised seeing them this far down the river. They are out of their territory. Pirates generally don't operate this close to Manaus."

Several minutes have passed. "Captain looks like they decided to move out of the way," Jasper said.

"This could be a trick of theirs. It appears the Pirates are moving out of our way to get us closer. They turn towards us at full speed when we are about to pass them by and then shoot several rounds across our bow, thinking we will stop. If they head towards us, Mate, put a round in their bow."

"Looks like they may let us by," Captain Sixto said. "NO here they come!" Shots rang out from the Pirates as the boat raced toward them at full speed. Mate aimed and let one go. It hit the

Pirate boat's bow and blew their boat's front end into pieces. "They must be new at this. I don't think we will have any more problems with them." Captain moved the throttles forward to full speed and continued to Manaus.

"Scorpio, I meant to ask you how Angelique works out?" Mama Bear said.

"She is just great and smart. Her computer skills are exceptional. With the CIA and the Senator's help, she is getting close to becoming an American citizen. Angelique seems to be happy where she is. Oh, she is in love."

"She is what? In love. What does she know about love?"

"Well, Mama Bear, probably the same way we did."

"Oh, yeah. I guess that is the way it works. Is it serious? Who is the lucky guy?"

"Yeah, it is serious. There may be a wedding at the base someday. Oh, it is Joker."

"Well, I should be happy for her. I guess I'm not surprised it would be one of the guys. Joker seems to be a good person."

"Now, I have a question for you. Tell me about the hooker and nun. How did that combination develop?"

"I'm not totally sure," Mama Bear said. "I think the nun was helping battered women, and the hooker was part of the group.

Now, they work together to move people out of dangerous areas. I talked to Bingo about it. I think that is where your team can help. Maybe help them out of these areas, or your team removes the bad guys, creating a safer situation."

"I'd like to meet them and talk more. But from what you said, it sounds like taking out the bad guys would be the easiest way." Scorpio responded.

"Maybe we can set that up, a phone call anyway. I'll check in with you later when I get something scheduled," Bear replied.

Captain said, "Okay, we can begin to see the city. We should be at the dock in about 45 minutes."

The team started to get their gear together.

Captain pulled into the marina and up to the dock as planned. Mate jumped out, tied off the boat, and headed to get the van. The team unloaded the gear.

"Captain and Mama, again, it was a pleasure working with you. Also, Mama, let's follow up on our discussion on the ladies," Scorpio said.

"Sounds good, Scorpio. I'll talk to the ladies and see when we can do a video call. I'll get back to you later."

Scorpio gave a thumbs up.

Mate drove up and helped the team load the gear up. The State Department guys thanked the boat crew for their help and climbed in the van. The traffic going through town to the airport was unusually light for midday. Mate pulled into the airport and turned left towards the corporate hangars. A few minutes later, the van parked next to the Global 8000. The State guys got out, grabbed their gear, walked up the stairs, and entered the aircraft.

Scorpio said, "Thanks, Mate, it was nice to see you again. I'm sure we will see you again on another mission."

Mate gave Scorpio a scout two-finger salute and said, "Great to work with you again, and yes, I'm sure I will see you again."

The team was securing the gear, and the engine came alive. A couple of minutes later, the pilot got clearance to taxi to the runway. After an engine run-up and check-out, the pilot received clearance for takeoff. The pilot eased the Global onto the runway and pushed the throttles forward. Within seconds, the Global raised off the runway, and the gear came up. Reaching 2,000 feet, the pilot turned to a heading of 320 degrees for the first leg of their trip back home.

Scorpio turned around in his seat and said, "Good job, guys," He gave a thumbs up. "You State guys, you doing okay? Need anything?"

"No," one of them said. "We're alive thanks to you guys, whoever you are. How long before we land?"

"About ten to eleven hours, we will land at Dallas airport," Scorpio said. "Once we clear customs, we will taxi to the corporate hangars, where a State Department team will meet you and take you home. So, sit back and relax. In case you are interested, sandwiches and beer are in the cooler."

"Oh, god, I'd love another beer," one of the State guys said.

Scorpio smiled. He was ready for one, also.

Several hours had passed. Most were asleep. Scorpio looked out the window and could see the sun was going down. Scorpio thought it would be dark when they landed in Dallas, looking at his watch. Maybe another hour. He got up and went to the flight deck. "How's it going?" He asked the pilot.

"Going well. We had a good tailwind. We will be on the ground in about thirty minutes. Should be at the base around 3:00 a.m."

"Sounds good. After clearing customs, we must go to the corporate hangars to deliver the State people." Scorpio headed back to his seat, and as he passed by the cooler, he picked up another beer. He takes out his phone and dials a number. It rang a couple of times, "Hello Boss, just letting you know we are almost to Dallas and have the State guys. They are doing well. Our guys are okay, also. We should be home around 3:00 a.m."

"That's good news. See you when you get to the base. I'll let the Senator know. Have a good rest of the flight." He hung up the phone and called the Senator to inform her.

It wasn't long before the landing gear went down as the Global descended into Dallas, Fort Worth International Airport.

"You, State guys. When going through customs, we are oil workers. As you're new, I'm sure the Customs Agent will ask about you. Just tell them this is your first break from the rigs."

"That easy to get through customs?" one of them asked.

"We often go through this place. They know us, so we don't spend much time on the ground," Scorpio answered.

After the touchdown, the tower directed the pilot to customs at the north parking corporate facility. Ground personnel referred the pilot to the required parking location a few minutes later. The engines shut down.

Scorpio got up and turned to the State guys. "Stay seated. We will be here only a few minutes before moving to the corporate hangar." He walked over, opened the door, and let the stairs go down. "Hi, how are you doing today?"

"Doing good," the customs agent said as he boarded. He looked around, "Oh, you guys have another oil rig shut down?"

"Yeah, a good time to take a break and let the guys see their families," Scorpio said.

"I won't keep you long. I'll get the pilot to sign the form and send you off." The agent said.

A few minutes later, Scorpio closed the door, and the engines began to ramp up. The Global started to taxi, turning to the corporate hangar. As the aircraft taxied towards the hangars, the pilot could see someone waving at him by a couple of limousines. The pilot turned towards him and saw several people leaving the cars. In a couple of minutes, the aircraft was parked near them, stopping. The pilot was letting the engines idle. Scorpio again went to the door and opened it, letting the stairs go down.

"Good evening," Scorpio said, "I have a couple of guys sure anxious to get home." He walks down the stairs with the State guys right behind him.

Their wives and kids came running over to them and hugged them. One wife told Scorpio, "I don't know who you are, but thank you for bringing them home alive." One of the officials also thanked Scorpio, shaking his hand.

Scorpio started up the stairs when several said, "Thank you." Scorpio turned and said, "You are welcome," waving at them. He closed the door.

The pilot began to taxi to the runway and was in line with three other aircraft for takeoff. Once airborne and cleared the traffic pattern, the pilot turned to a heading of 250 degrees for the first leg home. A couple of hours later, the Global touched down at the base runway. It was 3:12 a.m. The team was glad to get home – the Global parked by the operations building. Scorpio opened the door, and the stairs went down.

"Good morning," Boss said. "The chef has a great breakfast ready."

"That sounds great. It has been a while since we had a good meal," Scorpio said. "Grab your gear," he told the guys and waved at the pilot, "come in for breakfast. You had a long flight also; take a nap before you head home."

"I'll go for that," the pilot said.

A couple of hours later, everyone sat back, enjoying the conversation. The pilot remarked, "You guys get fed like this all the time?"

"Most of the time, yes. But you need to be here for seafood night and BBQ night. That is a real feed," Jasper said.

"Oh, by the way, Boss, I spoke with Mama Bear about our two ladies who want to be part of the team. It is not about being on the team but needing our help." Scorpio said, finishing his coffee. "These two ladies travel among many factions throughout most of

South America. They provide medical help, including to the terrorists."

"Now you are talking about the hooker and nun, I assume? Assisting the terrorists is my only issue. Why would they do that?"

"Well, Boss, yes, on the ladies. Because they provide medical help for everyone, they get a free ride anywhere in the region. The thing is that corrupt officials run several areas they help. These evil thugs torture, rape, and kill civilians to get money and other valuables from their victims. The ladies tried to relocate some of the victims, but they were found, which didn't help. The thugs find them, and most are then killed. Mama Bear is going to arrange to meet them or talk by Skype. Mama thought they might ask if we could remove a few individuals."

"Interesting. I'm sure their work is appreciated and essential. But this could become a high-risk problem and jeopardize our real mission." Boss said.

"Agree with you, Boss. Until now, our missions are through the CIA and funded by them. I'm unsure if anyone supports the ladies' work or will be a pro bono."

"I guess you will know more details after you talk to them. Maybe the team needs to discuss it before discussing it with the ladies?"

"Yeah, that would be good to get everyone's input. We are doing well, money-wise, so I don't think the pro bono will make any difference. Well… it depends on how many missions and costs to do them."

"Scorpio, Mama Bear, is on line 1," Zula said.

"Okay, thanks." Scorpio walked into his office, picked up the phone, and pressed line 1. "Hello, Mama Bear."

"Hey, I just talked to the two ladies, and they would be available to Skype tomorrow around 2:00 p.m. your time. Are you open to that?"

"Sure, the Boss is here also and will join us. Maybe a couple of the guys will want to meet them."

"Okay, we will call tomorrow. See you then." Bear hung the phone up.

Scorpio walked into the conference room. Everyone was there having a drink except for Jane and Angelique; they were still working on a computer program. "Just let you know Mama Bear will Skype us tomorrow at two. We will be introduced to the ladies and talk about what they want us to do. Also, I want you to be thinking about this. Their mission may be pro bono. Any questions?"

"You mean we may not get an R&R after their missions?" Star inquired.

"Hey, that is a good question," Cosmo said.

"Ah, maybe we need to hear their proposal first. If we do this pro bono, the CIA may not support it, and probably the Senator won't know. My concern is, would doing their mission bring problems to our doorstep?" Jasper questioned.

No one said anything. Jasper got up, went to the bar, and fixed another drink. He turned around, "Well, any thoughts on that?"

"I'm not sure if I follow you," Cosmo said.

"Let's say we do several of these missions." Jasper paused to add some ice to his drink. "Don't you think someone will get the idea they need to find out who we are, and if they find that out, what prevents them from knocking on our door and throwing a grenade in?"

"Jasper has a good point. Our projects have been through the CIA so that any follow-up would lead them there. In the case that Jasper is questioning… well, it is a possibility," Boss said.

"There are several things we need to study. Tomorrow, we might learn more about what we may get involved with and if we accept their projects," Scorpio said. "Maybe we do one, but I understand what Jasper is saying. If we hit several mission types, someone will want to know who we are and hire someone to investigate. I'm not sure we want that to happen."

The pilot got up. "Well, guys, spending time with you and having a great breakfast was a pleasure. Next time, try to arrange it so I'm here during your seafood night. Okay? Until next time, I'm heading home."

"Say," the Boss said, "I never knew where your home is?"

"Oh," the pilot said, "I live in Oklahoma, a wide spot in the road called Broken Arrow. My dad was from the Muscogee Nation, and my mom was from France. Talk about a combination! I know I don't look Native American, but I am. My Native name is Tomochirchi, which means 'causes to fly up.' But you can call me Bill. I run and own a flying service there. Thanks to you guys, I can stay in business. Thanks."

"Your family still lives there?" Jasper asked.

"No, both of my parents have passed on. My dad was a bomber pilot during WWII. The jacket I wear is his. I have a son, forty-two, a girl, forty-five – both flies." His eyes were aplomb as he continued, "and seven grandchildren. Now you know why I have grey hair. One is an attorney, and the other is my flight instructor. My wife is a full-blood Muskogee and is the boss."

Everyone laughed.

"I'm glad you are our pilot. Maybe we'll have you and your family fly out and have a seafood night with us. By the way, have you met the helicopter pilot we have used down south? He wears the same type of bomber jacket you have."

"Nope, never have met him. Like there isn't enough time to do that; maybe we could squeeze in a few minutes next time?"

"We can do that next time. We will let you know when we can have your family for a seafood night." Scorpio said.

"You got it. Just let me know when. Thanks, guys. I enjoy helping you. The work you do is important. Catch ya later." He waved, got into the Global 8000, and headed home.

Scorpio walked over to the bar and fixed a double. "Interesting. How come with all the flying Bill has done for us, we never took time to know anything about him?"

"I think because that is our rule, not to know who we work with," Cosmo said. "Be great to have them out sometime for a feast."

Angelique and Jane walked in. "Oh, I see you guys started happy hour without us," Angelique said.

"Yeah, I guess we did. You two get the programming done?" Scorpio asked.

"Sure did," Angelique said. "Boss, next time you come, you have to bring Jane. We had fun, and it was nice to talk to another female. Besides, your wife has some great ideas about running a business. We could use that. Oh, and some good information about men."

"Oh, crap, now I'm in trouble," Joker said.

Everyone laughed.

"Joker, it was all good stuff," Jane said.

"Boss, we are trying to plan for Angelique to go to D.C. to the CIA to install and train them on the tracking software. The problem is most of us are supposed to be dead. The FBI may be nosing around there," Scorpio said. "I think she is on your payroll. Maybe we can arrange a way to work that angle?"

"Yeah, we can do that. When do you plan that?"

"We're supposed to do that tentatively next week."

"Huh, not sure how to pull that off!"

"Well, I do," Jane said. "Angelique can go back with us, spend a couple of days, then you two fly out to D.C., do your thing, and come back. Then we bring her back here."

"Yeah, then Jane and I can do more work together." Angelique was excited about that idea. "That would work well."

"Boss, you got the feeling two women ganged up against you?" Scorpio remarked.

"Ah, yeah, I think so. The girls could be right. That may work."

The sun was coming up. Breakfast in an hour and a half, Scorpio said to himself, looking at his watch. He had worked up a sweat. He was in the lead, and his team was behind him. All were carrying a seventy-five-pound backpack on a ten-mile run. Scorpio began to pick up the pace for the last mile. He reached the team house and came to a stop. "Well," pausing, catching his breath, Scorpio said, "not a bad run. Just let you know we carved off seven minutes from our last run."

"Okay," Jasper said, "why are we trying to kill ourselves?"

"On our last mission hiking out, you all were dragging. I know we went almost seventy-two hours without sleep. But we have been slacking off the last couple of months. We must get back up to our normal level and stay that way. We don't need to kill someone because we are not in shape. We never know what kind of situation we may get involved in. Need to make sure we are ready." Scorpio was explaining.

"I'm hitting the showers," Bingo said. "Looking forward to the chef special."

After breakfast, the rest of the morning was spent finishing up gear inventory and what supplies were on hand. Angelique requested that part of her job be keeping track of equipment and the team's mission status.

"Guys, we have about twenty minutes before Mama Bear and her two ladies will be on the videophone. Oh, Cosmo, could you route that to our large screen T.V.?"

"Yes, all ready to go, Scorpio. I think that will be great, and we can all participate in the call."

Everyone found their way into the conference room. Boss and the girls were there. Scorpio asked, "Cosmo, how does this work?"

"As soon as Mama Bear calls in, the computer will route the signal to the T.V. We should see them immediately."

Everyone was ready. "I wonder what our hooker and nun will look like?" Bingo wanted to know.

"What do you mean?" Star asked.

"Will the nun and the hooker in a short skirt and high heels be in her habit?" Everyone chuckled.

You could hear a pin drop when the image came on the T.V. There were Mama Bear and two beautiful ladies. Which was which? Everyone was thinking.

"Good afternoon, Mama Bear. Nice to see you," Scorpio said.

"Good afternoon, Scorpio. It's nice to see the team as well. I want to introduce," pointing to her right. "This is Sister Karen." She appeared to be about five feet tall, medium build, a brunette, and forty years old. She wore a camouflage jumpsuit with a machete strapped to her left side. "And to my left is Madam Elizabeth. She prefers to be called Lizzy." Lizzy was slightly taller than Sister Karen. She looked a little younger, a blonde, and wore a camouflage jumpsuit, her machete strapped to her right side. Both looked like they would not take any guff from anyone.

"It is nice to meet you, ladies. I go by code name Scorpio, the team leader, and my team will introduce themselves." Each member said their code name and what their assigned job was.

Sister Karen spoke up. "Why do you have code names? Your assigned jobs are interesting. But do understand, considering the type of work you do."

"Sister Karen, we go by code names in case during a mission we are caught, then nobody knows the real names. We have two other folks here at the base. Angelique, our computer support, and Jane, the boss's wife. They are working on computer problems."

"We know Angelique," Lizzy said. "We have met her on a couple of occasions. We're happy she is with you and understand she is working on becoming an American. How is that going, Angelique?"

"It is going great, Lizzy. Not too much longer, I hope. Hey, it is good to see both of you again."

Cosmo said, "Just wondering, are you experts at using your machetes?"

"Cosmo, yes, we are experts, but mostly use them for protection in the bush and cutting through the jungle. Oh, sorry for the outfits. We just came out of the bush a few minutes ago and didn't have time to change and put lipstick on."

The team laughed. "No problem, we didn't dress up for the occasion either," Scorpio said. "Lizzy, your accent makes me believe you are from New York City?"

"Yes, sir, the big apple. I ran an underground brothel there. That was eight years ago. Now I'm with the sister."

"Sister, what part of the world are you from?' Bingo asked.

"I was born in Canada. After high school, I decided God was my life and went to the monasteries at St Joseph's Carmelite Monastery in Florida, and there was a nunnery you might call a convent. I was there for a few years and came to Brazil six years ago. I met Mama Bear, and a year later, I met Lizzy. We teamed up to help the unfortunate people in Brazil and neighboring countries."

"Not to be nosy," Jasper said. "But Lizzy, how did you get started in your profession?"

"Well, I was twelve, and my boyfriend kept trying to get in my pants."

"That's young to be dating to me."

"Well, my dad didn't exist anymore, and my mom was what I would call a barfly."

"Okay, well, I understand, but my original question was how you got started."

"One night at the drive-in theater, we were in the back seat making out. He tried to get in my pants again, and I said NO! Well, he pulled out a condom and a hundred-dollar bill. I said what is that for. He told me the condom was to protect me from getting pregnant."

"That was considerate of him," Jasper said. "And the hundred?"

"The hundred was to get laid. Well, I thought about it. Gee, I can make money with what I have between my legs, and I don't have to have a degree."

Everyone chuckled.

"Anyway, that grew to the point where several ladies worked for me. We provided a service to high-end clients, $1000 per trick or more, depending on who the client was. That's how it started. The rest is history," Lizzy commented.

"What about you, Sister?" Jasper questioned.

"Well, it didn't start that way for me. My mom made me go to Sunday school, which I hated. I wasn't sure if there was a God. One day, a good friend of mine was in a car accident. He was in a coma for several weeks before his family decided to take him off life support. I spent most of every day by his side. When life support was removed, most of his family left. I stayed holding his hand and leaned over and kissed him. I said a prayer, asking God to spare him. He was too nice of a guy to die young. Almost an hour later, I could feel his hand move. I looked up, and he opened his eyes and looked at me. His first words were, "Hi beautiful, it is nice to see you.""

"Whoa, Sister." Jasper continued, "That must have surprised everyone there?"

"Yeah, true. But to make a long story short, I decided to give my life to God, and as Lizzy said, the rest is history."

No one said anything for several minutes.

"How do you see our role with your team, Sister?" Scorpio finally said.

"There are times we try to relocate people to safer areas. Village officials beat people for various reasons. We find that it does not always work. Right now, we have a village near the headwaters of the Negro River. The village has about 700 people. They work their butts off trying to live. A few years ago, six guys came and took over the village. They take whatever the people earn through extortion and threats to kill them."

"Don't they have any law enforcement officials?" Joker asked.

"These thugs are the law," Lizzy said. "Sister and I have had our lives threatened. But so far, we get by and come and go as needed because we provide medical help. But every time we go back, we find some folks missing. We're sure they are dead."

"Like I already said, what is our role?" Scorpio repeated himself.

"We don't condone what you do," Sister said. "But we see no other way these people can have a future without these thugs gone."

"So, you are contracting us to remove them?" Jasper said.

"I don't know, I guess so," Lizzy said. "But that is another problem. We know you don't do this for free. This work is a business, and you expect to be paid."

"But you don't have money," Scorpio stated.

"How much would you normally get paid for a job like this?" Sister asked.

"Maybe a couple of million, I guess, depends."

"DOLLARS!"

"It costs money, Sister—money to get there and back, to get up the river and back. Sometimes, we must pay people off to be quiet about the mission. Sometimes there is collateral damage."

"What do you mean, collateral damage?" Sister asked.

"Sometimes we may have to kill someone not part of the original mission, just because they get in the way, or we can't leave a witness."

"Oh my god! I don't know if I can be part of this."

"Yes, oh my god, it happens. If you ask us to take these thugs out, there is only one way: kill them. If you can't be part of that, we can't help you. Unless you have a better way?"

"Can I say something?" Mama Bear asked.

"Yes, Mama, we trust your judgment," Lizzy said.

"You girls must understand that these guys will put their lives on the line. They could get killed themselves. It isn't just walk in, bang, and leave. Oh, no pun intended, Lizzy on the bang-bang." Everyone laughed. "There is a lot that goes into a mission like this. The Captain and I will do our part pro bono this time."

"Our team talked earlier," Scorpio said, "and we would also do it pro bono depending on the mission. However, we don't want to get into a routine of doing these assignments. It could get to a point where we become the hunted. But we need to know where they are, how we find them, and other logistics to get the right people."

"I guess I don't understand what you are saying," Sister said. "Become the hunted?"

"If we take on several of these mission types in the same area, potential targets will want to find and kill us before we get wise to them. As I said, we don't want to be the hunted."

"Oh, yes, now I understand. Lizzy and I don't expect we would have many of these requests. We have been doing this for several years, and this is the first time we think they must be removed before many more people go missing."

"Sister, we understand your position with God," Cosmo said. "I believe in the Book of Exodus 21:23-27 it expresses the principle of reciprocal justice measure for measure."

"Yes, you are right, Cosmo, but what about Matthew 5:38-40 about turning the other cheek?"

"The Bible is full of contradictions. Leviticus 24:19-21 Whatever anyone does to injure another person must be paid back in kind. Romans 12:19: Vengeance is mine; I will repay, saith the Lord."

"Okay," Scorpio commented. "Thanks for the Bible lesson. The bottom line is if we do this mission, the terrorists will die, and maybe one or more of us may, too. But this is what we need, and

Mama Bear may help you as she knows the area. But we need the exact location, number of targets, where they are, their routine, and what type of protection they have. If you can get that, then we can schedule a mission."

"Sounds good," Mama Bear said. "The Captain and I can get some of the information. The girls must return to the village and document the other information. Then, we will have another video conference. That work, Scorpio?"

"Yup, that works. Girls, are you with us?"

"Yes, we are. Thank you, Scorpio, and God bless you and your team. Talk to you later," Sister said.

The video ended. Scorpio got up, walked to the bar, and fixed a double scotch on the rocks. Walking back to the table, he said. "I think we need to do some pre-work. Cosmo, you pull up the imagery of the headwaters of the Negro River. Jasper, you head up a study team and gather whatever you can find about the area. Maybe you can find something about this village. We will see what we have tomorrow and design a basic plan." Scorpio was finishing his scotch. "Once we get whatever the girls and Mama Bear come up with, we can decide what to do."

The phone rings in Scorpio's office. Scorpio walked over and picked up the phone, "Hello, yes, it is Scorpio, this T.J.?"

"Hi, Scorpio. Yes, T.J. is here. We are calling about Angelique coming to Washington. We are anxious to get the tracking program. We were hoping next week would work?"

"We have talked about that. Maybe the end of next week, let's say Thursday. The boss will probably escort her there."

"Thursday will work, say around 1:00 p.m. Let me know the airline and arrival time, and I will send someone to meet them."

"Okay, T.J., I will get back to you by tomorrow. Talk to you later." Scorpio hangs up.

Scorpio walks back into the conference room. "Boss, how does next Thursday work for you in taking Angelique to Washington to meet with T.J. and the CIA on the software?"

"I think we will plan on flying out Wednesday afternoon, and Jane will fly home. After taking care of the CIA, Angelique will fly home with me. She is on our payroll, so it would be a good idea for Angelique to become familiar with the Company before people start asking questions. She can work there for a couple of weeks. She can stay with us. We have an extra bedroom. I know Jane will enjoy the time with Angelique."

"Sounds like a great idea. That will help her cover. Tell me your flight information, and I will pass that on to T.J."

"Scorpio, Boss, I just got a message from Mama Bear. She wants a video conference this afternoon. A couple of hours from now, maybe 4:00 p.m. will work. Bear has the information we need," Bingo said.

"Okay, go ahead and set it up. Let everyone know."

Several minutes later, everyone was in the conference room. Scorpio said, "Before Mama Bear calls, I wanted to take time and review what we have. What questions do we need to ask? Cosmo and Jasper, what did you come up with?"

Both presented their findings. Cosmo said, "We have a potential plan, but we need the information. Hopefully, Mama Bear will give us the key to moving ahead with a mission."

"Thanks. Any questions?"

About then, the T.V. came on with a message: 'video connection complete – Press start to begin.' Cosmo reached over and did just that.

Mama Bear and the girls came into view. "Hi, guys," Mama Bear said. "We're ready. I think we have everything you need."

"Good to see you, ladies," Scorpio said. "Oh, you didn't have to dress up. Are you sure you are the same two ladies we spoke too before?"

They just laughed, "Yes, we are the same Scorpio. Thanks for asking. We don't always get cleaned up for men, but you are so handsome we didn't want to scare you again," Lizzy said.

"Oh, don't say that. You get these guys hormones riled up, and they won't be able to think straight." Everyone laughed. "Okay, what do you have for us?"

Mama Bear said, "Lizzy, present what you and Sister found."

"Good to see you guys also," Lizzy said. "We have eight targets, six prominent people; the other two are professional hitmen. They live in a two-story cabin on the edge of the village on the north side. It is on a small hill overlooking the village. No windows on the first floor and only one door. The upper level has a deck with a large door into the cabin and no stairs to the deck. There are two windows on each end and no windows on the backside." She paused, looking at her notes. "Oh, yes, there are cameras, two of them. One on each end of the cabin pointed towards the village. I think that's it."

"Don't forget the map," Sister said.

"Map… Oh, yeah, I have a sketch of the inside of the cabin the cleaning lady gave me. I'll hold it up so you can copy it, as we cannot fax it. The first page is on the first floor. As you can see, it is just one big room with the stairs going up in the center. You got it?"

"Yeah, I got it," Scorpio said, "let's see page two."

"Here is page two. The second floor looks like four bedrooms, two on each side, with a hallway down the center with the stairs entering the second floor in the back wall center. Oh, and the cleaning lady said the bedroom doors open to the inside, except the northwest corner. For some reason, it opens out, and several weapons are in that room. She didn't know what kind they were. She just said they were big guns with long barrels. There were several strange-looking things she didn't know what they were. But she said they had short legs, and one side said FRONT TOWARD ENEMY. The northeast bedroom had two sets of bunk beds, the southwest bedroom had a single and double bed, and the southeast bedroom had two sets of bunk beds. It also had a table with radio communication type gear."

"Claymores," Scorpio said. "Thank you, Lizzy. That information is the key to this mission. Without it, we could have walked into a trap. Thank you for your detailed report. Mama Bear, what is your and Captain Sixto's schedule for the next two weeks?"

"We can be available anytime; just give me a date and time, and we will make it work," Mama Bear said.

"Okay, let us study this for a couple of days and see what we come up with. Also, we already have a detailed satellite picture of the village and see the cabin you mentioned. I will get back to you on a plan and schedule." Everyone said their goodbyes, and the video session concluded.

"Okay, it looks like we have enough information. Let's all study it, and then in a couple of hours, let's have a planning session and see where all your ideas come together," Scorpio said.

Scorpio and Boss walked into the computer room. Angelique and Jane were so involved in their project that they didn't see them walk in. "Are you two ready for a break?" Boss asked.

"Oh!" they both exclaimed, surprised by their entering the room. "Yes, what's up?" Jane asked.

"Well, Angelique and I are flying to Washington, D.C., next Wednesday so she can install and train the CIA folks on the tracking software. Then we'll meet you at home. Having her work out of the Company office for a few weeks would be good. She has been on the payroll and probably should show for the record she does work for us for her cover. She can stay with us."

"Angelique, you okay about staying with us for a while?" Jane asked her.

"Am I okay? Holy crap, YES! That would be so much fun. I enjoy working with you, Jane, and you can show me much more that would help us at the base."

"Well, that's the plan then," Scorpio said.

Scorpio was in the meeting room, looking at the maps and imagery. He looked at his watch; it was about 20 minutes before Mama Bear would do another video phone conference. The rest of the team walked in, making small talk. The T.V. was coming on and downloading the conference information. Before long, there was Mama Bear, Lizzy, Sister, and Captain Sixto.

"Hi," Scorpio said. "Good to see you all again. The team has developed a plan we would like to share with you and get your feedback. Jasper, go for it."

"Good to see you," Jasper said. "Here is the plan. We fly out in two days and land around 7:00 a.m. in Manaus. On Wednesday. Have Mate pick us up as usual. We take the boat up the river about a mile past the village. From that point, we work our way back to the backside of the village. Locate the cabin. That should be around midnight the next day. Check out the camera locations. We think they are used to monitor daily activity in the village. If not, then we will make some changes then. Two will enter the front door. While six of us enter by the deck and assume it is a patio door. Because there are claymores, we must be aware of trip lines at both entries. The two that enter from the main door will secure the first floor and be prepared to take out anyone trying to escape down the stairs. Once the six are in the second story, two per door, except where the weapons are. We think that is their weapon stash; most likely, no one stays there at night. Each two-person team will use a pin camera and check out the status. If we're lucky, they will all be asleep." Jasper paused, looking through his notes and finishing his coffee. "If that is the case, we ease the doors open, walk in and take them out."

"Now that's the easy part," Scorpio said. "We won't know several factors until we execute the mission. The security camera, doors locked, wire traps, if they're sleeping, and other factors we won't know about until we are there. Follow me so far?"

"Yes," Mama Bear said. "Let's say for now that is how it goes. Then what?"

"After we make sure we account for all the thugs. We burn the place down. That should make the locals happy. If possible, Mama Bear contacts someone in the village. Maybe Lizzy or the Sister would know who that would be. My thinking is we could meet with them. Show them how to keep their village safe and take care of any other thugs who may want to continue to run the village. We'd like not to have to come back again. Maybe the village people have had enough of the past and want to run it their way."

"Okay, that'd be great," Mama Bear said. "Now, what happens if they're not all accounted for or have other security personnel?"

"Those are things we must be ready for and plan how we deal with at that time. But we have been doing this for a lot of years. We have found not many missions go as planned. Always, some little thing comes up. But we usually deal with it quickly and move on. Before we leave, we want to ensure the village people can secure the village and protect it. We won't be back to do it again."

"Understand," Lizzy said. "Both Sister and I know several people that would fit that bill. Several would step up to protect the village from this happening again. They need the equipment to do it."

"I could arrange about 300 AR-15s and ammo within a couple of days," Captain Sixto said.

Everyone was surprised. "Captain, where would you get that in a short time?" Jasper inquired.

"I have a weapon cache about twenty-five miles from the village. Terrorists have been bringing weapons in for the past four years. They don't keep track too closely. I have been skimming a few off their shipments and gathering weapons from the pirates."

"Hey, Captain, I didn't even know you did that!" Mama Bear said

"That was something I kept to myself, figuring someday it would be needed for a good cause."

"How much do you hope to collect for this good cause?" Scorpio asked.

"In this case, nothing. Villagers must be willing to take on the responsibility to keep the village people safe from the bad dudes."

"This is good," Sister said, "I don't condone killing, but this may work out better than Lizzy and I had hoped."

"Okay, let us move forward with the mission, and with God's help, it will go smoothly," Scorpio said. "Mama Bear and Captain, we'll see you in a few days." They said their goodbyes.

"Jasper, better get the pilot informed that we are returning to Brazil," Scorpio said.

Jim was looking out the window. "Angelique, there is the Washington Monument. We are about to fly over the Pentagon and land at Ronald Reagan Washington National Airport." Jim looked over at Angelique. She was smiling from ear to ear, and she was excited. Their flight was touching down. Ten minutes later, they were taxiing up to their gate. They grabbed their bags from overhead and walked into the jetway to the terminal building. It wasn't long before Jim spotted T.J. by the outside door.

"Hi, T.J."

"Hi, Boss and Angelique. Sure, good to see you. We have a couple of rooms outside the CIA grounds at the hotel. I have a car out front waiting for us. I thought we'd drive through the city on the way so Angelique could see several sites. We're meeting the Director tonight at your hotel for dinner. Angelique, we have everything you requested ready to go in the morning. Also, Boss, you said your flight home was 4 p.m.?"

"Yes, that is the plan. Angelique made her program user-friendly," Boss said.

"Yes, it is elementary and runs great," Angelique said. "Oh, what's that over there?"

"That is the White House," T.J. responded.

"I know we don't have time this trip, but someday, I'd like to spend several days here. Lots of history, and I love history."

"Well, I know we will probably be back. Maybe after you become a U.S. Citizen, Jane and I can bring you here for a few days and visit all these places," Jim said.

"That would be wonderful. Oh, sorry, T.J. What were you saying about the software?"

"We are excited to see it. Oh, here is your hotel. Get checked in and freshen up, and meet me in the bar. The Director will be here shortly."

"Okay, T.J., we will see you in about fifteen minutes," Boss said.

A few minutes later, Boss and Angelique walked into the bar. The boss saw T.J. sitting at a table with several other guys. One looked like the Director. Not sure about the other one, he thought. They walked over to where the others were sitting.

T.J. stood up and said, "This is the Director of the CIA and Agent Johnson of our computer security unit. And guys, this is Boss. For security reasons, we will leave it at that. This is Angelique, the computer whiz that goes into our system and plays games with it." They all shook hands.

"Well," Agent Johnson said. "Angelique, I don't know how you got into our system. I'm sure anxious to find out how, and to track us was amazing."

"Agent Johnson, it was easy to get into your system. Your security program did what it was designed to do, except for one thing."

"What's that?"

"Well... once it detects a bad guy coming into your system, it sends it to the spam folder to secure the message, and it doesn't do anything with it."

"That's right, that is what it is supposed to do. It earmarks the intruder and puts it in a folder to keep it from getting into the main system."

"Yup, and it was easy to play with once I figured that out. By the way, I can fix your system to make it more secure."

"Oh," T.J. said, looking at Agent Johnson, "I thought our system routed what Angelique said as bad guys to a secure place on the server?"

"But T.J.," Angelique said, "it does. That is why it took me a couple of hours to figure it out."

"COUPLE OF HOURS! Is that all!" Agent Johnson exclaimed.

Angelique laughed, "Yup, but don't be hard on yourself. I got into the Russian system yesterday. They made the same mistake." She giggled. "You are all trying to make it so hard to get into your systems. You made it easy."

"Okay, Angelique," the Director said. "Can you explain what you mean by making it hard that made it easy?"

"Sure, but I want a glass of wine first. Take a minute to relax my mind. Then I will give you a lesson in computer tracking 101."

The Director was taken aback, "Oh, Okay… Well, we better get that wine. By the way, you want to work for the CIA. I could use a gal like you, and it pays well. I like your attitude."

"No, I don't think so. It is not about money, but I like where I'm at. Thank you anyway."

After some small talk, Angelique finished her wine a few minutes later. "Okay, are you ready for your lesson in Tracking 101?"

"We're all ears," the Director said.

"Well. Once a bad guy tries to get into the system, it is picked up by a security program, earmarked as a bad dude, and sent to a spam folder or whatever you want to call it. Once there, the system doesn't let it get outside the file because it now has an earmark. Works great. I love earmarks; they are so stupid."

The director looks at Agent Johnson, "Are you getting this? You follow what she just said?"

"Yeah, kind of," Agent Johnson said. "Okay, it has an earmark. That is how it is identifying it to keep it secured."

"Yes, that's right, that is why I could get around that. What I did once I figured out the earmark stuff. I sent a series of small apps. Of course, they were picked up, earmarked, and sent to the bad guy file. Love it. Then my last app had the key to the others." She stopped to take another sip of her wine. "This is pretty good stuff. What's the name of it?"

"Huh?" The question took Agent Johnson back. "Oh, I'm not sure, just a red wine."

"I could use another one."

The Director waved the waiter over, "Would you get this young lady another glass of wine, please?"

"Yes, Sir."

The Boss was trying not to smile or laugh. He knew Angelique was playing with them and having fun doing it.

"What were you saying about your last app?" Director asked, being caught off guard by the wine question.

"Oh, sure." Angelique was having fun playing with the Agent. "Of course, that app was earmarked as well. Again, it was sent to the secure folder. My last app builds a program from parts of the other apps, like determining its location. Like a GPS, it also builds a program to do the other functions I need for whatever purpose I want."

"Wow, now wait a minute. This new program or app is still on the secure server," the director said.

"Yes, right. But because it was built in that environment, it never got earmarked. So, I can go wherever and do whatever I want. Everyone uses earmarks to tag something. That's why it is so stupid!"

"Yes, but it is still in the secure server." Agent Johnson said.

"Yes, until I tell it what to do, and because it does not have an earmark, the security system thinks it is part of the system and lets it do whatever it wants. Zip-pa-dee-doo off it goes."

"I'll be a suck-egg-mule!" Agent Johnson exclaimed.

"Oh, don't be hard on the mule. So, that is how the basic program gets created. It uses part of the security system, routing data, or other files I want to use already on the computer. It's pretty simple from there. I can do whatever I want and own the computer at that point. The security system checks it, but because there are no earmarks and it is built with parts that have been approved, well… that's it. You'll see tomorrow how well it works. And if interested, I can fix your earmarks."

"Yes, how do you fix that? We have spent millions on this system to keep it the most secure globally," the Director said.

"Well, I'm sorry to burst your bubble, Director, but we have the most secure system in the world."

The Boss smiles, trying not to laugh.

"How do we fix our system to be the second most secure globally?" The director asked, smiling.

"Well, we start by buying me dinner. I'm hungry and can't think on an empty stomach."

"Let's get to it," the Director said. "Let's go to the dining room. By the way, Angelique, this place has one of the best buffets in the world."

T.J. looked at the Director, "Don't count on that. I have been at their base during seafood night. It is the best in the world."

The director just smiled, thinking he would have to make a trip one day.

Everyone was enjoying dinner. The director and Boss were making small talk, and Agent Johnson had his notepad making notes. Angelique enjoyed her dinner and took a sip of her wine, smiling. She thought this was so much fun playing with these CIA guys. She was done with dinner, sat back, and stretched.

"Okay, you ready to hear how you can fix your system?"

"Yes, we are," the Director said.

"I create a bubble around all earmarked files. This bubble has only one job. It is to guard. It is like a soldier marching around prisoners, left, right, left, right, etc. When something tries to escape, the guard kills it."

Agent Johnson peered at T.J. "Is she crazy?"

"Yes, she is," the Director said, "and I love it. We need a few more crazy people like her to improve this world."

"Okay, tell me more about this bubble," Agent Johnson said.

"As I said, the program only has one purpose. It protects everything around the earmarked program. It does not let anything in or out. The trouble is it never dies. The only way you can get rid of it is to transfer the whole file that contains the bad guys onto a hard drive. A CD or thumb drive will not work. The hard drive must be part of the computer, not a plug-and-play type. Once the file is transferred to the hard drive, you shut down the computer. Then, replace the hard drive with precisely the same type. Destroy the one you take out. That's about it." His eyes scanned the room.

"Questions?"

"Oh god, yes," the Director said. "Why won't a CD or a thumb drive work? And why do you have to shut the computer down to remove and destroy the hard drive? Can't you delete the file?"

"Nope, the security systems are developed to detect CD and thumb drives as devices to steal data. The system ignores it and does not allow it to copy or read from it. That includes external hard drives. That is why the hard drive has to be a built-in model. Also, the guards doing their job will not allow the file to be deleted. If you do not destroy the hard drive and install it somewhere else, it will automatically destroy the entire system, programs, and everything. So, don't try it unless you want to eliminate a system and the whole system."

"Why does it do that?" Director asked.

"Don't know."

"Why do you have to shut the computer down to remove the hard drive?" T.J. asked.

"When the system is not running, you can remove and replace the hard drive. The system does not seem to care. But if you do it while it is still running, it is a tizzy. It means it does not know what to do and may repeatedly get stuck trying to answer the same problem, like playing tic tac toe. There is no winner. The security system gets tired of playing the same game and shuts down the system. I'm not sure why yet. Someday, I'll figure it out."

"My brain is wearing out," the Director said. "Let's call it a night. T.J. will pick you two up tomorrow at about eight. That should give us enough time to get you to the airport on time. Angelique, thank you for a very entertaining evening. It has been a lot of fun, and I learned more tonight than I had in years; thank you again, and see you tomorrow."

Everyone said goodbye. Boss and Angelique headed to their rooms. On the way, Angelique said, "I sure enjoyed the evening. I can't remember when I had so much fun."

"I had fun, too. It was interesting watching you explain the process. You had a unique way of getting your point across. Have a good night. See you in the morning."

Scorpio was waking up. He looked at his watch. He heard the jet engines winding down for descent into Manaus. This will be an interesting mission—a couple of professional gunmen to take out.

The team was awakened by the noise of the landing gear going down. "Looks like we're about their guys," Scorpio said.

Minutes later, the Global 8000 touched down. Taxiing to the cooperate hangar didn't take long. The aircraft stopped, and the engines shut down. Scorpio opened the door, and the stairs went down. "Hi, Mate," Scorpio said.

"Hi yourself, back for another vacation, huh?"

"Yeah, right. Mama Bear and the Captain ready to go?"

"Yup, I just called them when I saw your airplane land and let them know we will be there in about 30 minutes."

"Hi Mate," everyone said, coming down the stairs.

"Good to see you too."

The ride through the town was in the middle of the morning traffic. Getting to the dock was almost a suicide drive. Mate pulled up alongside the boat. Everyone got out, grabbed their gear, and got onto the boat.

Mama Bear smiles. "Hey, good to see you. Have a nice trip?"

"Mama, I swear it gets longer every time we come down," Scorpio said. "We ready to go?"

"Yup, sure are," Mama Bear said. "Oh, we had a slight change." Lizzy and Sister walked out.

"Hi," Lizzy said. "We are headed towards the village. Mama thought we could get a ride if that's okay with you?"

"Oh, well, what is the plan?" Scorpio asked.

"You had mentioned after the mission was complete, you wanted to get people together and meet with them."

"Yes, Lizzy, but we don't want them to know about it until the mission ends. Getting them involved before could jeopardize the mission by having too many people knowing about it."

"We understand," Mama Bear said. "The ladies are due to be at the village, so I thought I would get them nearby so they could walk to the village. Therefore, not to raise any suspicion that they are late."

"Okay, so they don't say anything about the mission until it ends."

"Yes, I understand," Lizzy said.

"Hey, we're ready to go," Captain Sixto said.

"Hi, Captain, yup, we're ready. Let's get out of here," Scorpio said.

Before long, they were going upriver. Scorpio sat back. He enjoyed the river. It was relaxing. The vegetation was beautiful. The wildlife was unique in how they all appeared to get along, except when hunting. He put his feet on the edge of the boat, leaned back, and before long, he dozed off. Most of the rest of the team took advantage of getting a nap.

Scorpio jumped and grabbed his 9mil. "Wow, I guess I was dreaming. Are we slowing down?"

"Yeah," Captain said, "we're pulling over. This is where the girls get off. They are about an hour's walk from here. They should get there before sundown."

"We will go about another five miles," Mama Bear said. "By the time we hike to where we want to be, it will be dark."

"Okay, guys, let's ensure our night vision and commo gear are working before starting our hike," Scorpio said.

The boat pulled up next to the river bank. "Okay, girls, have a good walk and say hi to Tarzan for me," Captain said.

"Will do, Captain. You all be safe, God is with you, and we will see you later, Scorpio," Lizzy said.

"Who is Tarzan, Captain?" Jasper asked.

"You know who Tarzan is, don't you?"

"I know the funny book Tarzan and the movie Tarzan."

"This one is the real one."

"Captain, you pulling our leg?" Jasper asked.

"Yeah, Captain, is this jungle gossip?" Bingo wanted to know.

"No, really, there is a Tarzan. Have Lizzy or Sister tells you about him. They know him better than anyone," Mama Bear said.

Jasper and Bingo laughed, "I think we are being set up!"

It was several minutes later. Captain steered the boat towards a small cove. Mate tied up the boat and started to camouflage it with brush. Fifteen minutes later, they had all their gear on and ready for Mama Bear to lead them to the backside of the cabin. It was beginning to get dark. A couple of hours later, they were near the cabin.

Mama Bear stopped. "Scorpio," she whispered into her mic, which was the size of a pin. A superior design Scorpio had made. It could be used in a crowd without knowing they were communicating with anyone. The earplug receivers were so small they were placed inside the ear next to the eardrum, making them invisible. The device that made the system work was about the size of a cigarette pack carried in the pocket and had a three-mile range.

"Yeah, I hear ya, Mama Bear."

"The cabin is on our left, about a hundred yards. Let us proceed to that large tree near it. That gives us a better view and still has the cover."

"Jasper, you and Cosmo recon the cabin and meet us at the tree."

"Roger that," Cosmo said.

The rest of the team lay down near the tree. "The thugs have a great view of the village from here," Scorpio whispered. Scorpio looked at his watch. Fifteen minutes have passed since the two started the recon. They crawled over to the tree a few minutes later and joined the group.

"What did you find?" Scorpio asked.

"There is a camera on both ends of the cabin. They are attached to the corner facing the village. They are only for daytime use to monitor the village. The door is unlocked. A tripwire runs about four inches off the ground in front of the door. It is a filament line and hard to see. There is a flower pot on the right side, and it has a claymore hidden in the flowers. There was a light on in what we called the radio room and a T.V. in the southwest bedroom. The windows in the other bedrooms didn't show any lights. There is a place where the deck is only six feet off the ground. The entry is a double glass sliding patio door. There is a generator, but it is not being used. Four five-gallon gas cans are full, and it smells like diesel."

"Okay, Jasper, Cosmo, Bingo, Joker, Star, and I will get on the deck and enter through the patio door. Cosmo and Bingo, you take the lead and check for tripwires. Star and Joker, you are taking the northeast bedroom. You will take the southwest bedroom, Bingo and Cosmo, and Jasper and I will take the southeast bedroom.

Barber and Zula, you enter through the main door. Watch out for the tripwire. Captain and Mama Bear will keep the outside secure. We check if the doors are unlocked once we are by the upstairs bedrooms. Once we are ready, I'll say go, and we execute the plan. Make it fast. Don't let anyone out. If someone does, Barber and Zula, it will be up to you to stop them. Captain and Mama, if somehow someone gets out of the cabin, it will be up to you to stop them. Okay, everyone understands your assignment. And any questions?"

Everyone checked in, understood the plan, and was ready. "Okay, let's get to our places," Scorpio said.

They moved out. Cosmo and Bingo boosted Jasper, Joker, Star, and Scorpio onto the deck. Scorpio turned around and helped Cosmo and Bingo onto the deck. Okay, you two check the patio door. A few seconds later, Bingo said, "The door is unlocked, but we have a tripwire. It goes to a claymore." They disconnected the tripwire and opened the door slowly as they looked for additional traps. "Okay, the door is open. Tripwire is disconnected." They entered, got to the bedroom doors, and checked the locks.

Meanwhile, Barber and Zula entered through the main door after disconnecting their tripwire. They checked the room. It was secure. Captain and Mama Bear took positions to cover the outside exit.

Meanwhile, Scorpio asks, "Status of locks?" All reported they were unlocked. Star said, "Have a problem. I hear someone in the weapons room. Now what?"

"Think for a second," Scorpio said. "Okay, the room Jasper and I have is the radio room. Most likely, there is only one person in there. I'll take it. Jasper, you take the weapons room. Let me know when you are ready. Check the lock."

A few seconds went by; everyone was ready. Scorpio said, "Okay, on three: one, two, three."

Everyone proceeded, shots rang out, and the mission was complete within a minute. "Everyone reports," Scorpio said. Everyone reported everything was okay. "All the bad guys accounted for?" That was confirmed. "Did any of the bad guys return fire?" There was a pause. Finally, each team confirmed no return fire. "That is what I like to hear. Okay, let's meet at the main door."

Shortly, they all gathered by the front door. Scorpio said, "Grab the gas cans we found by the generator and dump them inside. Burn the place down."

Eight minutes later, there was a massive fire. It could be seen from the village. People were coming out into the streets, clapping. As the team walked into the village, Jasper said, "What do we do with the ammo and claymores we took out of the cabin?"

"We will give everything to the village police that we will form," Scorpio said.

Both Lizzy and Sister came running up. "All your guys okay, Scorpio?" Sister inquired.

"Yes, we're all okay. No more bad guys."

"The village people are gathering at the village center," Lizzy said. "That would be a great place for you to talk to them. Everyone will be able to hear you."

"Sounds good. Lead me there," Scorpio said.

There were several hundred villagers at the center. Lizzy handed Scorpio a microphone. "We had an announcement system put up when we saw the fire," she said.

Everyone applauded when Scorpio stood up on a makeshift platform. "Ladies and gentlemen, I'm happy to report that the threat to your village has been removed." Everyone applauded and cheered. "You have a choice. You can do nothing to protect your future or appoint village officials and police to protect you from future thugs. We will not be back. It is up to you what your future is."

"We need your help!" Someone yelled out.

"We are willing to stay here for a couple of weeks, train you, and help you establish yourself." Lizzy handed Scorpio a note. He read it. "I understand you appointed your governing officials and security a few months ago." Scorpio was looking at Lizzy and the Sister. They both were smiling. "I have a list of 137 volunteers to form your protection unit. Is that true?"

Everyone yelled, "YES!"

"Okay, here is the plan," Scorpio said. "Beginning tomorrow at 8 a.m., we will begin your training. We will meet here at the village center. Once this meeting is done, I want to meet your governing officials. Everyone okay with that?"

There were loud cheers and applause. "YES! YES!" was the response.

Scorpio leaned to the Captain, "How long will it take you to get the weapons from your cache?"

"If I had a couple of your guys, I could be back here before your training in the morning."

"Good, Star and Bingo, go with the Captain. See you in the morning."

Boss, T.J., and Angelique walked into the CIA secure computer facility. Several computers were set up, and a large T.V. was set up in front of the room. Employees from various CIA departments were waiting for the demonstration.

The Director walked up to the front of the room. "Ladies and gentlemen, I am pleased to introduce our guest—Boss, his code name, and Angelique, an amazing young lady. I enjoyed having dinner last night with them and learned more about programming than I had in my previous twenty years. Angelique, the T.V. is programmed to this computer" pointing, "so everyone can see and follow along with you. Please explain how it works. These folks have experience in programming and will probably have questions as you demonstrate the system. We have already loaded the program you gave me."

"Thank you, Director. You have a cool place here." Everyone chuckled. "You have someone try to hack into this computer. It is easier to explain in real-time." A young man sat beside her on the adjoining computer.

"Yes, that is me. I'm John."

"Hi, John." They shook hands.

"Oh," John said. "Just to let you know, we did a security update on the system last night, so things may differ from the last time you got into the system."

"That's okay. It won't make any difference."

The young man smiled, thinking, you won't get into it this time. "Okay, I'll start."

Angelique said. "This program is like a gate guard. When someone comes knocking at the door, the guard is alerted. As you can see, I split the screen to show you the process and the programming routines simultaneously. So now we are waiting for John to come knocking."

John was typing several commands.

Angelique sat back, watching. "When the program detects the knocking, you will see it here," she pointed to the screen. "Oh, Boss, I made some changes from the last time you saw this, so it won't look like the one we used before."

"That is okay."

Angelique, pointing, "the top of the screen, the word in red," the word 'ALERT' was blinking in red. "That tells me John is about to get into the system I am on. When it stops blinking, he is in the system."

Everyone was focused on the T.V. screen.

"As you can see, John is now in the system. My program, as you see, is doing a few calculations. These calculations determine the access speed, security system protocols, and formats. I see you made some protocol changes, but that won't make any difference. The essential calculation is speed. So, when my apps are sent, they enter at the same rate, not alerting your security system that someone is sneaking in. Okay, there goes my first app. You notice the protocols check the app for what I call live cells. You'll find that in the computer book called Protocols for Dummies." There were a few giggles in the group.

"Angelique," someone from the group said. "Will a change in the protocols stop the app?"

"Not likely. Anyway, I haven't found anything that would work. Again, speed is the key. But your security system gets confused if you change the speed up and down."

"Is there a way we can get around that?" Someone else asked.

"Maybe I haven't been concerned with that as yet. The problem is that changing speeds affects everything on your system, which would be a real challenge."

"I'm not following what is happening now," John said.

"Well, my first five apps are entering the system right now. Your security system thinks they are invaders. So, the system earmarks them to be sent to the junk file or some file you have set up for such things."

"Yes, but that file is secure; don't let anything get out," John said.

"Yup, you're right. Anything that is earmarked cannot leave your secure file. Once the apps are in that file, your system doesn't care what it does. Okay, now my last apps are going through the same routine. Now, in the same file. Now, the last app signals the others to send the newborn to it. I'm not sure where that term came about. It's some computer magazine, I guess. But the newborn is just a couple of commands. It doesn't mean anything by itself, so it doesn't alert the system. But my last app will turn it on once all the controls are combined. This little guy computes the location of the coordinates, like a mini-GPS, and sends it back where the app came from."

"But the apps were earmarked, secured in the file, and can't get out," John said.

"Yup, sure is. However, the newborn app does not have an earmark. Earmarks are attached by security when something that does not belong there is detected. Then, it is sent to the secure file or whatever the file is called. However, the newborn app does not have an earmark because it is already in a secure file and protected before being built. When the newborn app is working, it creates a bubble around it. Like many guards marching around the app, making sure none of the earmarks from the other apps get into the bubble. And because it is in a secure file, nothing outside can help. You see, my program goes in circles. So, if something tries to change or delete, it gets lost because it keeps going in circles."

"I'll be damned," John commented.

"Now, those coordinates have been received and converted to an address. The address is at the top of the screen. Is that where we are at?"

There was silence in the group. "Sure, the hell is," John replied.

"Now, this next part was fun. It sends a message to your system, asking you to turn your camera on for this computer. It will take a few minutes. Your security system could care less because it wasn't trying to invade the system. Just ask the system to look at us."

They were all staring at the TV.

"There we are. You can wave at yourself if you like." Angelique was giggling.

No one said anything. "Well, Angelique," the Director said, "I think we are all stunned and unsure of what to say."

"Director, you don't have to say anything, but maybe 'job well done' would be okay," T.J. said.

Someone started clapping. Within a few minutes, everyone clapped and said, "A job well done."

"Can you make our system secure so this can't happen?" Director questioned.

"Yes, maybe. What I mean is I can make your system more secure and fix several problems with how your system processes information. But that being said, someone may still find a way into your system. However, I can make it difficult for them. Plus, you have this system to find them."

"Do you think anyone else has this capability?" John asked.

"If you mean the tracking system, probably not. But if you mean the best secure system, well, only one place,"

"Where is that?"

"Our base."

"And where is that?" John was pushing to get an answer.

"Well, John, if I told you, I would have to kill you." She said, looking into his eyes with a severe expression. "The problem is I would have to kill almost everyone in this room."

No one said anything. You could hear a pin drop.

The Boss cleared his throat, "She can do that. I've seen her work."

"That's okay. No killing is needed. T.J. and I are the only ones who know where the base is, and that is how it will stay," the Director said.

"Angelique, you are an amazing programmer. I sure wish you were on our team," John said.

"I already tried to hire her, with no success," the Director said.

"Director, if you get into a bind sometimes, maybe we can loan Angelique to you. But we're never going to let her get away," Boss said.

"Okay, I'll keep that in mind. Maybe we could get her for a few weeks to get our system as good as yours, plus train our folks?

"Director, I'm sure we can do that."

Scorpio just finished his second meeting with the village-appointed officials selected by the village people to form a government. Scorpio thought they had things organized with the people in mind. The volunteers who created a police unit showed up for their meeting with Scorpio. He was pleased with the village people who wanted to make things secure and live their lives without being ruled by thugs.

"Scorpio," Star said. "We are back with a load of weapons, ammo, and other gear. We took them to the police station, or what will be the station."

"That is good, Star. You and Bingo have provided training to Afghanistan's soldiers, so you two will be the primary trainers. So, get the rest of our guys to help you and do what you need. Afterward, I'll talk to these volunteers and send them in your direction."

"Okay, I'll be ready in about thirty minutes," Star said.

Scorpio walked over to the group and climbed up in a wagon. The village didn't have cars or trucks but only wagons and mules—no roads outside. However, three well-groomed trails provided access to the village. The main trail went to a dock at the river.

"It's good to see so many willing to provide protection. How many of you know how to fire weapons?"

All raised their hands. "Where did you learn that?"

Most said they served in the Brazilian or Venezuelan military. Others learned from their family members before coming to the village.

"Over there," Scorpio pointed, "I have a team of trainers. They will train you on the AR-15s and some explosives. Has anyone ever used an AR-15?"

There was no answer.

"You'll get plenty of practice and training hand to hand, providing first aid and other defense needs. Who is the head of your unit?"

"I am, Sir." An older man said.

"What experience do you have?"

"I'm a retired major. I served in the Brazilian military. I was in charge of what you would call the MPs for twenty-six years."

"That's great. Are there others that have military experience?"

"Yes, Sir, we have three captains and some NCO ranks in the group."

"I don't understand," Scorpio said. "How did the bad guys take over the village?"

"We had no weapons, and our family's lives were at stake in other places. We tried once, and several of them were killed by the thugs who worked for the guys here."

"What do you think might happen now with your families?"

"We don't know," the major said, "however they were paid by the guys you killed, so their money source is gone. I think they will find other work."

"Okay, let's hope so. Maybe those families can come here. Major, it sounds like you can form a good outfit. Let's get you all checked out on the AR-15s. Also, Major, you know better than us what training you need. So, let's you and I talk more about that. The rest head over there where my guys are. You have a couple of the best trainers; they are ex-marines."

Over the next two weeks, the training went well. Everyone was excited. They now had a way to protect themselves from pirates and other bad guys. Other major concerns were addressed during the meeting, such as outside support and arrangements with the Captain and Mama Bear for different needs.

The team was packing up, getting ready to head back to Manaus in the morning, when the Major stopped by with a couple of his guys.

"Scorpio, thank you again for risking your lives to give us ours back."

"You are welcome. I'm glad it worked out well. I think the training went well. Your guys know what to do. Both the Captain and Mama Bear can always get ahold of us if needed."

"I'm sure we will do just fine now that we can defend ourselves. The village folks are planning a celebration in your honor tonight. It's an old-fashioned BBQ Brazilian style. Lots of drinks and food. It is intended for four this afternoon at the village center. Everyone is excited to send you off with a party. Your team is always welcome to rest if you get up this way again. We would love to have your team as our guest anytime."

"Thank you. We will be at the center on time."

They got the gear down to the dock and ready to load. "Let's put those under the bow and the rest in the storage unit in the stern." "Okay," Scorpio said, "we're ready. It is almost four, and it's time to get some great food and drink."

They all agreed and headed to the center. On the way, Lizzy and Sister joined them. "Lizzy, it was great meeting you and Sister," Scorpio said. "This operation worked out better than expected.

You two, keep up the good work you do. Ah… Let's say that you are now doing."

They laughed. "Yes, Scorpio, we plan to."

They entered the Center. There were flowers and music, and everyone cheered them as the team entered. It was a party.

The mayor said, "Sister, you and Lizzy were responsible for bringing us help. We love you both. Thank you from the bottom of our hearts for bringing us this team and securing our freedom. Sister, before we enjoy this great meal, would you say the blessing?"

"Thank you, mayor. It would be an honor," she paused, "Dear Lord, bless those who brought this meal to celebrate this moment in our new freedom. Bless Scorpio and his team for risking their lives for our freedom and protecting them on other missions. God bless our people in their struggles and guide us in our future. In God's name, Amen."

"Thank you, Sister," the mayor said. "Now, let us celebrate our freedom. Everyone, take time this evening to thank Scorpio and his team."

It was a grand celebration. People thanked the team for their new life. It was almost midnight when Lizzy and Sister walked over to the team.

"You all about ready to head for home?" Lizzy asked. "We want to thank you again for your help. We know the village people will always remember you and what this team did for them."

"Thank you, Lizzy and Sister. It worked out okay," Scorpio said. "Oh, we were wondering who this Tarzan guy is?"

"Oh," both ladies giggled. "Most think he is a myth because Hollywood made a movie from several books. But he is real."

"Lizzy and Sister, we have a hard time believing that. I remember the movie was made about 80 years ago."

"That may be true, but we do have a Tarzan today. He was about nine years old when he and his dad were flying over the area not far from here. Their plane crashed, and he survived. We can show you the crash site. There is nothing but a few wing and tail pieces anymore."

"I suppose you will tell me a bunch of monkeys or baboons raised him," Jasper said. "And that he flies through the trees."

"No, not quite. Monkeys and baboons didn't raise him. He was raised by a tribe called Tikuna. This tribe is the largest in Brazil and lives in the western Amazon. About 40,000 are left, and they avoid contact outside their area, except for us. We wandered into their village by mistake. We were taking a shortcut. Anyway, that's how we met Tarzan. He is a great hunter. He is a white man and is now about seventy.

"The tribe calls him Tarzan because he is strong and has a way of communicating with many animals. He speaks English, French, and the Tikuna language. We have talked to him several times. We were not allowed to bring anyone with us or take pictures. We were there to provide medical help, mostly training them to deal with minor wounds. The tribe found ways to create the needed drugs from different vegetation types. So, that's what we know about Tarzan."

"Interesting story. Next time we are in the area, I'd like to see the crash site and find interesting artifacts. But for right now, we need to be getting back. We have already extended our authorized schedule," Scorpio said.

"Oh, that reminds me, the pilot will land at the airport early in the morning, so we need to get downriver," Cosmo said. "It will be daylight in a few hours."

Jim headed to his office to check with Angelique about her citizenship appointment. Jim walked into his office, "Hi Angelique, have you recovered from your CIA trip?"

"Oh, Boss. Ah, Jim. I guess I can call you Jim outside the base? Yes, I have recovered. It was fun. I did get a nice note from the Director thanking me again and still offering me a job."

"So, are you going to become a CIA Agent?"

"No, Jim, I owe you and your team my life. I don't plan on leaving the team. I think a lot about all of you."

"Thanks, Angelique. But this is your life. You decide what you want to do with it. You are not obligated to the team. Everyone wants you to be happy and do what YOU want with your life."
"I know, Jim, but I enjoy what I'm doing and doing things for the team. I want to be part of that mission. Also, I feel honored that you and Jane took me in and helped me become an American."

"Oh, that is what I'm checking on. Any word on your hearing?"

"Oh, yes, Jim. Today, I was informed by the Director everything is complete, and all I have to do is go to the swearing-in next Monday at the courthouse here in Helena. On Monday, a group is scheduled to be sworn in, and I was told to be there. I'm so excited. I will be an American citizen."

"Oh, wow, that is great. The team will be happy to hear that. What kind of party would you like to have, and what to feast on?"

"Are you serious?"

"Absolutely."

"Jim, I wish to be at the base and have the chef make his special seafood dinner. Have the team there, your pilot and his family, Jane and you, the Senator, the Director, Agent, and T.J. Is that too much to ask for?"

"Probably, but you're worth the effort. I'll get on it."

A couple of days went by. Jim was in his den, reviewing information needed for updates on the base—the phone rang. "Hello," Jim said.

"Hi, Boss, Scorpio, just calling to let you know we're back. The mission was completed and was very successful. I'll send you a complete report, and Lizzy and the Sister were great. I met many great people, and it was an amazing trip. How are things with you?"

"We're going to have a celebration at the base next Friday. Angelique is now an American citizen. It happened on Monday. I asked her what she'd like to do for a party. She wanted it at the base with everyone involved in saving her."

"That's great news. Friday is seafood night. Who all is coming?"

"Jane and I, the Director, Agent, T.J., the Senator, the pilot, and his family. I just confirmed the Captain and Mama Bear. Our pilot is flying down there, picking them up. What do you think of that?"

"I think it will be one hell of a party."

"I also arranged for the pilot to stop in Vegas to pick up the Senator, Director, Agent, and T.J. on the way here. They will be at the base Thursday around noon; we will arrive late afternoon. I think Angelique will be surprised. Oh, by the way, there is talk of another mission coming up. So, that is on the schedule for Friday morning. Then afterward, the celebration will begin.”

“Okay, I’ll get the team to polish the place and put up some balloons and other party stuff. What about a mission? Any clue what it may be?”

“No idea. Hoping the Senator will give us some information.”

“Well, okay, see you Friday.”

“Sounds good, and I’m glad you are all back. See you Friday.”

Scorpio was briefing the team regarding the party for Angelique on Friday. Everyone was excited for her and decided to decorate the conference room with pictures of places she had worked. Mama Bear can help with that and enlarge her U.S. citizenship certificate.

The chef said, “This is going to be fun. I know she doesn’t like cake but loves eclairs, so I’ll get busy making a few dozen. Being seafood night, she loves the Alaskan King crab. I’ll have extra.”

Bingo walked in, “Scorpio, I got a one-page e-mail from the Senator about a possible mission in Panama. Some island has thugs holding a yacht for ransom. Not much information on the yacht, but I have a map of the island and where the yacht is anchored. Could we pull up the classified satellite, get a detailed image, and see what we have?”

"That would be a good idea. That will give us something to work on before the Senator arrives tomorrow. Maybe we can find out more information about the yacht," Scorpio said.

The team was busy getting the place spruced up and ready for the party. Some cleaned the guest rooms, and others refreshed the minibars in the rooms with their favorite drink. The grounds outside were cleared of dead branches, and the team planted a few new bushes around the entryway.

Scorpio said. "The place sure looks better. I wonder what the Boss will say. The building and grounds look like a professional building, not a dump. However, we may have to downgrade it when the party ends."

"How come?" Star asked.

"It was not to look like a nice place," Joker said. "Try not to have the building attracting nosy people."

Everyone gradually worked their way into the meeting room and to the bar, fixing their favorite drinks.

Bingo came in, "Hey, Scorpio. I downloaded images and found out an oil company owns the yacht. It is a large 180-foot yacht and can accommodate twelve guests and thirteen crew members. A private firm chartered the vessel. However, I don't have any details on how many were on board. Maybe the Senator could provide that. I found the manufacturer and downloaded the deck/floor plans.”

“Thanks, helpful information. Anything about the island?

“The island is near Panama. Within sniffing distance of the isthmus. The island is long and narrow and has several beaches. It is for sale, but there is no structure according to the sales document. However, I was able to get a real-time image. The image was timed fifteen hours ago. I also ordered a thermal scan last night and should have it in a few hours. Maybe we’ll get a good reading on the number of people.” Bingo rolled out the image to show Scorpio. “The yacht, as you see, is on the north end. The island is pretty flat. The thermal may give us a better idea of the best area to enter the island.”

“I think that will give us a start. I hope the Senator will have the missing details. Have you heard anything from the pilot? He was to pick up the group in Vegas and be here this morning.”

“Yeah, he called in. Scorpio said he would leave Vegas shortly. Should be here top of the hour,” Bingo said.

“That’s good. It gives us a little time to talk about the mission. Angelique and the Boss should be here about 2 or 3 this afternoon.”

Star and Cosmo walked in. Cosmo said, “Bingo, I think this is what you have been waiting for a thermal image.”

"Just came off the printer. It looks good. I think you have been hoping for lots of detail," Star said.

"Roll it out," Scorpio said.

Cosmo rolled out the 3-foot by 3-foot thermal image. All four were looking at it, "the detail is amazing," Scorpio commented.

"Looks like we have three guards with weapons on the yacht; there could be more inside. Maybe they are holding the hostages on the vessel," Cosmo commented.

"Yeah, look at this," Star was pointing. "Looks like a tent. Maybe a storage box next to it. I count six guys. Five more are scattered along the beach, maybe guarding at different points on the island, all carrying weapons."

"That makes fourteen guards that we know of. I'm sure there could be one or two inside the yacht," Scorpio mentioned.

"We would have to skydive on a moonless night or come in underwater. A boat would be heard by the sound and seen during the daylight." Scorpio said.

"We could," Cosmo thought out loud, "take a boat to the island and leave it a mile or two offshore. Come in on the rebreathers. That would get us onshore. Then, we monitor with the real-time satellite on the thermal channel. We will see where everyone is and go from there."

"Good idea, Cosmo," Scorpio was saying.

"What's a good idea?" The Senator asked as she walked into the meeting room.

The Senator, T.J., the Director, the pilot, and his wife walked in. "Good to see all of you," Scorpio said. "Hi, Mama Bear and Captain. Good to see you also. Hi Bill, this your wife?"

"Yes, Scorpio. Her name is Abeque, which means 'she stays at home.'"

"Scorpio, it is nice to meet the person that keeps my husband busy," she said.

"Nice to meet you also."

"Okay, where is our new American," Mama Bear asked.

"Angelique, Boss, and his wife should be here in a couple of hours," Scorpio said. "We were talking about the Panama mission. We just got fantastic imagery showing the island, yacht, and worst guys."

T.J. and the Director looked at the imagery, "This is excellent. I heard we had this capability but have never seen any of the imagery," T.J. said.

"While we wait for the person of honor, you can enjoy some goodies the chef put out and help yourself at the bar." Scorpio said, "The chef promises another great seafood night. Angelique will be surprised. I didn't tell her who was coming for sure. Senator, do you have any information on the Panama problem?"

"Yes," Senator said while fixing her drink. "Several CEOs from various financial corporations chartered the yacht. An oil company owns the vessel itself. There were nine crew personnel and twelve guests. While the yacht was about 150 miles from Panama, they were boarded by terrorists or drug runners. A gunboat stopped the vessel of these thugs. Another ship nearby reported fourteen heavily armed guys boarded the yacht."

"Where were they heading?" Cosmo asked.

"They were to go through the Panama Canal, and then North is all we have," the Senator said. "But we don't know why they changed their destination and anchored on the island."

"So, what is it they want?" Scorpio asked.

"They are demanding twenty million in U.S. dollars. They say they will blow up the yacht if anyone tries anything. They say they will release them once the money is received. However, we don't know who gets the money or where it will be delivered."

"Senator, you have any idea where this group came from?"

"Director, you want to answer that?"

"We, meaning the CIA, believe it is the same group that operated near Japan a couple of years ago. They had the same MO. They operated in a couple of other places as well."

"How did that end?"

"Well, Scorpio," the Director said. "Not too good. Once they were paid the ransom, the terrorists let them go. However, their ship blew up a few minutes later, killing everyone."

"You think that is going to be the case here?"

"Yes, we do. That is why the Senator called you."

"What about the Seals or other teams?"

"Scorpio. A lot is going on regarding this incident. Just too much politics. We don't believe we have the time to work through that."

"Director, how much time do we have to execute a mission?"

"Scorpio, not much, maybe a week at the most."

"Well, the plan now is the team will fly into Panama City, Panama. Take a boat and cruise by the island about two miles away just after sundown. We go overboard with scuba gear rebreathers and use the new version of the Yamaha XL Sea scooters. Then we go to the island's south end. Once we crawl ashore, we unpack the satellite monitor and bring up the thermal channel. We map out where the bad guys are."

"How do you do that?" Senator asked.

"The thermal channel should pick up their body heat. Then, we can locate their positions and determine the best method to remove them. Then go towards the yacht and plan a method for that."

"You cannot do that before you go, meaning plan?" The Senator asked.

"We can't make the final plan until we know where everyone is. We have to be on the ground to do that. Most of our missions are that way," Scorpio explained.

"What gear are you taking?" the Director asked.

"Besides the scuba gear and satellite monitor, we take the commo gear and long guns, and everyone will have a sidearm. The weapons will have silencers. We have night vision and a medical kit. We will all be in black. That's about it."

"I heard of the rebreathers, but are your scooters capable of a round trip?" Director asked.

"These new ones can go up to six mph and have a range of two hours at that speed. There should be no problem," Jasper said.

"Regarding a boat, I can arrange that," Captain Sixto responded. "I can hang out about 5 miles out and pick you up when ready."

"Scorpio, I don't see any dock. It looks like the yacht is anchored, so how will you get on board without being seen?" T.J. asked.

"We will have what we call stick-on steps. It is the same thing that glass installers use to hold onto the glass. We stick them on the side of the hull and pull ourselves up, probably here…" Scorpio, pointing at the yacht, "Looks like the best place and provides some cover. There will be a couple of my guys posted here and here," again pointing at the lavish structure that was soon to take form of a sophisticated, classy rendition of Scorpio's vision. "They will cover the ones going up the side of the yacht. That has to be on both sides at the same time."

"Why is that?" Senator asked.

"It is a large vessel and may or may not make any difference. Best to, err, be on the safe side. Going up one side may slightly move the vessel, dipping to one side. That may alert a guard that something is different, especially if there is no wave action. By going up both sides, it will keep the vessel stable."

"Glad you are doing this. I would not have thought about that," the Director said. "How are you going to handle it once you are on board? You still have people that may get killed by the bad guys. Plus, they could have explosives ready to go if needed."

"The way we go up on the yacht and the placement of windows, we can reach the top deck without anyone seeing us," Scorpio said. "Once on top, we know we have two guards. We have to make a plan once we are there."

"Okay, so when can you go?" Senator asked.

"We can leave in the morning, drop you all off in Vegas, and Captain and Mama Bear can go with us to Panama to handle the boat." Scorpio said, "I assume, Captain, you could arrange for the boat today?"

"Show me the phone. I'll get it done."

"Scorpio," Star said. "Angelique, Boss, and Jane just pulled up."

"Okay, turn the lights out. We will surprise her when she walks in," Scorpio said.

"Jim, the team has been busy cleaning up the place. It is about time. Oh, I see the Global is here. Did the pilot come?" Angelique was asking.

"Oh, I don't know. It looks pretty quiet today. Maybe everyone is coming tomorrow," Jim said.

"Oh, maybe they forgot or couldn't come," Angelique said.

"Well, let's go in and find out the plan."

"Yeah, okay." They walked in. "How come the lights are off?" Angelique wanted to know.

"I don't know. Maybe they are out on a walkabout and turned them off before leaving."

They walked into the meeting room. Lights went on, "SURPRISE! Congratulations, Angelique, you're an American." Everyone was saying.

Angelique just stood there with her hands over her mouth, tears running down her cheeks. "Oh my god, Mama Bear!" Angelique ran over and hugged her. She hugged everyone, crying at the same time. "Sorry, I'm not crying. I'm just so happy that you all are here."

"We're so glad you are with this team. Everyone at the CIA told me to tell you that you are always welcome," the Director said.

"That's right," T.J. confirmed.

Everyone was hugging with tears in their eyes. That went on for several minutes. "How about a glass of wine," Cosmo said. He was handing one to her.

"Yes, Cosmo, thank you."

There were more congratulations and visiting with everyone. The chef walked into the meeting room. "Okay, everyone. Angelique, this is your favorite dinner, seafood night. I even have extra crab. So, fix your drink and come and get it."

Everyone was enjoying the dinner and conversation. The pilot stood up. "Scorpio, may I say a couple of words?"

"Absolutely."

"Thank you, and first, I want to thank Angelique for becoming an American. Angelique, I have known you through Mama Bear for several years. I'm so happy you got out of the dreaded camp and are now with the most incredible team ever. Sorry, Director and T.J., I know the CIA agents risk their lives every day. Secondly, I have flown with this team on various missions, some I wasn't sure I would see home again. This group of guys does impressive things to save people without any recognition. I know that is not why you do this work. I toast this team and thank you for your work."

"Hey! Hey!" Everyone said.

"I'd like to make a toast also," the Director said. "To congratulate Angelique for her interest in making computer systems work better. I also want to toast Jim," He stopped briefly. "Boss, you call him Boss. Thank you, sir, for your insight into forming this team. I wish we had the freedom your team has in executing missions. We would get more done. While I'm the Director of the CIA, I will do whatever I can to assist your team. Thank you."

Scorpio stood up. "Thank you, Angelique. We're so happy you are with us. Boss, I know there have been some rough times for you. Especially losing part of the team is part of the job. We know that. Oh, and just to let you know, we're leaving in the morning for Panama. We have another rescue. I'll tell you more later. But now we want to celebrate Angelique in becoming a citizen. Thank you, Angelique."

The party went on for a couple more hours, and everyone called it a night. Scorpio and Boss discussed the mission scheduled for the following day and then called it a night.

Scorpio was relaxing. The seats in the Global 8000 were specially built like recliners. Sleep was essential before a mission—Scorpio looked at his watch. We should be in Panama City around 5:00 or 6:00 p.m. The trip already seemed long. They dropped the Senator, Director, Agent, and T.J. off in Vegas and the pilot's family in Oklahoma. However, it was worth it, Scorpio thought. It made Angelique happy. She sure has been a great addition to the team. Scorpio got up and walked to the flight deck.

"How are you doing?" Scorpio asked the pilot.

"Doing okay. Sometimes I wish I had a co-pilot."

"Joker and I are checked out on the Global 8000 if you need a break."

"I remember that, but I just put it on autopilot and play checkers on my iPad."

"Okay, but who is watching for other aircraft?"

"Oh, I never showed you this. Right here is the coolest thing. Once I turn it on, it is a unique 360-degree radar. Anything within

200 miles and 2000 feet below or above us alerts me on the radar screen. Even if I fall asleep, it will wake me up."

"What happens if there is a change in oil pressure, the RPM changes, or other problems that can occur?"

"Well, Scorpio. Once I turn the system on, it records all the instrument's settings, and if there are any changes, this light comes on and buzzes, wakes me up."

"That is nice to hear. Now I will sleep better." Scorpio chuckled, putting his hand on the pilot's shoulder, "As I said, I can take over if needed."

"Thanks, Scorpio, but I'm okay. Oh, we should be landing in about two hours."

"Okay, thanks." Scorpio walked back to his seat. Most of the team was waking up. "Just let you all know we are about 2 hours out. Captain, what kind of boat do we have for the mission?"

"It is a nice boat. I have used it a couple of times. It is a seventy-five-footer walk-in dive platform with plenty of room for the gear. You can get in the water without spattering, or clamoring nor can they see you."

"Is it ready to go?"

"Yes, Mate is on the boat and will have it serviced and ready to go when we arrive. Don't worry about the boat being ready."

"Anyone has questions? You ready for this?"

The team all replied with a thumbs up.

Scorpio sat down and leaned back to relax, looking at his watch -- about forty-five minutes before landing. This is the first time the entire team has been on a water rescue mission with rebreathers. He thought of several firsts on this mission besides the rebreathers, the first boat rescue, and new commo gear for underwater communication. The training will be tested over and over on this mission. Scorpio smiled. He thought, I'm proud of these guys and know they will do their job.

The Global began its descent. The landing gear could be heard falling and locked a few minutes later—another smooth landing. Scorpio got up, "Okay, listen up. We all know what to do. Keep focused, and let us make this our best mission."

The Global pulled up next to the corporate hangar. Mate was standing next to a van, waving at the team. Scorpio opened the door, and the stairs went down. "Hi, Mate."

"Hi, Scorpio. Good to see you again. The boat is ready."

"Hi, Mama and Captain Sixto."

The team loaded the gear into the van and climbed in, taking a seat. Mate took off towards the marina. Fifteen minutes later, they pulled up next to a boat.

"This our boat?" Cosmo asked.

"Yup, sure is," Captain said.

"Nice, too bad we will only enjoy it for a few hours. It looks like a great way to take a vacation," Joker said.

"Yeah, I like this boat. I would call it a yacht. It is too fancy to use on the river, and this baby is too classy to mount a .50 caliber on the bow," Captain commented. "We have about an hour before it is dark enough to head out. Water is calm, and there is no moon, making it better."

"Okay, let's get the gear checked out and make sure the gear is working before we get in the water," Scorpio said. "Then, let's take a few minutes and review how we're starting the mission."

"It's time we head out. It will take about an hour to get to the drop-off point," Captain said. "After dropping you off, I'll go out another five miles and hang out until I hear from you." An hour later, "Looks like we are almost there. According to my radar, we are about 1.8 miles offshore, and your heading will be eighty-two degrees; the bottom's depth is ninety-three feet."

The team walked to the dive platform and looked at Captain Sixto. He said, "Okay, go. Good luck."

The eight-man team went into the water. The team leveled off at twenty feet below the surface. They did a commo check, then picked up the heading of eighty-two degrees on the scooter compass and took off.

About twenty minutes later, Scorpio said, "I see the bottom; it appears about ten feet below us. We should be close to the surface in a couple more minutes." They followed the bottom; they were now six feet below the surface. Scorpio stopped. He said, "Settle on the bottom, and I'll take a look."

Scorpio eased to the surface, eye level with the ocean; it was calm, and the shore was about fifty feet from him. He scanned the shoreline. They were on target, and he settled back on the bottom. "Okay, we just have a short distance, then let's crawl ashore, and the beach covers about twenty feet before getting to the vegetation."

It took about ten minutes to get everyone into the vegetation. They removed the dive gear and camouflaged the scooters with the surrounding vegetation. "Cosmo, fire up the monitor and see what the thermal imagery says," Scorpio said. "Everyone's night vision working?"

Everyone gave a thumbs up. Cosmo said, "I see seven guys around the island with weapons, three onshore by the yacht and one on the yacht. The other three must be in a tent near the yacht. I have the coordinates of the guards."

"Okay," Scorpio said, "here is the plan. Each one of you takes a coordinate that is your target. Find your target and then check in. I will be by the yacht to make sure no one walks away. Once everyone checks in, we will plan on taking them out simultaneously. Then come to my location as quickly as you can. Any questions?" Everyone gave a thumbs up. "Okay, let's go."

Twenty minutes later, everyone was checking in. "Alright, on three, we shoot… one," Scorpio was saying.

"Abort, abort," Star said.

"Who aborted?" Scorpio asked.

"It's Star. My guy was checking in."

"Yes, so was mine," Cosmo said.

Everyone was saying the same thing. Scorpio looked at his watch. It was the top of the hour.

"Scorpio, this is Joker. My guy said he was making his hourly check-in."

"Alright, it looks like we have an hour to make the kill and get back to where I am. Here goes, one… two… three." There was silence.

A couple of minutes later, everyone checked in that their target was down, and they were on their way to Scorpio's location.

Twenty minutes later, the team joined Scorpio. "Cosmo, see if you can get behind the tent, use the pin camera, and see what you find."

Cosmo crawled through the vegetation. Several minutes later, he was beside the tent. He slid the wand a couple of inches under the tent. Cosmo whispered, "I have one person sitting next to a radio and one sleeping on a cot. The one on the radio is talking to someone. I'll bet there is someone offsite behind this kidnapping."

"Okay, thanks," Scorpio said. "Stay in place and report any changes. Okay, we have to take out seven: two in the tent, two by the yacht on the beach sitting on the log, one on top of the yacht, then two in the vessel somewhere. Does anyone have any ideas?"

There was a long pause… Jasper said, "Cosmo could take the tent guys out. Bingo and I can sneak up behind the two on the log and take them out. The guy on top looks like he is half asleep. Once we take the log guys out, maybe Barber and Zula can use the climbers and go up each side of the boat and get behind the guy, pulling him back while killing him."

"Yeah, that may work," Joker was saying. "Maybe Star and I could make our way around to the stern while Barber and Zula get in place. Once they take their guy out, Star and I can get on board and crawl to the slider door. Then we have to see from there what we do."

"Okay, let's do it, but take the log guys out first. They are close to the tent and may hear the silencer from Cosmo."

Several minutes later, Bingo and Jasper were crawling up behind the two on the log. They were within four feet. Bingo and Jasper stopped and looked at each other. They could hear one of them snoring. They smiled while taking out their long knives. They were slowly getting up, first on their knees and then on their feet. Nodding at each other, they took one step toward the two on the log. They quickly put their hands over the guard's mouth while inserting the knife into their chest, pulled them back to the ground, and held them until their life drained. Bingo whispered, "Okay, Cosmo, you're clear."

Cosmo looked at the monitor, and nothing had changed. He eased up the bottom flap of the tent. He aimed at the radio guy and squeezed the trigger, making a whooshing sound. The guard fell forward onto the table. The guard who had been sleeping sat up. "You say something?" Cosmo squeezed another round off, and the guard fell back on the cot.

"Okay, I'm clear here," Cosmo said.

"Okay, guys, make your move on the yacht," Scorpio said. At the same time, he aimed at the guard on top of the yacht. He thought he might have to take the guard out if the guys couldn't arrive in time.

Barber said, "Zula, I'm ready to take the first step."

"Okay, on three: one…two…three," Zula said. Both made the first step, then the next, until they reached the top. They slowly peered over the top, looked at each other, and nodded okay. They looked over to the guard sitting on the edge, looking towards the stern, but he was asleep.

"He is a big guy," Barber whispered in his commo mike.

"Yeah, I'm bigger than you. I'll grab him. You stick your blade into him," Zula said.

They both crawled on top and eased towards the guard.

Zula looked at Barber. Barber said, "Let's do it." Zula reached out and grabbed the guard. The guard woke and said, "What the hell." Zula held him while Barber finished the job. "Okay, Joker, you and Star are clear," Zula said.

Joker and Star pulled themselves on board and crawled to the slider doors that led into the main lounge. Once at the door, they peered in using night vision and saw one guard sleeping on the couch. One was standing in the stairwell that led to the room below. The guard was carrying an AR-15 and playing on his cell phone. Joker looked at Star and said, "Take the one sleeping. I'll bag the one in the stairwell." "Okay." Star opened the slider about a foot. "Ready, now." Two shots were made. Star opened the slider the rest of the way. They rushed in and down the hallway, opening doors. They found the hostages tied up with hoods over their heads.

"Scorpio, this is Star. We are in, and all targets are down; the place is clear." Reaching over, he took the hoods off the three in the room, "You, okay?"

Joker went through the other rooms doing the same thing. "Scorpio, we have several hostages, I think seven. They all seem okay."

They had all the hostages in the main lounge when Scorpio walked in. "Are you all okay? Anyone needing medical help?"

"No, sir," one said. "Who are you?"

"We're your ticket home. Are any of you the captain or crew?" Scorpio asked.

"Yes, I'm the Captain. I don't know what happened to the crew."

"Were they taken off the boat when you were taken over or later on?" Scorpio asked.

"When we were boarded, they were taken by the pirates then."

"Were they tied or freely boarded to another boat?"

"I don't remember. I don't think the crew was tied up, not sure."

"Was this crew your normal crew?"

"No, I never had this crew before. The charter came so fast we couldn't get our normal crew."

"Did this crew do their job? They appeared to be professional?"

"No, they were not well trained. I would never again use them."

"Well, Captain, I don't think you have to worry about that. I suspect they were part of the pirate's crew. How did you hire the crew?"

"That's interesting. Now that I think about it. They just walked up and told me the owner hired them to crew the vessel. I didn't think about checking them out."

"Jasper, did you contact our boat?

"Yes, Scorpio, he is on his way. Be here in a few minutes."

"Captain, when our boat arrives, it will follow you back to Panama's marina. We will stay on board until we get back. I have a couple of qualified guys to crew this vessel."

"Okay, thanks."

"Bingo, Zula, and Jasper gather up our gear and get it on board," Scorpio said.

He turned to Joker, "Fire up the engines. When Captain Sixto and Mama arrive, we will head out once the gear is on board."

"Okay, I'm on it. I'll have the engines fired up shortly." He reached over to start the engines when he noticed a thin wire coming out of the back of the radar panel and running along the wall. "Check, Check, Check. We have a booby trap. It looks like the yacht is wired to be blown up."

"Everyone stands still," Scorpio said. "We are standing on a bomb. Let us go slow and disarm this crate!"

They were still looking for explosives when Captain Sixto came up alongside."

"Captain, stay clear," Scorpio said. "This yacht is loaded with explosives."

Sixto put his boat in reverse, "Okay, can we help at all?"

"No, I'm afraid if your boat is next to this one, it may trip a trigger device, and we all will go up," Scorpio stated.

Everyone was moving slowly about the yacht, disarming the explosives. After about an hour, Scorpio said, "I think we have them all. We found nine devices, all wired to the main trigger, that appeared to be controlled by radio or cell phones. So, they probably have someone in Panama City that can set this off."

"I think we're clear," Bingo said. "We can't find anything else. We even checked under the yacht as well. All the hostages are okay also."

"Okay, thanks, Bingo." Scorpio reached for the satellite phone and dialed a number. It rang a couple of times before the Senator answered. "Hello, Senator."

"Hi, Scorpio; how is the mission going?"

"We have your guys, and the bad guys are history. Regarding this mission, we discovered that the crew was probably part of the kidnappers. We found the yacht wired with explosives. We have disarmed them. The trigger was wired to be set off by radio or cell phone. I think there was a third-party connection—it may be something the FBI needs to investigate. I don't know how you will handle it. But the people chartering the yacht were set up, I'm sure of that."

"Okay, I'll pass that on. Where are you now?"

"We're getting ready to head back to Panama. If you want to dig them up, we buried the bad guys near the spot where the yacht was tied up."

"Okay, Scorpio, stay where you are at. I'll let the FBI in Panama know and see what they want to do. They may have been contacted about this. I'll get back to you shortly." Senator hung up.

"Okay, guys, we stay in place until the FBI gets back to us."

Several hours went by when the satellite phone rang. "Hello," Scorpio said.

"Is this Scorpio?"

"Yes, who is this?"

"This is Special Agent Richard with the FBI. I'm the district agent in Panama. Senator called and brought me up to date on your mission. Are you in control of the yacht? What is your status?"

"Yes, Sir, all hostages are okay. The yacht is disarmed. We're just waiting on orders."

"That's great. We know the person behind this and have him under surveillance but have been afraid to approach him, knowing he may be able to trigger the explosives."

"I say you can pick the son of a bitch."

"Okay, stand by."

It seemed like forever before Agent Richard said, "Okay, Scorpio, we got the guy. He held up a cell phone and said he would blow up the yacht. Well, he dialed a number and looked out the window. He was probably waiting to see an explosion that didn't happen. Good work, Scorpio."

"What would you like me to do?"

"Senator said the bad guys are all dead."

"Yes, we buried them in one place if you want their bodies."

"Mark the place, and I will have a team pick them up. Are you able to bring the yacht to Panama?"

"Yes, it is gradually becoming daylight . We should be there in three hours."

"Okay, thank you, Scorpio. We will meet you at the marina."

"Okay, see you soon."

"Scorpio, we are all set to head out," Jasper said.

"We have all the gear onboard?"

"Yes, including the dive gear. We didn't leave anything behind except the bad guys," Jasper said.

"Okay, let's go," Scorpio replied.

Both boats cruised alongside each other. They pulled into the marina almost three hours later, and Sixto tied up at their assigned slip. Scorpio pulled into the adjoining slip. A couple of guys who turned out to be the FBI were waiting. It took a couple of hours for the team to tell the FBI agents what they knew and where they could find the buried guys. The team grabbed their gear and headed to the van. Mate was waiting, "You have a good mission?"

"Yes, any mission you return from and don't lose anyone is a good mission. This was different. But it turned out okay, and the FBI has some work to do. But we're ready to go home," Scorpio said.

Several minutes later, Mate pulled the van up next to the Global. The pilot was waiting at the foot of the steps. The team exited the van, grabbed their gear, and headed toward the stairs. The pilot said, "Welcome back, glad to see you. Oh, it looks like some of you got close to your work. Or is that your blood I see on your jumpsuits?"

"No," Zula said. "Not ours."

"There are clean outfits in the back, next to the shower," the pilot said.

"Yeah, thanks. Sometimes you have to get your hands dirty," Jasper said. "It still was a good mission."

The team was getting the gear tied down as the Global taxied for takeoff. Once airborne, the pilot turned to a heading of 338 degrees for the first leg toward home. Several hours later, most of the team was sleeping. Scorpio's phone rang, and he looked at the number.

"Hello, Senator, what's up?"

"Just following up on a couple of things. I had a good meeting with the FBI and CIA regarding your mission. They were pleased with how it was handled. Looks like they were working on the case before your mission started. I shared the information you gave me about the crew. They said their investigation was leaning towards a corrupt crew. Your team just confirmed it. Also, they told me about the third party. He planned on blowing up the yacht. Anyway, Scorpio, great job, thank you."

"Thank you, Senator. Keep me posted on any FBI and CIA results on the guy they captured. I would be interested if they found out who this guy was. I'm betting on a foreign adversary. Maybe a pissed-off shareholder," he chuckled.

"Okay, sounds interesting. The FBI also thought about the adversary idea. But the CIA is not sure yet. Why do you think that, Scorpio?"

"We went through all the personal effects of the bad guys. There was no identification on anyone. However, their radio gear and weapons were Russian-made. I'm not saying they were Russian, but they were probably connected to Russia. I did pass that on to the FBI at the marina."

"Okay, Scorpio, I'll let you know what I find out," The receiver went back into its cradle.

Scorpio couldn't sleep, so he walked up to the flight deck. "How are we doing?" He asked the pilot.

"We're doing great. We should be landing in Dallas in about ninety minutes. The weather at home is clear skies. We should be landing at the base, probably around 10:30 p.m. I don't expect any delays at customs. Here, you take over. I need to stretch my legs and get some coffee. We are on autopilot, and I see nothing ahead of us on the radar. I'll be back in ten."

"Okay, no rush," Scorpio said. About then, his phone rang, "Hello, Senator."

"Scorpio, where are you? What are you doing, and when will you land in Dallas at customs?"

"Well, right now, I'm flying the Global. The pilot had to take a break. We should be on the ground at Dallas in about hour fifteen."

"You guys fly too? Well, okay, the CIA will meet you there. They have something for you to look at. Not sure what it is, but it must be photos of something."

"Okay, they must not have dug up the bad guys. Thanks for the call."

The pilot returned and sat in his seat, "Thanks, Scorpio."

"You are welcome. Oh, the Senator called. We're meeting the CIA at customs, so we will be delayed getting home," Scorpio said while getting out of the seat. "I'm going to have a beer and put my feet up for a few minutes."

It wasn't much longer, and the Global started to descend. The jet engines slowed down, and 10 minutes later, Scorpio could hear the landing gear going down. He looked out the window and could see Dallas spread out over several miles. The Global made a left bank and descended steeper into a smooth landing. He pulled up to customs near the corporate hangars and stopped a few minutes later. Scorpio walked over to the door, opened it, and the stairs went down.

"Hi, Scorpio," the customs agent said, knowing Scorpio for several years from past trips.

"Hi yourself, good to see you again. How have you been?"

"I am fine. Are you in trouble? A couple of CIA agents are here waiting to talk to you."

"Oh, no trouble. We did some work for the CIA and planned on meeting." Scorpio walked down the stairs and walked over to the CIA guys. T.J. was one of them, he noticed.

"Hi Scorpio," T.J. said. Shaking hands.

"Hi, so what is going on?"

"Well, Scorpio, instead of making a trip to Panama to dig up bodies, we thought we'd talk to you when you got back to the States. We have some pictures to show you. Do you recognize any of these guys?" T.J. asked.

Scorpio went through each one carefully, studying each one. "Yes, I recognize every one of them. We buried them all. Who are they?"

"Two of them are retired snipers of the KGB, and we think they ran the show. The others are not sure. We don't have much information on them."

"I don't get it. Why kidnap these folks?"

"They all are top financial backers of major projects and special programs to help people in or around Russia. Their lives have been threatened many times."

"Well, I think that chartering a yacht with no way to provide security was stupid, but what the heck, maybe they learned something," Scorpio commented. "Maybe the next time they do something stupid, they will put more thought into it and have security."

The customs officer walked over. "Okay, the paperwork is done. You can take off anytime you want," he said.

"Yeah, Scorpio, we have what we need to know. Thanks, we will call if we need anything else," T.J. said.

"Okay, guys, let us load up and go home," Scorpio said as he walked up the stairs to board the Global.

A few weeks later, Jim enjoyed his coffee while looking out his office window toward the mountains. He loved the time hunting as a kid in the wilderness areas of Montana. The phone rang, and Jim looked at the phone I.D.

"Hi, Senator, what's up?"

"Boy Jim, do I have a mission for you!"

"Oh, now that sounds interesting. Any place I know?"

"Yes, sure do. It's in your backyard!"

"Now you have my attention."

"Do you know a place called Spotted Bear?"

"Sure do, Senator. There is a Spotted Bear Ranger Station where the Spotted Bear River and the South Fork of the Flathead River join—a breathtaking location. I used to fish and hunt there many years ago. So, what's so important about this area?"

"Well, Jim. We have a nasty dude, or should I say a vicious individual. Goes by the name Carpetbagger. But he is far from being a carpetbagger. No one knows his real name, and he should be named slippery dick, as the FBI almost captured him many times. They never get close enough to arrest him. He is personally responsible for over seventy-five murders of women and children. The FBI thinks this may be a job for your team -- nail his ass with a bullet between his eyes."

"Okay, but what does Spotted Bear have to do with him?"

"This guy likes to hunt, mainly in Africa. But this time, our contact believes he is going early archery big game hunting around the Spotted Bear area. We think the 1st through the 3rd of October. We know this guy has inside contacts in the FBI. That's why we picked you guys. We are sure he doesn't have a clue about your team. Therefore, you're the choice of weapons. I sent you the latest picture of him and his bodyguard and some background on his activities. See what your team comes up with."

"Okay, Senator. I'll get back to you later." Jim opened his inbox and found a document from the Senator. After reading a few pages, his phone rang. He was looking at the I.D. while picking up the phone. "Hi, Scorpio. I assume you are calling regarding the latest message from the Senator?"

"Sure, am Boss. Have you read it yet?"

"No, I just started, but from what I have read, this guy is an absolute sweetheart."

"Yeah, you can say that again. According to the information, he enjoys torturing his victims for fun. The pictures are clear but are seven years old according to their date."

"So, do you have any thoughts on approaching the mission?"

"Yeah, we have a couple of ideas. I'll take Jasper and Bingo with me. Bingo has been in that area a few times on fishing trips. We plan to make reservations at the Diamond R Ranch and arrive a few days before our targets. We'll register as Terry, John, and Don Patterson. Our story is we're brothers from California. We were stock investors taking a break before we started a new company. We hope to get the plan together on the mission after we get there."

"Sounds like a good start. Bingo, have any thoughts on where they may hunt?"

"Yeah, kind of. He remembers his dad did an archery elk hunt there several years ago. The Spotted Bear Lake area was his choice. But who knows until we get there what the plan will be."

"How are you guys getting there?"

"We are taking the Global to Kalispell, Montana, and renting something at the airport. I guess the ranch is about a two–three-hour drive. We'll stop in the nearby town, Columbia Falls, to get fishing licenses on the way up."

"Oh, you don't want to forget your fishing gear!"

"Yeah, Boss. Bingo has that covered. Oh, and he will show us how to fly fish the next couple of days, so we will know what we're doing when we fish!"

"Scorpio, that is a *damn good* idea!"

"So, when do you plan to go there?"

"Well, according to the Senator's information, the target is supposed to be there on the 1st. So, that means we need to leave in four days."

"Okay, enjoy your fishing trip, and let me know when you head home. Also, good luck hunting."

It was a busy couple of days for Jim—new contracts for a three-story apartment building. But what was really on Jim's mind was fishing at Spotted Bear. He wondered if this were a mission he would like to be on. Well, he thought, Scorpio might have said something about that if he thought it would be. I need to leave that decision to Scorpio.

Jill walked into Jim's office. "Jim, there is a gentleman here to see you."

"What's his name?"

"He didn't say. He said he was a friend."

"Okay, send him in." Jim walked over to the coffee pot and poured a cup.

"I'll take one of those if you have extra!"

Jim turned around. "Oh my gosh. Yeah, I have an extra cup." Jim poured another cup, walked over, and said, "Nice to see you, T.J."

"Good to see you also."

"So, what are you doing here? This is unusual."

"I have family in Bozeman I haven't seen in years. So, I decided to drop by and chat while I was in the area."

"What's on your mind?"

"I had mentioned we had a project we wanted you to take on."

"Yes, I remember that. But you know we're not in a secure area."

"Yeah, but I don't expect your office to be bugged. Besides, I'll keep it short." T.J. closed the door.

"Okay, what's this big project about?"

"Remember President Reagan?"

"Yeah, the 40th president, so?"

"Remember a project called Star Wars?"

"Yeah, a proposed missile defense system intended to protect the United States from attack by ballistic strategic nuclear weapons. If I recall, President Clinton scrapped the project in 1993."

"You are up on your history. What else do you know about it?"

"I think several things made the United States scrap it. One was 30 billion spent on the concept's development, with a projected project cost of 800 billion. Many thought it was a Reagan bluff."

"What do you think?"

Jim looked at T.J. "You mean about a bluff?"

"Yeah."

"Well, probably Reagan was the only one serious about it."

"This is the most classified project this government ever had. Only about seven people know the details of what I will tell you. I'm one of them, and you will be the eighth. The President doesn't know, and no damn politician knows. None can ever be trusted with this information."

"Oh, shit." Jim got up and walked over to his desk, opening a drawer and pulling out a bottle of bullet bourbon. "I think this discussion has changed from coffee to bourbon." Jim walked back to the table with a bottle and two glasses. He set the glasses down and poured two drinks with about five shots each. He handed one to T.J. Then Jim downed his and filled his glass again. "Okay, what is the rest of the story?"

"Well, Jim." T.J. raised his glass, downed his drink, set the glass next to the bottle, and looked at Jim. Jim picked up the bottle and refilled T.J.'s drink. They sat there just looking at each other, and several minutes passed.

"Well," Jim said.

"Jim, we have had a couple of guys working on this forever. They're getting old now. The project has been paid for by nickel and diming other projects. So, it has been 50-plus years, and we have a system. Well, almost. The problem is people are wondering where this extra money is being spent."

"I could imagine."

"So far, some of it has been covered by a covert operation, which is always classified."

"T.J., I don't understand what this has to do with the team or me?"

"You have an ideal place to move this system to. The cave."

"This system must be huge and a problem to move," Jim replied.

"Jim, that was a problem ten years ago. Now that we have it on a computer system, we can move it in pieces without anyone getting suspicious."

"I'm sure you need a large communication dish that can't be seen?"

"That was another problem, but we have two communication satellites that can receive commands from an eighteen-inch dish."

"How could you test this without someone knowing about it?"

"Jim, did you hear about North Korea having a rocket blow up after launch and Russia's launch from a sub that blew up when it came out of the water?"

"Seems there was something about that on the news."

"Yes, that was us."

"What about people operating this system?"

"Yeah, Jim, that is a significant problem. But one we have to deal with later. Right now, we need a place to hide this system. Your cave is an ideal place."

"When do you need to move it?"

"Well, yesterday would have been great. However, it would take about three to five weeks to get it out of the Pentagon and to your location."

"Okay, move forward with it. I understand the importance. We'll figure the rest out once it is in place. I'll have to discuss this with the team, but I know they'll have no problem with it."

"Jim, this project could save the world from nuclear destruction."

"Yes, T.J., I understand that. I know several steps must be resolved once the system is in place. So, move forward. Please let me know what you need from our end to get the system in our cave. Oh, how does this system work?"

"I'll cover that later."

"Okay, we're here for you."

"Thanks, Jim. I'll be in touch." T.J. raised his drink and finished it. He got up and left.

Jim just sat there, taking a deep breath. Oh boy, he thought. Wait until Scorpio hears about this.

Scorpio looked over at Jasper. "This is a beautiful country. Fall is here already."

"Yeah, Scorpio. Bingo, do you remember any of this?"

"Sure do. We're on Eastside Road, which is what most people refer to, but it is Forest Service Road 38. The other side of the reservoir is referred to as Westside Road or Forest Service Road 895. Parts of that are paved but more winding. There are more campsites on that side. We'll go back that way and cross the Hungry Horse Dam. The bridge you just crossed is the Upper Twin Creek. This was one of several areas that were good for fishing. Diamond R and the ranger station, not much further."

"Bingo, is this the road you described where a section is a single lane, and the edge drops down to the river?"

"Yeah, Jasper. It used to be. When I researched this trip, I saw that part of the road was rebuilt in 2022. So, you don't have to worry about falling off the road into the river." Bingo chuckled.

"Jasper, maybe parts of the road were paved a year ago?"

"I don't have any information on that."

"I do," Bingo said. "I worked on the Flathead Forest survey crew in the Seventies. They had a major fire in this area. Lots of money was left over, and the Ranger decided to have the road paved going into the Spotted Bear Ranger Station instead of losing the funds. At least that's what I understood."

They all chuckled. "That doesn't surprise me," Scorpio said. "You need to spend the money if you have it because you may not have it next year."

"I think that is how it works, Scorpio," Bingo replied.

"Does this look like the ranch on the left?" Scorpio questioned.

"Yup, this is it," Bingo said. "All these years, and it hasn't changed much. Oh, the office and restaurant are off to your right."

"I see they have horses!"

"Ah... Jasper. This is a ranch." Bingo smiled.

"Oh... Yeah... I guess I would expect that. I wasn't thinking."

"Well, this will be another adventure for your city folk..." Bingo chuckled again.

They pulled up in front of the office and got out. A young lady walked out. "You must be the Patterson brothers."

"Yes, ma'am," Scorpio said. "I'm Terry, and this is Don and John."

"I'm Kate. I work part-time. The owners are in town getting supplies. Your cabin is over there. It is labeled cowboy. The bath house is there." Pointing toward the center of the ranch. "The restaurant is here, and the deck overlooks the Spotted Bear River. We have beer and wine. That's about it. Breakfast is at 8:00 a.m., and dinner is at 7:00 p.m. We're not open for lunch, but we have lunch material out during breakfast if you want to pack a lunch."

"Looks quiet here, slow time?" Bingo questioned.

"We have several doing an early archery hunt and have two pack trains in the 'Bob.' We have two guys coming tonight interested in doing a hunt close by. I think they probably hunt the Spotted Bear Lake area. At least that's what they said."

"Okay, thanks. We will see you at dinnertime," Jasper replied.

The team drove over to their cabin. "Who's Bob?" Jasper questioned.

"She was referring to the Bob Marshall Wilderness. There is another wilderness area called the Great Bear Wilderness just north. Both areas have great fishing and hunting. The hiking isn't bad, either. It's a beautiful country, and in some areas in the wilderness, white men haven't set foot on it either. That's how big it is."

"Okay, tour guide Bingo. With that, when do you recommend we go?" Jasper asked.

"Well, I suggest during dinner, if those other two guys are here, we talk about going up Meadow Creek and try fishing. At least those two guys will think we were uninterested in where they were going. But in reality, we will head to Spotted Bear Lake."

"Yeah, I understand. Let's study the imagery and maps to ensure this is planned correctly."

After a few hours, the team was ready. "Well, I wonder if those two gentlemen arrived." Jasper looks at his watch. "Looks like it is almost time for dinner."

"Yup," Scorpio said. "So, let's go to dinner and see what we find out."

The team walked towards the dining room. Bingo said, "It looks like we have another car here. You think that may be our target?"

"I guess we will see," Scorpio said, walking into the dining room.

The team entered the dining room and noticed a lady and a guy sitting at a long table. They were wearing U.S. Forest Service uniforms. Two other guys were seated+ at a smaller table off to the right near the fireplace. The team walked over to the long table.

"May we join you?" Scorpio asked. "The Forest Service working late?"

"Tonight, we are. We stopped to get a soda before heading back to Kalispell. Kate said she had plenty if we wanted to stay for dinner. That sounded great," the lady said.

"I noticed you are both wearing sidearms. I didn't know the Forest Service carried guns," Jasper said.

"Jasper, the Forest Service has a law enforcement branch," Bingo said.

"Yes, the gentleman is right," the lady said. "The Forest Service agency is under the Department of Agriculture. Our agency and the National Park Service, Bureau of Land Management, and the Fish & Wildlife Service have armed agents to enforce land management laws."

"Sounds interesting," Jasper said. "You after bad guys way up here in the boonies?"

"No, we were here to brief the District Ranger on a case we had worked on. You guys here for the early hunt?"

"No, we are brothers who don't get together often, and we got this wild hair about coming to Spotted Bear to fish for a couple of days," Jasper said.

"How did you pick Spotted Bear?" Lady Agent asked.

"The short story is that we were sitting in a bar in L.A. That's where we live. Every year, we pick a place to do something fun. This year, it's fishing. The bar had a large map of the U.S. We threw a dart at the map, walked up, and saw Spotted Bear. The rest is history," Jasper said.

"Where are you going fishing?" One of the other guys asked.

"We're going to Meadow Creek or down to Twin Creek a little closer. It depends on how we feel in the morning," Bingo answered. "You guys here to fish?"

"No."

"You must be going to hunt?"

"Yes."

No one said anything for several minutes. The lady agent finally said. "Well, we need to hit the road. You guys have a good time during your fishing trip. Of course, you have a license?"

"Sure do. Need to see it?" Bingo asked.

"No, we trust you." They headed out the door.

"Well, let us turn in. It may be a long day tomorrow," Scorpio said, getting up. "Thank you, Kate, for dinner. See you in the morning."

The team walked back to their cabin. Scorpio closed the door and said, "Those are our two guys. They match the picture we have. So, how do we do this?"

"Scorpio, we get up early. Kate said the coffee was on at 6:30. We grabbed a cup and lunch fixings. We have other rations if we need something. Head out. Like to be on our perch at least a couple of hours before they show up," Bingo said.

"Sounds good to me, Scorpio," Jasper said. "That would give us plenty of time to be set."

"What happens if they don't show up?"

"Well, Bingo, we'll try another day."

"Okay, see you in the morning. I'm going to crash," Bingo said.

It was a long night for Scorpio. He thinks it may have been better to set up an ambush along the trail or run them off the road somewhere and then blast them. He finally dozed off. Bingo woke him up.

"What is it, Bingo?"

"It's 5:30."

"Already?"

"Yup, sure is."

"Damn, it is cold in here."

"Yeah, Scorpio, it is 38 degrees. Should warm up in the high 60s today."

"Wish we had told the FBI to handle their problems."

"Gee, Scorpio. You are getting to be a grumpy old fart."

"Bingo, you may live long enough to be my age, then you will be the grumpy old fart."

"You probably are right. Let's hope we can get the job done today. Jasper has all the gear broken down and in our rucksacks. He is over getting coffee. Let's join him. Coffee may be what is needed right now."

They walked over and joined Jasper and Kate. They made small talk and one more cup of coffee, then headed back to their cabin. Getting ready to go, Scorpio said, "I'm ready. You guys ready?"

"We are forgetting one important thing," Bingo said.

"What the hell is that, Bingo?"

"Scorpio, we need to take our fishing poles. I feel those two guys will watch us leave and make sure we are going fishing."

"Yup, you are right, Bingo. Grab the fish nets, also. Let's go."

They left the cabin, walked to the road, and turned towards the ranger station. The trail is at the end of the road to Spotted Bear Lake. After a few minutes, Jasper said. "You think we were being watched when we left Diamond R?"

"I do," Bingo said. "I looked out of the corner of my eye when we walked by their cabin. I swear I could see someone watching by the curtain in their window. But I don't think they followed us to ensure we took the right trail to Meadow Creek."

"Once they have breakfast and warm up a little, they will probably take off." Scorpio continued, "Sure hope they decide to do the lake and not hike elsewhere."

A couple of hours later, Bingo said, "Okay, there is the lake over there. This trail goes that way around the lake. According to the

imagery, we take off up the hill and should find this clearing."
Bingo pointed to the imagery.

"Looks right to me," Scorpio commented. "Let's do it."

An hour later, they picked out a good perch at the clearing.
Scorpio said, "Okay, Bingo, you take out the bodyguard, and
Jasper, you take out the bad dude. I'll spot."

They pulled their gear out of their rucksacks and pulled out their
weapons. They assembled the long guns and got settled in their
spots.

About four hours later, Bingo said, "At least it warmed up, I was
about freezing my ass off."

"I know what you are saying, Bingo," Jasper responded. "Bingo,
I'm confused. I look at the mountains. The falls are beautiful. But I
thought deciduous trees were the only ones that changed color.
However, I see pine trees changing colors. I thought conifer trees
were pine trees with needles that don't change color?"

"Well, Jasper, you're mostly right. However, Larch trees also
have needles, but it is the only conifer I know that also changes
color and loses its needles. There might be others, but Larch is the
only one I know."

"Sure, makes it pretty." A long pause. "I think the place I picked
is a little slippery with this moss."

"You can select a better place if needed," Bingo responded.

"If you do, you better get to it, as our targets just entered the opening near the lake," Scorpio said.

"Yeah, I see them," Bingo said. "My range finder says 1976 feet. Easy shot."

"Are you ready, Jasper? I have my guy."

"Got it. I'm ready."

"Okay," Scorpio said. "On three: one, two, three."

"Oh shit."

"Jasper, what's this oh shit stuff?" Scorpio questioned.

"My arm slipped on the moss as I was pulling the trigger. I know I hit him, but don't think I killed him."

"Nope, you didn't," Bingo said. "I see him crawling towards the trees. I'll take him out."

"Wait, wait!" Scorpio uttered. "Look over to your left, about 150 yards. What do you see?"

"I see a bear."

"Bingo, not one, but I see two, and they appear to be large grizzly bears."

"What are you thinking, Scorpio?"

"Well, guys. Let us see what they do."

"Scorpio, I see a cub and the mother near the trees to the right of our guy, about 50 yards."

"That's even better," Scorpio whispered. "Our guy is between them."

"Crap, Scorpio, look at that guy stand up looking. He is a big bear. He is not happy having our guy between him and his cub."

"You want me to finish our target off?" Jasper said.

"No... Let's see what Mother Nature has in mind."

"Huh, I don't follow you," Jasper questioned. "Our papa bear is walking towards our guy."

"Yeah," Scorpio smiled. "Let's watch the show."

"Scorpio, I still don't follow you?"

"Jasper, we have our guy between a papa bear and a cub. Mama Bear is not happy either. I'll bet you $1,000 bucks the Papa Bear will take care of our target. Like I said, let's watch the show."

"Our guy is scared shitless," Bingo exclaimed.

"Yeah," Scorpio leaned against a tree and lit up one of his Cuban stogies. "I think he will get some of the same torture he gave to the women he killed."

A few minutes later, Bingo said, "What a hell of a way to die."

"Bingo, you think the bear will eat him?"

"Well, Jasper. Grizzly bears are one of two species that like hunting and eating a human. But that is rare. In this case, papa is protecting their cub. That is a good reason why the bear will attack, kill, and probably eat part of him. They will probably chew on the other guy as well."

"Okay, Mother Nature did our job. Let's head back. I want to try fishing at Twin Creek. I have never caught a fish before," Scorpio claimed. "Be something new for me. Might be fun."

They were fishing at Twin Creek three hours later, draining into the Flathead River's South Fork. Each was casting their line into the water.

Minutes later, Scorpio stared at the river, not thinking about fishing when, "Hey, I got one," Scorpio yelled.

"You sure did," Jasper said. "It is a giant of a fish. Must be at least four inches long."

Everyone laughed.

"Go ahead and laugh. This is the first fish I have ever caught." Scorpio was smiling like a kid at Christmas time.

Later, they sat at the dining room table, enjoying spare ribs, baked potatoes, corn, homemade bread, and a glass of wine.

"This is good, Kate. Thanks for an awesome dinner," Bingo remarks.

"Yes, that goes for all of us," Scorpio praised Kate.

"Wonder what happened to the other guys? They were expected to be back by dinner time," Kate questioned.

"You never know about hunting… what can happen. Maybe they ran into some game and tried to drag something out." Bingo said, smiling.

"You could be right. I'm headed back to the cabin. Thanks again, Kate. We will leave early, before breakfast, so we will grab a coffee and head down the road."

"Okay, Terry. See you all in the morning. Sure, you don't want breakfast? I can have it ready by six if you like."

"Well, okay. If you don't mind getting up early."

"Not a problem, Terry."

The team waved at her on the way out the door and headed to their cabin. "What do you guys think about the mission?" Scorpio asked.

"I think it went well," Bingo answered. "Be interesting when they find the other two guys."

"Yeah, let us get packed and hit the sack," Jasper commented.

They all slept well that night and were up early. Jasper looked out the window and saw several pickups in front of the office. "Hey, guys. Something at the office seems like a lot of activity."

Scorpio looked out the window. "Okay, guys, let us go over and have coffee. It is almost six."

A few minutes later, they walked into the restaurant. They noticed the Forest Service law enforcement agents sitting and having coffee. There were two others with them. Their shoulder patches said Fish and Game Law Enforcement.

"Good morning," Scorpio said. "You guys are up early."

"Good morning, Terry. " It was an early start for us," the lady said. "Kate just told me you guys are heading back this morning. Giving up fishing?"

"No, ma'am, we had fun and were scheduled to leave this morning."

"Terry, do you mind if I ask you a few questions?"

"Not at all. What's up?"

"Do you know anything about the other two guys that were here?"

"No, they only said two words to us. Why?"

"Did you notice anything different about them?"

"Not really. They weren't very friendly. As I said, they only said two words. We only saw them at breakfast the first day."

"Yeah, that is what Kate said also."

"Why, they lost or something?"

"No, not lost. We had one of the packers come out last night and came across them dead by the trail at Spotted Bear Lake."

"No shit! What happened?"

"Well, Terry. We're not sure yet. The packer said they looked like grizzly bears mauled them. One was pretty much gone, and the other was worked over. However, the packer thought he had a bullet hole. Anyway, we're getting ready to go and investigate and bring their remains out."

"Sounds like you guys will have an interesting day."

"Did you guys go up Meadow Creek?"

"Yeah, we did but got tired walking through brush, so we returned, got the car, went down to Upper Twin, and fished."

"Kate did say she saw you guys getting the car about mid-day. How long were you at Twin?"

"Not sure, but we were back by dinner time, maybe 3-4 hours."

"Did you hear any gunshots while at Meadow Creek?"

"No, none."

"You catch anything?"

"Yeah, he did, a monster," Bingo said.

"Hey, they are giving me a bad time because it was only four inches long."

They all laughed.

"So, what's with all the questions?"

"Oh, nothing. Just curious," the lady said.

"Well, we're headed home. I'm sorry your day won't be a pleasant one. I don't think picking up body parts will be much fun."

"Thanks, Terry. I'm sure it won't be pleasant either. You fellows have a good trip home."

"Thanks, and thanks, Kate. We enjoyed our time here and hoped to be back again."

"You are always welcome. See you next time," Kate waved at them.

The team walked out, got in the car, and left. Several minutes later, Scorpio said. "Did the shell casings get picked up?"

"Yeah, Scorpio. I also brushed out the tracks when we left," Bingo said. "Do you think she was suspicious about us?"

"Ah... I don't think so—just typical questions. She was feeling us out. Oh, I like this road better."

"We will cross the Hungry Horse Dam in about an hour. It is a good road," Bingo remarked.

"Is there cell service along this road? Like to inform the pilot that we're on the way."

"Not until we get close to the Dam. Are you concerned about anything?"

"No, not really, Bingo. I always feel better when we are airborne."

"Do you think the agent will check us out?"

"If she does, she won't find anything. I paid Kate in cash. The driver's license and car rental information are not traceable."

A couple of hours later, they pulled into the airport, turned the car in, and boarded the Global. The pilot inquired, "Have a good mission?"

"We sure did," Bingo said. "Scorpio caught a fish. We would mount it, but it would be too big to get it on the airplane!"

"*No shit Kaku!*" Pilot responded.

"Yeah, no shit. It fits in my pocket. So enough said."

The pilot looked at Bingo, and Bingo winked at the pilot.

"Okay, let us get out of here," Scorpio commanded.

"Yes, Sir." It wasn't long, and the pilot had the Global airborne.

Two weeks later, Jasper was reading a request from T.J. that the Senator had sent to the team.

Interesting, usually someone calls about a mission before sending the details.

"Hi Jasper, look out for information from T.J. The Senator sent a request to us. I talked to her late last night."

"Well, Scorpio. I'm just reading about it. Interesting mission. If I get this right, several mercenary soldiers, possibly from Russia, are held up on an island near Venezuela. They have seven captives. I'm not sure where from as yet. But this group has shoulder-held missiles and set up portable radar. A special team from Venezuela tried to get on the island but was blown out of the water, and everyone was killed. T.J.'s message says our government will not get involved. I wonder why?"

"Jasper, probably about some political bullshit," Scorpio answered.

"Yeah, that's right, it's always the case."

"Let's call T.J. and see if he can share other information." Scorpio dialed a number and pushed the speaker button. It rang a couple of times.

"Hi, Scorpio. I bet you are calling about the island mission," T.J. said.

"Right on, T.J." Scorpio took a drink of coffee. "There are a lot of unknowns."

"Yes, I didn't have much information to send you. It was more of an alert. But I now have more data."

"We're all ears. What do you have?"

"Well, we are not sure whether these guys are Russian. Anyway, the seven captives are high-level individuals from the UK. They were meeting in Wales. How they were captured and why they were taken to this island is unknown. I have some guys in the area trying to find out more information. I'll send the coordinates of the island."

"So, what do you want us to do now?"

"Scorpio, I realize you need more information. But maybe look at the location and see how you could get on the island. Keep in mind that these soldiers have the gear to take on an army if needed."

"Okay, we will pull up some imagery. But it would be nice to know how many soldiers are involved and their types of gear. The other is why we are requested?"

"I'll get back to you as soon as I get the additional information. It shouldn't be very long. My guys have been working on this for several days."

"When did this happen?"

"The group was taken captive about two weeks ago. They were just located four days ago when a team of Venezuela special service tried to get on the island. They didn't make it."

"Okay, we will take a look and wait to hear back from you." Scorpio terminated the connection.

Bingo walked in. "Here is the imagery of the area. I overheard the conversation and pulled up satellite data available. This one has the most detail."

"Oh, crap. Look at the detail," Scorpio said. "The island is a pretty good size. Looks like small bunkers, maybe a 2 or 4-man type."

"Yeah, about every 400 or 500 feet apart. But just on this end of the island. I count six tents, maybe a 6-man type. I see a shadow, which appears to be from a portable radio tower. One large tent in the center."

"Yeah, Bingo, I think you are right. Scorpio, look at the other end."

"I was looking at that, Jasper. From the pattern of the tracks, they have mines planted."

"I wonder if we can locate the mines if we get an earlier image?"

"Good idea, Scorpio. I'll check it out."

The rest of the team walked in. "What's up, Scorpio," Barber asked.

Scorpio filled everyone in on the potential mission.

"Scorpio," Jasper walked in carrying some new images, "this new satellite we have access to is great. Look at this," pointing at the pictures. "This one looks like when they started installing the mines."

"Wow, look at the detail," Zula said.

"That's nothing," Jasper commented. "Look at this image. It's the next day, and you can tell from the tracks and the covered areas where all the mines are located."

"Scorpio," Star said. "It would be easy to calculate each location's GPS coordinates."

"Cosmo, you're the expert on this stuff. Can you make a map showing the locations of the mines, tents, and anything else we need to know about? Including the GPS coordinates of each?"

"Sure can," Cosmo said. "Take me 2-3 hours. I could have it together."

"Go for it. Also, the rest of you research everything you can find about these guys, any background data, training, whatever you can find."

"You got it, Scorpio," they said.

"Bingo, give T.J. a shout and get anything he has on these guys that may help."

"Okay, Scorpio."

"Let's shoot for tomorrow afternoon to get back together and review what we have gathered. Maybe enough detail that we could do the job." Scorpio sat back, put his feet up on his desk, and, grabbing another stogie, plunked it in his mouth. I love this job, but he thought it would be nice to retire and work on my bucket list someday.

It was a long night. Finally, they called it a night and hit the sack. It was early when Scorpio walked out onto the deck with a cup of coffee. He was proud of his team and how well they worked together. He started thinking about retiring. Cosmo or Jasper could take over as the team leader and be good at it.

Cosmo walked out on the deck carrying a coffee cup, "I hope I'm not interrupting your deep thoughts, Scorpio."

"Oh, no, it wasn't important for now. How did you do on the map-making project?"

"Real good, have to say." Cosmo smiled, "I forgot how much fun photogrammetry was."

Scorpio was looking at his watch, "Breakfast must be about ready. I can smell the bacon. Let us get everyone together. Chow down and get to work."

After breakfast, everyone gathered in the conference room. Angelique had organized everything on the big table.

"Well, what do you have here, Angelique."

"You know me, Scorpio. I like to be organized. I took everything everybody gathered and put it in a report. The photos are in order by date, and the subjects are written on the whiteboard. I thought we could review what we have on each item. When we're done, we may have the big picture."

"Well done," Joker said. He was so proud of her and in love with her.

"Okay," Scorpio smiled. "Cosmo, explain the map you made."

"The map may not be to scale, but it is detailed with everything on the island. The tents, approximate size, the bunker locations, and after studying all the images, measuring everything and ensuring all is accounted for."

"What are the numbers by each item?" Zula asked.

"I started writing down information on each item, and it didn't take long before I knew it would be a mess. So, I numbered everything." Cosmo reached for a stack of papers and handed out a copy to everyone. "Each number on the map corresponds to a number on these sheets. By each number is a written description of that item with as much detail I could find about them."

"This is quite a detailed list. You got this from the pictures?" Star asked.

"Pretty much." Cosmo paused, taking a drink of coffee. "Oh, the stick figures count for every individual. Oh, but you know the location where I have them doesn't mean that's where they are now. I just did that to keep track of the number of people."

"What is this by the big tent? It looks like a squad in formation," Joker said. Everyone laughs.

"That is the number of people I think are in the big tent. Seven are the captives, and three are guards. This tent," pointing on the map. "This is the radio tent, the antenna located next to it.
The bunkers usually have two soldiers; maybe a couple may have one, and a couple may have three. And some bunkers don't have anyone."

"Cosmo, how did you come up with the number of soldiers?" Scorpio asked.

"That was hard, but we have thirty-two to thirty-five soldiers when comparing the images. I'm 95% sure that it is between those two numbers."

Everyone was studying the map. "Cosmo," Angelique asked, "what are these funny-looking puppy paws?" She pointed to the map.

Everyone laughed. "I assume they are the mines," Star said.

"Yup, right on," Cosmo replied. "And I triple-checked the coordinates. I didn't want to be off on those locations."

After a long pause, Scorpio asked. "Anyone have questions about the map?"

After another long pause, Star said. "Looks like a great job. You get an 'A' in my book."

"I think we all agree with that," Scorpio said. "Bingo, did you have anything useful regarding the soldiers?"

"Yes, T.J. had a lot of stuff. I don't have a clue where or how he got his information, but he said the soldiers are x-military, Russian. But they were all booted out of the army for various reasons. Basically, they are all misfits. Most are drunks or on drugs, not well disciplined, unorganized."

"Anything on equipment, training?" Joker asked.

"I would say just basic training stuff. They weren't in the army long enough to get advanced training."

"Any information on why these guys were picked and who picked them?"

"Well, Scorpio, that is a little fuzzy. T.J. thought Russia hired them. He thinks this mission was a long shot at being successful. So, these guys were hired in case they were all killed. That way, they wouldn't lose any of their guys on the mission."

"Not sure about what they were thinking?"

"I didn't either, Scorpio. But T.J. just laughed about it. His thought was that this group of captives was from several different countries. High-level folks. Their job was to plan a mission to take out the president of Russia."

"I don't understand. If that is the case, why hire a bunch of misfits and not have their best guys go in and kill them? Why kidnap and haul their asses to this island? And use a bunch of misfits for the job?" Scorpio was confused.

"T.J. wasn't sure, but the KGB planned the idea."

Scorpio got up, walked to the bar, fixed a double bourbon, and sat down. "Why don't you all have a drink? Maybe that will help us determine the reason for the island gig."

It only took a few seconds before everyone agreed and went to the bar. Several minutes later, they were all back around the conference table. No one said anything. The phone rang.

Scorpio looked at the ID. "It's T.J.," and he pushed the speaker button. "Hi, T.J.. What are you up to?"

"Well, this little voice told me to call you regarding the mission near Venezuela. I figured it could be a little confusing."

"Well, we all agree with you on that point."

"I figured so. How can I help to make it clearer?"

"T.J., why the island thing? Why not just kill this group during their meeting?"

"My inside guy told me that was what the KGB wanted to do. But the president wanted them to be kidnapped and put somewhere where he could blow them up."

"Wow, now that doesn't make any sense at all."

"Well, Scorpio, it didn't to me either. But then my guys told me that the president was still pissed off about the Ukraine war that happened years ago. He wanted the top guys all in one place to kill them when he was ready."

"Ready for what?" Scorpio was about ready to fix another double.

"Well, Scorpio. The president is holding them hostage and demands one billion dollars for their return. That would pay back most of the money he lost during the war."

"Okay, so someone pays the billion. How would he blow them up? Whoever will pay the ransom would want some guarantee of getting their money's worth, wouldn't you say?"

"Yeah, that is why it is taking so long to agree. Oh, by the way. His method of blowing them up is, you won't believe this."

"T.J., I would believe about anything at this point."

"Well, the president has a submarine parked offshore a few minutes away with a short-range missile. But it is big enough to obliterate the island."

"*No Shit Sherlock*!"

"Elementary, but yeah, no shit, Scorpio. But he doesn't know that we know that. The concern is that the explosion would be big enough for the tidal wave to take out several other islands plus all the low-lying lands over thousands of miles, thus killing thousands."

"Damn! So... what the hell are we supposed to do? We get there, this bunch of misfits calls on the radio that they are in trouble, and the submarine captain blows them to hell. And we join them."

"Yeah, it is a tricky situation. So, have you done any planning as yet?"

"Yeah, we found out they have mined the island's east side. There are between 32 and 35 soldiers or, should say, misfits. That is about as far as we got so far."

"Wish I could be of more help. My guy was supposed to contact me yesterday to bring me up to date from the Russian side. But I have heard nothing. We have an alternative contact point scheduled in about three hours. Hopefully, he can make that schedule."

"Would be nice if he tells you that the submarine sank."

"Well, you never know. I'll get back to you in three hours, regardless if our contact is on schedule. Hang in there. I know you will come up with a plan." A faint call disconnect tone could be heard as Scorpio placed the handset back.

"Anybody have any ideas?" Scorpio asked.

"I know you guys are well-trained and equipped," Angelique said. "I know your skills and dedication to your mission, but I got an idea."

"Please share that," Cosmo said.

"Well, it depends on the wind and other factors you must figure out. But skydive at night with the gear you need. Maybe just several miles out, they think the aircraft may be an airline flying by. You land in the ocean about ½ mile from the island on the east side. You crawl ashore, then using your handheld GPS with all the coordinates of the mines loaded, navigate your way through the minefield. They probably wouldn't have any guards in that area. Well, that's about as far as I got."

"Not a bad beginning, Angelique. Does anyone have thoughts?" Scorpio asked.

"Yeah, once we navigate the minefield, and if there is little or no light, we could sneak up to each bunker and take out the guys. We know about these misfits. They will probably be drunk or out from drugs," Barber said.

"What about night vision? What happens if they have that?" Zula asked.

"According to the map, the radio tent is far enough away from everything else. We could take that out first, maybe?" Star questioned.

"We still have a lot of unknowns," Scorpio said. "What type of light do they have? Do they have night vision? Do they contact someone on a scheduled basis? Is there a code word and other stuff we need to know?"

"According to my watch, T.J. should be calling in about ten minutes," Scorpio commented. "I think I need to refill my glass and think before T.J. calls."

Several minutes later, the phone rings. Scorpio looks at the ID. "It's T.J.," pushing the speaker button. "Hi, I hope you got some good stuff."

"Hi, you also. Yeah, I have some worthy information. This is probably the biggest mistake the KGB or maybe the president has made. Anyway, this bunch is not only misfits but also idiots."

"Well, that's good." Scorpio smiled.

"This is how things went down," T.J. said. "The KGB had a highly trained group go in to do the kidnapping. They didn't think the hired soldiers could do it without screwing it up. Anyway, they delivered their captives to an airport. I don't know yet which one. But they met their misfits there and loaded everyone on an unmarked airplane. We think it was a military type. Anyway, they dumped them off on the island."

"Well, at least the KGB did one smart thing for their side," Joker said.

"But, Scorpio, this is the best part. According to my guy, after the guys boarded the aircraft and took off with the captives, they found several walkie-talkies left behind. But they did take a radio. They didn't take any night vision stuff because they didn't know what it was or how to use it."

"Great, at least you had some excellent news. Anything regarding these guys checking in on a schedule with anyone," Scorpio wondered.

"Oh, yeah, almost forgot. They were supposed to check in with the sub every six hours. On the clock, at 1200 hours, then 0600 hours, then 1200 hours, and so forth. The other thing is that we have a stealth sub-chaser aircraft in the area and can now track them. I have requested the clock tag on them. I'll have more on that later."

"What about the ransom, and how long do you think we have before we need to have the mission completed?"

"Scorpio, they agreed on the billion but are far from doing it. I guess you probably have a four, maybe a five-day window starting tomorrow. I could give you more time. If you decide not to do it, let me know. I'm unsure what else we can do, but let me know. Later." Hung up the phone.

"Any other thoughts?"

"Scorpio, I think we can do it," Cosmo said. "I have the Global coming, and he will be here tomorrow about mid-day. The Dash-8 will be in Panama."

"Sounds like a go. What Angelique came up with is a good start. They do not have night vision, which gives us a good chance. We will have to plan the takedown after we're there. We need to take the radio out shortly after one of the check-in times. That will give us time to pull this off. What about pick up?"

"The Dash-8 has long-range tanks. After we bail out, he could land in Venezuela, refuel, and hang out over us until we give him the green light to the land," Cosmo said. "The strip on the island is gravel, but from what we can tell, it is in good shape. After all, that is how they got on the island."

"Okay, Angelique, I want you onboard the aircraft. Make sure we have all the medical stuff you think we need. Alright, let's get the show going. Get the gear ready and loaded as soon as the Global gets here. Oh, any word on where the pilot is at?"

"No, Scorpio, I'll call him and find out," Bingo went to the commo center.

When Bingo came in, the team had the gear ready to load. He said, "The pilot is about thirty minutes out."

"Let's double-check on the gear, parachutes, weapons, commo gear, handheld GPS, night vision, and you might make sure your bowie and other close-quarter weapons are sharp," Scorpio said. "This will be one of those missions where we may get a little dirty."

The Global taxied up to the team house. "Hey," the pilot said, leaning out the window, "we should have a good flight. Got a nice tailwind."

"Sounds great," Jasper yelled back over the engine noise.

It was a smooth flight. About halfway to Panama, Scorpio asked, "Hey, everyone awake?"

Everyone responded with "Yes."

"Okay, I just want to go over the mission again. We jump out of the Dash-8 at 22,000 feet. The pilot said we should have about an eight-mile-an-hour wind to our backs when the chutes open. We will freefall down to 8,000 feet and open. That may be adjusted once we know the wind over the drop zone. Our descent angle will put us around a mile from the beach at that altitude when we hit the water with the present wind conditions. Dump our chutes and harness."

"Scorpio, I got the latest forecast for the area," Star said. "Looks like no moon, which is great. The wind's out of the east hasn't changed."

"That is good. We could get closer to the beach depending on our position and how dark it is. We should be able to tell what kind of lighting they have. Then swim the last ½ mile. Once on the beach, we fix our silencer and get our GPSs going."

"Scorpio, it may be good for us to study the area as we come in. Once on the beach, we compare what we saw and tune up our plan," Jasper said.

"Good idea," Scorpio said, feeling the Global starting a descent. Several minutes later, they touched down.

"Gentlemen, just letting you know your pilot on the Dash is ready," the pilot said. "I'll pull up next to it, and it will be an easy transfer. I wish you luck and a safe return."

It wasn't long before the Dash-8 was taxiing out for takeoff. Once airborne, the pilot came on the intercom. "Hi, guys. I am glad to have you back on board. I loaded the coordinates into the laser system—so it's the same plan as before. The yellow light will flash. Once it goes steady, the door will open. Greenlight, you go. Also, the wind has increased by ten mph at altitude. So, I recalculated your opening position. I think you want to be open around 5000. That would give you a good angle and far enough out that no one will see you when you hit your spot in the ocean."

The team was gearing up and checking and double-checking everything. Scorpio looked at the group, "You ready?"

They all respond with a thumbs up.

The intercom clicked on. "Gentlemen, we're about 10 minutes from the yellow light. I will depressurize in a few minutes."

Everyone was ready. Scorpio looked at Angelique. "We will see you later."

"Yes, and you all stay alert. No one getting wounded." She walked over and kissed Joker. "You keep your ass safe."

It seemed like it was forever before the yellow light started blinking. A few seconds later, the door was open, and the green light went on. Out the door, the team went.

Scorpio was last out the door. His laser was working, showing his altitude and the position of the others. According to his laser, he made a slight turnabout of twelve degrees. He looked around, and in the distance, he saw small spotlights on the ground. It must be where the bunkers are located. His attitude was passing through 8000. He thought it was another five to six seconds, and the laser would open the parachute. Then he felt the harness tighten up, and the chute was open.

Scorpio looked around. Everyone was close to the same altitude. He spoke on his mic. "You guys hear me, okay?"

Everyone responded.

"Okay, I think it is dark enough to get closer to the beach before entering the water."

"I think so, Scorpio," Jasper said. "We have plenty of tailwinds. We should turn into the wind and flare out, not to make a splash. Be like stepping into the water."

"Yes, good move," Bingo said. "Looks like we will be only a couple hundred feet from the beach."

"You think we can make the beach?" Star asked.

"Yeah, probably," Scorpio said. "But we have a few mines close to the water, and the tide is up. I don't think we should change it."

A few minutes later, they entered the water. "Everyone hears me, okay?" Scorpio asked.

They all responded. The wind was strong enough that it formed small waves that rolled over their heads, obstructing their view for a couple of seconds.

"Okay, let's stay low in the water and crawl to the beach's edge. See what our GPS tells us about the location of the mines."

Several minutes later, they had a good picture of the mines. Jasper downloads a new image of the area. "I have the photos, and it looks like nothing has changed."

"That's good," Scorpio said. "According to my watch, it's almost 1:30. It won't be daylight for a while, and maybe we will have them taken care of before the sun comes up. We have more than four hours before they check in again."

There was a long pause; everyone was studying the photo and data from the GPS. Cosmo said, "Looks like the only light is at the big tent, the radio tent, and a couple of the bunkers."

"Let's crawl through the minefield. The first mine looks about twenty feet in front of us – the next one is about 7 feet to its right. Jasper, you take the lead. We all follow until we are past the minefield," Scorpio said. "Then we'll plan the next step."

It didn't take long for them to get through the minefield. The GPS locations let them move reasonably fast. Ten minutes later, they gathered around Scorpio.

"Okay, this is what I think we can do. Jasper and Cosmo, you take the radio tent. Evaluate and let me know your plan. That is where I can coordinate the other tasks. Joker and Star, you two check out the big tent. Barber, Zula, and I will take the first bunker. Let's check in when we're in place."

Scorpio and the team were near the first bunker several minutes later, only to find it empty. They could see the next bunker and only saw one guy sitting on the edge, looking half asleep.

"Scorpio, this is Joker. We're in the big tent. Our camera shows all the captives in what appears to be a cage. There are only two guards. Right now, they're both sleeping in chairs."

"Okay, Joker, standby."

"Scorpio, this is Cosmo. There are only two guys in the radio tent. They are playing cards—no one else. We can see the bunker to the west, and it looks like two guys. Neither looks very active."

"Roger that," Scorpio said. "Okay, here is the plan. My guess is none of the soldiers are good at anything. So, Cosmo, you guys take out the two on the radio. Then move on to the closest bunker and do your thing. Joker, take out the sleeping beauties, tell the captives to stay quiet and put. Then move on to the bunkers. We'll start taking the bunkers. At some point, one of the soldiers will catch on to what is happening, and then we need to be aggressive and get the job done. Check your watch, I have 1:47 a.m. At 1:50 a.m., we execute the plan. Good luck."

Cosmo and Jasper walked into the radio tent. The two guys turn to look when Cosmo takes them out. Jasper was at the door, watching for anyone that may come in their direction. Cosmo is looking at the papers and notes sitting by the radio. "I don't know much Russian, but this looks like a record of their radio traffic."

Joker and Star walked into the big tent. The two guards were still asleep. Joker looked at Star, "You think we should take them captive?" Star raised his .9 mm and shot them both. "No."

The captives were waking up and wanting to know what was going on. "It's okay," Joker said. "We're your ticket home. Stay in place and be quiet until we're done. We'll come back to let you out and get you home." They all smiled and didn't say anything.

Barber, Zula, and Scorpio took out the guys in the first bunker with their bowie knives and headed to the next. They were taken out without any resistance. Scorpio heard a shot off to his right. Then all hell broke loose. "Go right, charge the bunkers and take them out," Scorpio yelled.

There was plenty of gunfire. But it only lasted about fifteen minutes and then silence. Scorpio knelt and changed clips. "Barber, Zula, are you okay?"

"Yeah, fine," they both said.

"Joker, Star, your status?"

"Star answered, I'm fine, but Joker took a hit, left arm."

"Cosmo, Jasper, your status?"

"Cosmo, Jasper, your status?" Scorpio repeated.

"Star, look for Cosmo and Jasper. We'll head that way also."

"Scorpio," Star said. "Found Jasper. He is unconscious and looks like he has a head wound. Oh, here is Cosmo. We need the medic kit."

"Roger." Scorpio dialed a number. "Inside or outside the wire?" he asked the pilot.

"I'm hovering nearby."
"Okay, I need you on the ground ASAP. We need additional medical equipment. Have several wounded?"

"10-4, will be on the ground in about ten minutes."

"Star, go release the captives. They can help get our wounded to the airstrip," Scorpio ordered. Then he dialed a number on the satellite phone. Two rings later, "Hi, T.J."

"Hi, Scorpio. What is your status?"

"We are on the island and have taken out the bad guys, and we have the captives."

"Good job. Everything okay?"

"No, I have three guys down. Our aircraft should be on the ground in a few minutes. It is equipped with emergency medical equipment."

"How serious?"

"One will be okay, but I don't know the other two. They are in serious condition. However, according to my watch, this submarine captain will make a scheduled contact in forty-two minutes. If no contact is made, he probably will plant a missile on the island as planned."

"We are ready for them. I have had a B-2 Spirit, a stealth bomber, assigned to your airspace since you have been on the ground. They have been tracking the sub. When the sub commander comes up near the surface to make contact, I will order that the B-2 present them with a package to take care of the problem."

"What happens when Russia hears about losing the sub."

"The sub won't have a clue what hit them. So many parts will be scattered on the ocean bottom that they will probably never be found."

"Okay, I have to run. Our aircraft is on the ground. Touch base with you later." Hanging up the phone. "Let us get on the aircraft," Scorpio said.

Dasher taxied over to them, and the pilot stopped. The door opened, and the stairs went down. A few minutes later, they were all on board. Scorpio told the pilot, "Let us get airborne and away from here before the bomber arrives."

"You got it."

"Scorpio," Angelique said, "looks like Joker's wound is a through and through to the arm. He will be okay."

"And the others?"

"Jasper has a head wound. It doesn't look serious, but it is hard to tell. It looks like a bullet struck the side of his head. He was still unconscious, maybe just knocked out. But Cosmo was hit twice, once in the leg and the other in the abdominal area. I need to do surgery ASAP, but we are bumping around too much. And I don't know if I can do what he needs."

"What do you need to do?"

"I won't know until I open up the area."

"Can he wait until we get back to Panama?"

"I don't think so."

"Then all you can do is your best. I'll talk to the pilot about smoothing out."

Scorpio went to the flight deck. "We have a serious problem. Angelique needs to do surgery ASAP, or Cosmo will die. We need to smooth out if we can."

"No problem, we are out of the danger area. I'll get her slowed down and smoothed out."

The pilot pulled the throttle back and dropped the flaps to forty-five degrees. The Dasher smoothed out.

Angelique and Barber were setting up the equipment when one of the captives came to help. "Can I be of any help? I was a surgery RN before I got into politics."

"Yes," Angelique said. "I don't have the training for what I will be doing. Any help will be grateful."

"Angelique, how am I?" Cosmo finally asked, slurring his words...

"Hi, glad to have you back. You have a serious wound. I need to do surgery, but..."

"But, nothing. I know you can do it. I know you will do your best. That is all I ask for."

"Okay, handsome. I'm going to put you out with chloroform, so good night." She started, "Scorpio."

"Yes."

"I'm going to be using chloroform. You might tell the pilot he should be on O2. We don't want him going to sleep on us."

"Okay, you got it. Angelique, you'll do okay."

It was several minutes into the surgery. "Oh," Angelique said, looking at the RN. "The kidney is ripped apart. It needs to come out."

"You're right, doing good. Keep going. I'll get a bag of plasma started. Do you have any blood on board?"

"No."

"Plasma will have to do the job."

The surgery went on for two hours. No one said anything. Then the RN said, "Great job. No bleeding and you have things together and ready to close up."

"Yeah, just about done. What are his vitals?"

"The BP is 102 over fifty-eight, and oxygen is eighty-six, rate, fifty-seven."

"Well, not quite out of the woods, but that is better than what it was a couple of hours ago."

"You did good, Angelique. He may need a transfusion when you get home."

"How are things, Angelique?" Scorpio inquired. "The pilot has been hanging out and can land anytime you are ready."

"We're okay, and we can land. But I'm mentally beaten."

"I understand," Scorpio putting his arm around Angelique. "You did great. When we transfer to the Global in Panama, it will be tight. Do you think Cosmo can sit up?"

"No, he won't be waking up for a while yet, either. He needs to lay flat. What about taking the Dash all the way to Dallas?"

"Good question." Scorpio walked onto the flight deck. "Hey, is it possible to go all the way to Dallas?"

"Oh, boy." The pilot was computing things and turned to Scorpio. "I think so, and it will be close. We will be on our reserve tank." Scorpio gave a thumbs-up and walked back to Angelique.

"Okay, you got it. With the Dash's long-range tanks and reserve tank, we can make it." A pause. "Well, the pilot thinks he can!"

"Let's hope so," Angelique responded in a concerned voice.

"We called and told the pilot to take the Global and head home. How is Cosmo doing?"

"He is stable, but it is too soon to know if he will make it."

"Scorpio, Angelique did a good job. Cosmo has a fighting chance," RN said. "But it will be several hours before we know the outcome."

"What about Jasper?"

"Scorpio, Jasper is awake and has a headache, but he will be okay. I need to change the dressing on Joker, and he will heal okay."

"Great job, Angelique," Scorpio said, hugging her. He returned to the flight deck and sat in the right seat. "How are you doing?" looking at the pilot.

"Well, I may have you take over for an hour or so. Having a hard time keeping alert."

"No problem. I'll make a call, then will give you a break."

The pilot gave a thumbs up.

Scorpio grabbed the satellite phone and dialed a number. "Hi, T.J."

"Hi, Scorpio. Are you in Panama yet?"

"No, due to the condition of Cosmo, we're headed home in the Dasher."

"Who was wounded, and what is their status?"

"Joker caught one in the arm, and Jasper took a flesh wound to the head. They are doing okay. Cosmos is stable, but we're not sure yet about the outcome. Angelique did surgery on him and saved his life so far. He may require a transfusion."

"Can the Dasher make it to Dallas?"

"The pilot thought he could but would be on the reserve tank."

"You have to go through Dallas customs. I'll have someone meet you there and get him to the hospital. I'll set it up as a wounded agent."

"Okay, T.J., that should work. I'll let you know when we get close to land."

"I'll call my friend, the FBI agent in Dallas, to make arrangements," T.J. said.

Several hours later, Scorpio looked over at the pilot. He sounds like a sawmill Scorpio was thinking, but he needed some ZZs.

"Dasher 1, 1, Niner, 6 Whiskey, this is Dallas approach, your status, over?"

The call surprised Scorpio. He was not expecting a Dallas approach call for at least another hour. "Dallas approach this is Dasher 1, 1, Niner, 6 Whiskey, at flight level 180, bearing 240 degrees, we're squawking 1, 4, 8, 0 we are about ninety minutes from Dallas, over."

"Roger, 1, 1, Niner, 6 Whiskey, after you land, you are cleared to hangar 12 to meet your medical service. Once you reach the outer marker, you'll have a medical emergency priority."

"Roger, Dallas, appreciate that. Dasher 1, 1, Niner, 6 Whiskey clear."

The pilot was waking up, "Ah, you say something? What's going on?"

"Oh, just Dallas approach, giving us medical emergency priority for landing when we hit the outer marker."

"Oh, that's nice of them. I'll take over now. Thanks, Scorpio. I needed that break. How are your patients doing?"

"I don't know. I'll go check." Scorpio got up and walked towards the back.

"Angelique, how are your patients doing?"

"Joker and Jasper will live another day. Not so sure about Cosmo. He is not doing well. He needs blood. The RN thought he might be losing blood somewhere. His vitals have fallen in the last hour."

"We should be on the ground in about forty minutes. We have landing priority and have a medical unit waiting for us."

"That's good news. I hope we make it in time."

Scorpio headed back to the flight deck but stopped; looking at the team, he said, "Everyone, we will be landing in a few minutes. Make sure everything is strapped down."

Before long, the Dasher touched down and taxied over to the hangar. There were several SUVs and an ambulance nearby. The Dasher pulled up near the SUV. T.J. was standing there with a nurse and a couple of first responders. Scorpio lowers the door.

"Hi, T.J.," Scorpio said.

"Hi, Scorpio,"

The nurse and first responders run up the stairs.

T.J. said, "So, how are your guys?" Looking at Scorpio.

"About the same, T.J. We must get Cosmo to the hospital. Not sure what his status is. Not doing well, I know for sure."

Before long, Cosmo was off to the hospital. T.J. said, "Don't worry about Cosmo; we have him listed as an FBI agent. I'll keep you posted."

Scorpio motioned the team to get on board, "Let us head home. Thanks, T.J., will be talking to you later."

It was several days later. Scorpio walked into the conference room. Everyone had a drink in their hand.

"Okay, just letting you know Cosmo is doing good. He should be out of the hospital in 3-4 days." He walked to the bar and fixed a drink. Then he walked over to the whiteboard and started drawing a map.

"What you have there, Scorpio, looks like the island from the last mission," Barber said.

"Yup, I just want to review what happened and see if we learned anything. My drawing is, as Barber said—a map of our last mission. When the shooting started, Barber, Zula, and I were making our way here," pointing at the map. "I put Star about here and Zula about here," again pointing at the map. "Cosmo and Joker were here, I think."

"Looks right, but Cosmo was found shot here," Barber said, pointing at the map. "If Joker was here," again pointing at the map. "Who was covering Cosmo?"

No one said anything. I have just looked at the map. Joker spoke up. "I think I screwed up. I should have been in the same bunker as Cosmo. But I was here when the shooting started." Joker points at the map.

"Cosmo must have moved on without you knowing it," Star said.

"Yeah," Joker said. "As I said, I screwed up. I didn't focus on our next move."

"How come? What were you thinking?" Star asked.

"Wasn't on the mission," Joker paused. "I was thinking about Angelique. Then, all hell broke loose, and refocusing on the mission took me a second. Cosmo was shot because I wasn't covering him as I should have been."

"Oh, no," Angelique said. "Hon, you must be mind, body, and soul on the mission at all times until the mission ends. That's why you guys train so hard." She paused, got up, and walked over to the window. "If I weren't here, that would not have happened."

"NO, you are not to blame. I'm responsible," Joker said. "You are right that the mission must be the only thing on our minds until it ends. Sorry, I take full responsibility. I screwed up. It will never happen again," Joker said sadly.

"Well, this brings us to a dilemma where we have never been before. One of the rules the Boss set up years ago was: if a member fails in their responsibility and a member is wounded or killed because of it, then a secret vote is to be taken by all the members. It only takes a single 'no' vote to remove a member," Scorpio said.

"Scorpio," Jasper said. "I remember that. It was a marble vote system. But I don't have a clue what that is."

"The Benevolent and Protective Order of Elks use the system," Scorpio explained. "Maybe they invented the method. I'm not sure why Boss selected it. However, it is where everyone takes one marble out of the bag, either white marble or black marble. They place it in a box. No one can see the other one vote. In this case, everyone votes except Joker. Once the vote is done, the marbles in the box are shown—either one at a time or dumped into a bowl. Suppose there is a black marble. Then you are done and have to leave. No ifs, and's, or but's about it, you go."

"Wow, it sounds like a crud way to vote," Bingo said. "But it works, I guess."

"When Cosmo gets back to the base, we hold a meeting, ensure everyone understands the charge against Joker, and vote. That is it," Scorpio said.

"I'm okay with that," Joker said.

For several days, everyone stayed busy cleaning equipment. Everyone practiced with the rebreathers and reviewed medical procedures with minor surgery for bullet wounds. The team's proficiency was at its best.

They heard the Global fly overhead. They walked onto the deck. Scorpio said, "Looks like Cosmo is back."

The Global taxied up to the team house. Everyone walked over to meet Cosmo. The door opened, and the stairs went down. The pilot was at the door, "Hey, I have a package for you." He stepped back, and Cosmo appeared. He was smiling and walked slowly down the stairs. Everyone was happy to see him. Joker hugged him, "Sorry, buddy. I screwed up. I'm glad you are alive and back with us."

"It's good to be back, and I feel great."

"I talked to the doctor yesterday. He said he probably would release you, but he said no duty for at least a month. So, you get to do KP," Scorpio chuckled. "Oh, the boss will be here tomorrow."

"We have a mission?" Barber asked.

"No, we are having a team meeting. Cosmo," Scorpio said, "come into my office. I need to explain our situation."

Everyone except Cosmo knew what it was about. They went back to work on what they were doing. The pilot was taxiing out for take-off and heading back home.

The following day, everyone was quiet, not the regular chit-chat. They sat around the conference table, having coffee, reading, or fiddling with the equipment. The Boss walks in. "Well, this sure is a sober bunch." He walked to the bar, fixed a bullet bourbon on the rocks, and sat down.

"Boss, I explained to everyone why we're here," Scorpio said.

"Thanks, Scorpio. When I developed the rules for the team, I thought about what happens if we lose someone because someone didn't do their job." Taking a sip of his drink. "I decided the fate needs to be determined by everyone on the team, including myself. The method I came up with was how we voted when I was a member of the ELKs. Before we vote, Joker can say anything he wants; then Cosmo takes his turn. Afterward, if anyone has a question, you can ask it. Any questions before we start?”

Everyone shook their heads no.

“Okay then. Joker, what do you want to say?”

“Cosmo, I’m sorry you were injured. I’m happy you were not killed because I didn’t do my job correctly. Also, I apologize to the team and the Boss because I failed to follow the rules. If you decide I should leave, I’ll go, but I am still proud of the team. If you decide I can stay, I promise this will never happen again.” Joker sat down.

“Cosmo,” Boss motioned his turn.

“I understand why there are rules; we depend on them to get the job done, and we all come home.” Cosmo took a sip of water. “I think we all learned from this. We can’t take a second and not focus on the mission. I was lucky, and I’m not dead.”

“Okay, does anyone have any questions?” No one said anything. Boss got up and walked over to a cardboard box. Took out a bag and a box. The box had a rubber cover with a slot in it. “This is how it works. One at a time, come over to open the bag. You will find white and black marble. You reach in and take one marble. The white marble Joker stays. Black, Joker leaves. You take the marble in your hand so no one can see which one you took. You lower your hand through the rubber slot on the box and drop the marble in the box. In this case, it only takes one black marble. Once everyone has voted, I remove the slide at the bottom of the box. I lift the box. If there are one or more black marbles, that's it. Joker leaves. Any questions?"

Everyone just looked at each other. Angelique walked over to Joker and sat next to him.

"Okay," Boss said. "I'll be first." He reached into the bag, picked a marble, and placed it in the box. Everyone, one by one, got up, walked over, and did the same. Everyone was focused on the box, and it was a solemn few minutes.

Once everyone voted, they all sat at the table, staring at the box. Boss got up, went to the box, and removed the slide from the bottom. Everyone could hear the marbles drop to the table. The boss grabbed the box, lifted it, and set it next to the marbles. Everyone stared at the marbles. Then they looked at Joker. The boss walked over to Joker. He reached out to shake his hand. "Well, it looks like you get to stay."

"You didn't think you'd get off that easy, buddy," Scorpio said with a glint in his eye and a smile about to break his joined lips.

Everyone smiled. Scorpio remained collected.

Scorpio was sitting with his feet up on his desk in his usual position, a Cuban stogie in his mouth, never lighting it, just chewing on it. He was involved in reviewing the team's equipment inventory and additional needs. The last primary mission was the Panama mission. Since then, there have been a dozen small projects over eight months. They mainly dealt with rescues involving kidnappers and the assassination of a murderous general in Brazil. The only additional equipment Scorpio was considering was the new imaging capability to detect individuals behind concrete walls. They did have a sniper scope that performed the same job, but he felt the new system would be a valuable addition. It was priced at six-nine thousand, but it would also work with their current laser system.

Jasper walked into Scorpio's office. "Sorry I'm interrupting you, but I just got this off the fax. It's from Lizzy. I'm unsure why she didn't call; maybe she could not. Anyway, it looks like some of the villagers we trained had several family members kidnapped by some of the remaining group members we took out."

"What does the message say?" Scorpio questioned.

"Ah, she said. We're in trouble; the village you helped out and trained is able to maintain security in the village. However, three of the top people got word that their family members were kidnapped by some of the groups that had previously controlled the village. They are demanding two million dollars; they say it is back pay. It goes on to say. I will call you tomorrow afternoon. The Sister and I are meeting someone to get additional information. Later. Lizzy."

"I wonder who they are meeting? I hope they don't do something crazy and get themselves captured."

"I don't know, Scorpio. Should we contact T.J. and see if one of his guys knows anything? He usually knows what goes on in different places."

"Yeah, Jasper. Good idea." Scorpio reaches for the phone and dials a number. It rang a couple of times. "T.J.?"

"Hey, Scorpio. I thought that was your number. I bet you are calling regarding Lizzy and Sister."

"Ah, yeah. But how did you know that?"

"Well, I have people on the ground in Bogota, Columbia, following a bad guy involved in extortion, murder, and child pornography. He also has ties with the group in the village you rescued. He reported and said two ladies joined the group, maybe for a meeting. He wasn't sure. I sent him pictures of Lizzy and Sister. He confirmed they were the two."

"Oh, crap! I hope they're not getting in over their heads. T.J. Lizzy sent a note saying this group kidnapped the family members of some of the top people. Lizzy said they were meeting someone to get more information."

"In that case, Scorpio. I think they just walked into a bee's nest."

"I hope not, T.J. You think this guy has kidnapped these people Lizzy was referring to?"

"Well... it is not his MO, but I don't know for sure. I'll get back to my guy, brief him on what Lizzy was up to, and see what he can find out. This guy is what you would call a stupid genius. I don't know how he gets information without getting into trouble. Somehow, he does."

"Okay, T.J., talk to you later." Scorpio hung up.

"Hey, Bingo!" Scorpio yelled.

"What's up?" Bingo asks, running into his office.

"Are you still communicating with the chief, ah... You know, in the village, we helped out?"

"Yes."

"Give him a call and see what you can find out about what Lizzy told us."

"I'm on it."

Scorpio was looking at imagery around Bogota. It was a waste of his time looking at this without knowing where they might be. He was wandering about when the phone rang. He reached over to answer it and noticed T.J. was calling. "Hi, T.J."

"Hi, Scorpio. Were you sitting on the phone?"

"No, not really. What's up?"

"Well, Scorpio. I have additional information on Lizzy and Sister, and they met with our bad guy. There were several cars in and out of the compound. We think our ladies were in one, but I can't be sure. Anyway, we haven't seen them for two days. My spies talked to the cleaning people, and they said the two ladies might have been taken somewhere in a car yesterday. But didn't know where to."

"So, T.J., our ladies probably joined the people who were kidnapped."

"I think you're right, Scorpio. Oh, hang on, be back in a minute."

Crap, I was afraid that could add fuel to the flame, he thought.

"Hey, I'm back, Scorpio. I have a saving grace. My guy in Ecuador reported in. He says the picture I sent about our ladies was near Ibarra."

"Great, so where in the hell is Ibarra?"

"It's a small town about forty miles south of the Colombia and Ecuador border."

"Okay, T.J., that means we have a fighting chance. Now what? And how come they are that far south?"

"I don't know why Ecuador was selected. My guy will get back to us in a few days when he finds out where they are tracked down. So, I'll talk to you then."

"Okay, T.J.," a long pause. "Bingo," Scorpio's empowered voice.

"Ya, boss."

"See what you guys can find out about Ibarra. It's a small town in Ecuador. We might be going there."

"Got it."

It was several hours later when the phone at the base rang.

Scorpio picked it up, "Hey, T. J., hope you found something."

"Yup, Lizzy and Sister Karen did walk into a bee's nest. My snitch says they are being held in a small cabin near Ibarra, Ecuador. The cabin is near River Carchi. However, the cabin is heavily guarded. He thought about 15 guys."

Bingo and several others got up and began a search for satellite imagery.

"Okay, T.J., any ideas?"

"My snitch, an aging yuppie, said to meet him at the El Triangulo. It is a nightclub off highway E35. That is East of Ibarra, and he will send the coordinates. There is a small opening about a mile north of the nightclub. You can skydive into there, and there is lots of cover to hide the gear."

"Is there a date when we are supposed to do this? I'd like a few more details on the cabin, how we get there, how we find this guy at the club?"

"Yes, I just got a drawing of the cabin. He will guide you there, and I also just received a few pictures of the area. I'll forward this to you, and you should have it in a few minutes. Oh, this guy is a regular customer. Just tell the bartender that you are looking for Santiago Sebastian 3rd. Regarding the date and time, that is up to you. I'll get that information back to him when you are ready."

"Okay, T.J., we will get on this shortly and get back to you soon," Scorpio responded, unsure about the mission. "Okay, guys, I need you in the conference room."

Jim was enjoying his new boat, a twenty-foot Bayliner. Great for fishing, water skiing, and just enjoying the lake. He took another sip of his beer while watching the fly floating. He only used a fly rod and didn't like trolling as he thought it wasn't challenging enough. He would often take the barb off the hook, making it more sporting, at least in his mind.

"Hon," Jane said with a cunning smile. "Are you with your team or off in Wonderland?"

Jim responded sheepishly, "Ah, no, just watching the fly."

"But hon, you're looking over there, and your fly is over here," she pointed.

"Well," he was blushing, "I guess you caught me. Yeah maybe. It's been several months since I have talked to them or seen anything in the paper."

"Maybe you need to get in touch with them, you know, a blast from the past!"

"Yeah, that would be cool," reaching for his phone and dialing a number.

It rang several times, and he thought maybe they were out on a mission when someone said, "Hello."

"Hello, this sounds like Jasper?"

"I'll be damned. Hi, Boss. It's great to hear from you. What are you doing right now?"

"Well, Jasper, I'm floating around on this beautiful lake in my new boat and having a beer with Jane. What are you doing?"

"That sounds like fun. Well, we're just planning a mission. We think Lizzy and the Sister are in trouble."

"What did they do?"

"We think some of the family members from the group we saved from bad guys are being held hostage. Lizzy and Sister met with them, we think in Bogota, and now are in a cabin in Ecuador."

"Is that the group you helped train?"

"Yeah, Boss, I guess we missed a couple of the bad guys. Lizzy and Sister thought they could negotiate with them but then became a hostage. T.J. has a guy on the ground who will guide us, so now we're putting a plan together."

"Hi, Boss," Scorpio said. "I thought I recognized the voice. So, you enjoying retirement?"

"Hi, Scorpio. Yeah, retirement is hard work. You have to decide where to go fishing or where to take a nap. You know, management decisions!"

"Must be nice."

"So, I hear our ladies are in trouble."

"Yeah, Boss. We have a plan roughed out. Probably take off tomorrow or the next day."

"What's your plan so far?"

"Well, Boss, we are having problems getting clearance into Quito, Ecuador. Our pilot recommends we take the Global to Bogota. He is often in and out of there and has a good rapport with the airport manager. We meet with the Dasher 8 and fly south along the border of Ecuador. The pilot thinks he can drift far enough south before ATC in Ecuador warns him, he is in their airspace. I think he made a deal with the devil. That's what he said. And I didn't ask him to clarify that as I didn't want to know."

"That sounds tricky. I hope his deal with the devil doesn't get you in trouble." Boss commented.

"We're thinking of doing this at night. We can open high and drift into the LZ if the wind favors us. We have looked at the LZ on the satellite imagery, which looks feasible. The walk to the nightclub is easygoing and has lots of cover."

"Nightclub?"

"Yeah, Boss. That is where we meet this guy, Santiago Sebastian, 3rd. He will guide us to the cabin. That is about as far as we planned to go. Once we reach the target location, we then plan the rest."

"Oh, one of those missions? How about getting out? What are your thoughts about that?"

"You remember our helicopter guy, the WWII bomber jacket?"

"Yeah, didn't he work out of Bogota?"

"Sure does, Boss. When we take off from Bogota, he will work south and land near the border. Our target is 38 miles into Ecuador. He will hang out near the border until he hears from us."

"Wow, lots of loose ends. When you return, give me a shout. I'd like to hear how it went."

"Will do, Boss." They hung up.

The morning started as usual. Scorpio was on the deck having coffee, watching the sun come up over the Nevada desert. Jasper walked out with a cup of coffee.

"Good morning, Scorpio."

"Good morning, Jasper. Things about ready?"

"Yes, Sir. The Global should be landing in a few minutes. The Dasher will be in Bogota as scheduled. The helicopter is on standby waiting to hear from us, and all the gear is ready to be loaded."

"That's great, Jasper. Thanks for making sure everything is ready. What about the team? Everyone got their head screwed on right and focused on the mission?"

"Yes, Sir. They have never been more ready for a mission."

"I hope so. I have a feeling this mission is going to be a challenge." Scorpio looked up. "There's the Global, right-on time. Let's get the guys moving."

The Global made another perfect landing and taxied up to the team house. The pilot opened his window. "Hey, Scorpio. You ready to go?"

"Yes, Sir."

"You see that black cloud," the pilot pointed. "That's one big storm. We need to be out of here in the next 45 minutes, or we will be stuck on the ground."

"We will be on board in ten minutes. Come on, guys, get loaded."

Everyone was getting the gear on board. Joker walked over to Angelique, "Don't worry. Love you."

"I love you too, and you better stay focused on the mission, or I'll kick your ass if you get wounded again."

"I promise I'll stay focused and think about you all the way home."

"You better."

"Okay, love birds, Joker get your ass on board," Jasper said.

It didn't take long before the aircraft was off the ground. The landing gear went up, and the Global turned southernly. Scorpio sat back in his chair, knowing this would be another long flight. He looked over to the guys, "You all better get some shuteye. You are not going to get much sleep the next several days."

Everyone knew what Scorpio was saying. They had all been there before. Several hours later, Scorpio woke up feeling the engines slow down. He looked out the window and recognized Bogota. He sat up and looked over at the guys. They were still sawing logs.

"Hey, sleeping beauties. Time to go to work."

Everyone was saying, "Yah, yah," as they got up and looked out the window.

"Scorpio," Jasper said, yawning. "How come the pilot picked Bogota and not somewhere closer to the job site?"

"Yeah, besides, Bogota is over 8000 feet ASL, Scorpio, give us nosebleeds," Bingo added to the question.

Everyone chuckled.

"The pilot felt the Bogota airport is so busy no one would question our presence."

They could feel the Global banking left when the pilot came on the intercom. "Gentlemen, we will land shortly at El Dorado International Airport on runway 13 Left. Short taxi to the corporate hangars. Make sure everything is tied down."

It wasn't long before the Global pulled up alongside the Dash-8. Scorpio was looking at his watch.

"Guys, we're about two hours ahead of schedule. So, take your time getting the Dasher loaded. Before we take off again, let's double-check everything," Scorpio said, standing between the two aircraft.

The pilot of the Dasher leaned out the window, "Hey, Scorpio!"

Scorpio turned towards the sound. "Oh, hi. You about ready to go?"

"Absolutely! We must be airborne in fifty-three minutes to stay on schedule. Also, I checked the winds. The way I have it figured; your exit point will be about twenty-eight miles into Ecuador. Set your lasers for the parachutes to open at 11,380 feet. Your standard glide slope should put you at least half a mile from the nightclub for your LZ. Should be no problem."

"That far into Ecuador, are you going to have a problem with their ATC?"

"Probably, but by the time I wander back on course, you all will be gone."

"Okay, sounds like a workable plan."

Several minutes later, the two Pratt and Whitney 150's turboprop engines on the Dasher 8 started to wind up to taxi speed. The pilot began to roll out of the corporate parking area. The pilot got on the radio, "El Dorado departure. This is Dasher Bravo 6, Niner, 4, Lima, leaving corporate parking for runway 31 Right for takeoff, over."

"Roger Dasher Bravo 6, Niner, 4 Lima. Hold on to the outer marker and contact tower on 118.25; departure clear."

"Roger departure, Bravo 6, Niner, 4 Lima clear." The pilot reached over and dialed 118.25 on one of four radios. "El Dorado tower, Dasher Bravo 6, Niner, 4 Lima on hold at outer marker ready for takeoff, over."

"Roger Bravo 6 niner, 4 Lima. Hold until inbound has cleared."

"Roger Tower, 4 Lima." The pilot hit the intercom button. "Guys, we're waiting for clearance. We have an airbus coming in, and once he is cleared, we will be airborne."

Several minutes later, the tower, "Dasher Bravo 6, niner, 4 Lima, you are cleared for takeoff, over."

"Roger tower, cleared for takeoff, Bravo 6, niner, 4 Lima." The pilot pushed the throttles slightly forward, turning on the runway and then pushing the throttles for full power. It wasn't long, and they were headed south toward Ecuador.

About an hour later, the pilot said, "Okay, guys, time to get your gear on. I'm flying parallel to the border between Columbia and Ecuador for about eighteen more minutes. Then I'll drift south, and you are on target when the doors open. Good luck with your mission."

"Okay, guys, you heard the pilot," Scorpio said. "Same order and plan as last time we made this jump."

"Bravo 6, Niner, 4 Lima, this is Ecuador ATC."

"Ecuador ATC, this is Bravo 6, Niner, 4 Lima, over."

"Bravo 6, Niner, 4 Lima, you are now in Ecuador airspace. What is your intention?"

"Ecuador ATC, this is Bravo 6." The pilot was trying to stall for another 2 minutes, and that would put him on target. "Sorry, I didn't realize I was in your airspace."

"Yes, sir, you're about twenty-plus miles off course. If you don't correct your course, I must send you some visitors."

"Well, guys, I've been had by the Ecuador ATC. I'll need to change course. The door will open in a few seconds. You still should be okay. Good luck."

Everyone was ready and standing in order by the door. Soon, the ready light came on, and the door opened. Scorpio was staring at the green light. It seemed like forever, but it was only a second, and the green light came on. Everyone went out the door, and the door closed.

Scorpio was looking for the laser to mark the LZ. There it is, he said to himself. He could see lights, probably the nightclub. The display on his visor showed everyone nearby, and his altitude was approaching opening altitude. Seconds later, he could feel the tug from the harness; the chute had opened. He looked around. Then he spoke into his mic. "You all doing, okay?"

Everyone answers back, saying yes.

"Okay, good. If we hold this heading, it looks like we will be about ½ mile from the nightclub across the road. I'm picking up the ground. So far, several trees are off to our right, about 50 yards. Our LZ looks grassy for the most part. You picked good Jasper."

In minutes, they were on the ground. "Okay, everyone good?" Scorpio asked.

Yes, that was the answer he got back. "Okay, let's get our gear packed and hidden until we pick it up later. Let's get our jumpsuits off. We don't want to look like we fell out of an airplane when walking into the nightclub."

Everyone chuckled.

It didn't take long before they walked across the nightclub's parking lot. Jasper said, "The front of this place looks like it could be a strip club!"

"Yeah, it does. But look at this black and white checker floor. That would drive me crazy after a few drinks," Scorpio commented.

They walked up to the bar. "Yes, sir, what can I get you?" The lady bartender asked.

"Yes, ma'am, we are to meet Santiago Sebastian 3rd."

"Oh, the Cholo. He sits with the white hat with the two ladies over there."

"Thank you."

"Scorpio, what did she mean by Cholo?"

"Well, Jasper, a Mexican term for a gangster."

"That's nice. Wonder if he is part of the group that has the girls?"

"I don't know, but let's keep alert. We may be walking into a trap ourselves." Scorpio was wondering.

They walked up to the gentlemen and ladies. The gentleman looked up. "What can I do for you?" A couple of other guys stood up at the next table.

"I'm Scorpio. We were to meet you here, and you are to guide us to a special location."

"Oh, yes. Well, grab a seat, grab a couple of ladies, and have a drink."

"No, Sir. We don't have time."

"We have all kinds of time, and it's only about a four-hour walk from here. Be daylight in a few hours and be easier walking."

"No, Sir, we will go now!"

"I'll tell you when we go!"

"Well, you stay here and enjoy yourself. We are gone." They start to leave.

"Just a minute. Where is my money?"

"You don't get a dime until you do your job," Scorpio said, getting impatient with the guy.

The two guys at the next table reached inside their jackets.

"Gentlemen, I have two guys over there in the dark corner, and they have you in their sights. If you remove that hardware, you will be dead; all of you. Sebastian, you and your two lady friends will also be dead."

The guy looked at his two bodyguards and said, "Relax, we don't want a shootout in the club. Okay, I'll show you the way, but when do I get my money?"

"When we reach the site, you get your money and leave."

"How do I know you won't kill me anyway?"

"You don't. But you do your job, get the money, and leave us to do our job." Scorpio was trying to explain the situation.

"Okay, let's get going," Sebastian said, getting up while kissing the two ladies and saying, "Keep your asses hot and purring. I'll be back soon."

After leaving the club, Scorpio looked at Bingo. "If those thugs follow us, take them out in the woods and catch up with us."

"You got it."

Sebastian said a couple of hours later, "It's about another mile to the cabin. It is just over the top of that hill," he pointed.

"Okay, once we get on top of the hill and see the cabin, you'll get your money, then leave."

They continued the hike, reaching the top of the hill; looking down through the trees, Scorpio could see a cabin. "Is that it?"

"Yes," Sebastian said. "Now, where is my money?"

"Not so fast," Scorpio said cautiously. "Jasper, you, Cosmo, Star, and Zula. Do a recon and see what you find."

"Okay, let's go, guys," Jasper said. "Shouldn't take too long."

"You don't trust me that it's the right cabin?" Sebastian commented.

"Yup, you are right. I don't trust you. But we will know shortly."

Bingo showed up.

"Well, what happened to you? Stop off for a beer?" Sebastian questioned.

"No, I'm just bringing up the rear. Scorpio, they won't be a problem."

Several minutes later, Jasper and his team were close to the cabin. Jasper said, "Cosmo, you and Star check out the front, and if possible, check out the tent we saw while crawling here."

"You got it, Jasper. Come on, Star, let's crawl over to the tree line and go from there."

"Zula, let's get next to the cabin." A few minutes later. "Looks like a good place for the pin camera. See what you got, Zula."

It didn't take long to look inside. "I see five guys and our girls, nothing else."

"Okay, let's get back to the meet-up with Cosmo and Star," Jasper said.

It didn't take long to meet up. "Cosmo, how did it go?"

"Okay, couple of tents."

"Let's get back to Scorpio and fill him in," Jasper said.

A few minutes later, Jasper and the team came back. "Scorpio, it is the right cabin. There are nine bad guys. I know there's more reported being there, but that is what we think is there now."

"Okay, Sebastian, here is your money, and now you can leave." Scorpio handed him an envelope containing money.

"Thanks, Scorpio. Nice doing business with you," Sebastian said while leaving.

"Okay, Jasper. What about the hostages and our girls?"

"We counted five plus our girls in the cabin. There was heavy brush up against the cabin so we could get a pin camera in—no guards in the cabin. One door and one window, and both are in the front. There are two large tents in the front." Jasper drew a map on the ground. "Cosmo, you can fill this part in."

"Okay, Jasper. The tents are where the bad guys stay. There were three on guard duty in the front of the cabin. The others were either sleeping or sitting around a fire drinking,"

"Scorpio looks like an easy take," Star said. "We could simultaneously take the guys out by the cabin and the fire. Throw a couple of grenades in the tent, taking care of the others."

"I think that would be a good plan, Scorpio," Zula said, agreeing with Star.

"Okay, Bingo, Star, you two take out the tents a few seconds after we blow the hell out of the others. Everyone on the same page?"

Everyone gave a thumbs up.

"Let's get into position, check watches. We execute the plan in seven minutes from...now."

Everyone headed into position, crawling the last several feet.

Scorpio checked his watch. Two minutes left, he thought. He raised his weapon and took aim, glancing at his watch—six seconds, 5, 4, 3, 2, 1 and squeezed the trigger. The sounds of the grenades were heard a few seconds later. Scorpio and Jasper rushed into the cabin. Everyone in the cabin jumped up as they didn't know what was happening. Instantly, Lizzy and Sister recognized them and ran to them, hugging them.

"Oh my god," Sister said. "I prayed you guys would find us. We sure did a stupid thing."

"Yes, Sister, you did," Scorpio agreed. "Is everyone okay? Anyone need medical attention?"

"No, Scorpio," Lizzy said. "Everyone is in good shape."

"Jasper," Scorpio said. "Contact the pilot. He can land the helicopter near the cabin."

"Already on it, Scorpio The pilot said he was on the ground just across the border and should be here in about twenty minutes."

"Sounds great, Jasper. Let's get all the gear and everyone ready by that opening."

"What about the bodies, Scorpio?" Sister was asking. "We should try to bury them."

"Sister, sorry. But that noise you hear is the helicopter. He doesn't have clearance to be in this country. He can't hang around, and neither can we. Don't worry. Mother nature will take good care of them."

Sister walked over to the bodies and said a prayer as the helicopter descended into the opening.

"Holy cow, Scorpio! It looks like Blue Ridge Helicopter got themselves a fancy dude for a helicopter," Jasper said.

"They sure do, Jasper. That's a Sikorsky S-92. I bet that cost him a pretty penny."

"Okay, people, we need to get on board ASAP," Scorpio was yelling over the sound of the helicopter.

A few minutes later, they were off and heading north towards Bogota at tree top level. Once in Columbia, the pilot gained altitude to be safer. The pilot motioned to Scorpio.

Scorpio leaned into the flight deck. "Hey, you sure have a nice bird. You win the lotto?"

"No, no lotto. We are lucky to work for you guys and can afford this baby. Oh, this is my son. He ensures I pull the right lever and push the right buttons." Chuckling. "We have long-range tanks on her, giving us about a 1000-mile range."

"1000 miles... That means we will have to refuel somewhere?" Scorpio questions.

"You're right, Scorpio. I have a fuel cache about 230 miles from here. It takes us about an hour and a half to get there. This is a nice aircraft, but I can only get about 190 MPH out of her."

"So, in about three or four hours, we are in Bogota with the fuel stop?"

"Yeah, Scorpio, give or take a few minutes. There are sandwiches and cold water in the cooler, enough for everyone. Help yourself."

Scorpio gave a thumbs up and then passed out the food and water. Everyone was happy to see it and enjoyed the treat. An hour later, Bingo motioned to Scorpio.

"What's up, Bingo?"

"Scorpio, I know we can't land at Bogota yet, but we sure are getting awful low over these trees."

"The pilot has a fuel cache. I bet that is where we are landing."

The Sikorsky began to hover, moved slowly over an opening in the trees, and settled down. They could hear the engine slow down to an idle. The rotors slowed to a stop. The pilot's son went to the door and opened it. He said, "We will be here a short time. Just going to put some juice in the tank."

"Can I be of any help," Scorpio said, walking behind him.

"Sure, help me pull this camouflage off this barrel."

It wasn't long before they started pumping gas into the helicopter. Several minutes later, the pilot's son said, "That should give us plenty of fuel to get us to Bogota. Let's get this covered up and get on board."

Scorpio follows the son up the stairs and closes the door. The rotors began to turn, and before long, the Sikorsky raised above the trees and continued to Bogota. Scorpio walked back to his seat.

Zula leaned over to Scorpio, "This is the only way to travel. It even smells new."

"Sure does, but that smell you smell is money. I'd say about 27 million," Scorpio said. He then laid back in his seat. He felt a kiss on his cheek. He jumped and turned to see who it was.

"Sorry if I scared you," Lizzy said. "Just wanted to thank you for saving us again. I guess we were rather stupid doing what we did. But how did you track us down? That had to be a miracle in itself?"

"Well, Lizzy, it's called the CIA. They know everything. You got lucky; one of T.J.'s guys spotted you at the Bogota airport. From there, we found where the bad guys had you. Then, they found they had moved you and the other hostages to Ecuador. From there, we just got lucky, I guess."

"I'm glad about that. The hostages were the family of some of those you saved several months ago. The bad guys you took out were the last of those who harassed the village. So, they shouldn't have any future problems."

"That is good to hear. So, the people in the village are doing great?"

"Yes, Scorpio. The village is doing great. Mama Bear comes through regularly with tourist groups, and they spend a couple of days. We have built a hotel, well, maybe more like a resort. Thanks to Mama Bear, that business has given several jobs to the villagers. So, it has been great. Thanks to you and the team."

"Okay, let you all know," the pilot said, "we will be landing in about 15 minutes. I have clearance to set by the Global. I talked to your pilot, and he said he is ready."

"Lizzy, what are your plans once we get to Bogota?" Scorpio asked.

"We have contacts. We can arrange to get back to the village, and then Sister and I will go back to do what we do: helping people."

"Sounds good. You and Sister stay in contact with us. Here is our secure e-mail address." Scorpio handed Lizzy a card. "Next time, let us know what you are up to. We'll check it out before you move forward. Okay?"

"You got it, Scorpio. Thanks."

They could feel the Sikorsky hovering near the Global and the gear going down. A couple of minutes later, the Sikorsky settled on the ground, and the rotor slowed to a stop. Scorpio opened the door.

"Okay, let's get our gear moved over to the Global. Lizzy, I have a van for you and your group to take you where you need to go."

"Thanks, Scorpio, we appreciate that. Thank you all for risking your lives to save us."

"Yes, that goes for all of us," one of the hostages said.

Scorpio leaned into the flight deck, "Thanks for the ride. This is a beautiful chopper you have. Hope we see you again soon."

"Thanks, Scorpio. Anytime." The pilot gave a thumbs up.

The team hugged Lizzy and Sister as they got into the van. Scorpio and his crew loaded up the Global and headed home.

Jim was sitting on the dock, having just finished fishing and cleaning the results of a productive day. He heard the phone ringing in his office. "I'll get it," Jane said.

"Hon, it's Scorpio."

"Okay, on my way up."

"He'll be here shortly, Scorpio. He was cleaning the fish he caught today." Jane passed the phone to Jim.

"Hi, Scorpio."

"Hey, Boss. I heard you had a good day fishing."

"Yeah, Scorpio, it was a nice day on the lake. So, when will you bring the guys up to spend time on the lake as our guests?"

"Well, Boss, we will do that one day. But I called to let you know we have our girls back. They are okay, but I think they learned a good lesson."

"Glad to hear that. Is everyone okay? No problems?"

"It was another long mission, and most had to be planned on the ground. But it was easy. Got rid of the bad guys and got our people back."

"That is what I like to hear."

"Me too, Boss."

"You have another mission coming up?"

"No, not yet. But you never know. Depends on the Senator. Oh, by the way, our love birds are getting serious."

"Oh, how's that?"

"You know, Boss. It didn't take long for you to fall in love with Jane."

"Yeah, I understand. I hope we will make it a big deal when they get married."

"Yes, Boss. That is for sure. With that, Angelique wants to tell you something."

"Hi, Boss. I want you to be the first to know. Joker asked me to marry him, and I said YES!"

"Congratulations, Angelique!"

"Yes, Angelique, congratulations," Scorpio also said.

"But that is not all! You and Jane have been my family, and I was hoping you could give me away. That be possible?"

"Absolutely, Angelique. I would be honored. Have you selected a date yet?"

"No, not really. Depends on your schedule."

"Well, it is almost the end of August. How about we do the wedding here, in Montana, at our place on the lake?"

"Oh, gosh. That would be wonderful."

"We have the team fly here, the pilot and his family, plus we have Captain Sixto and Mama Bear. Oh heck, why not Sister and Lizzy? Anyone else you'd like to have?"

"That pretty much covers it. So, just need a date."

"Say, Boss," Scorpio interrupts. "Depends on you, but how about next Saturday, a week from now? I'm not trying to rush it, but that is open for the team. I'll check with the pilot and could arrange to have the Captain and Mama picked up."

"Well, I think we could have things arranged for her by that time. What about you, Angelique? Are we rushing it?"

"No way, I'm for that."

"Okay, Scorpio. Keep me posted on arrival, and Jane and I will have everything ready. Angelique, I will have Jane call you when she gets home later today, and you two can work out the girls' stuff. Later," hanging up the phone.

The next few days flew by. Jane and Angelique worked out the details. Scorpio had the schedule worked out with the pilot. He reached over to the phone and dialed a number. It rang once, "Hi Boss, just letting you know the pilot will be here tonight with most of the group. The Senator and T.J. will be here early in the morning. We should be airborne mid-morning and at the Helena airport about noon."

"That's great. I have two limousines from Big Sky Limo's picking you all up. They will take you to the Residence Inn by Marriott. That will give you all some time to rest and freshen up. I have dinner and a band set for 7 pm, and the wedding will be at my place on the lake at noon. There will be a BBQ to follow. Scorpio, when was the last time you went waterskiing?"

"Gee, probably high school. That was a couple of years ago." They both chuckled.

"Well, you all can sit back and enjoy fishing and waterskiing. I have jet skis, or you can do nothing and sit by the beer kegs. I think Angelique wants to learn to waterski."

"Boss, it sounds like something overdue for the team. Great wedding and a good time."

"Okay, Scorpio, we will see you tomorrow."

That evening, Jane, Angelique, and Jim sat around a fire and relaxed. Jim noticed Angelique staring at the fire, but she was elsewhere.

"Angelique," Jim said. "You, okay? You seem far, far away?"

"Yes, Sir. I'm just thinking how lucky I am. I'm excited about seeing Joker tomorrow and looking forward to the wedding. But I'm sad my folks are not alive to see me getting married. But you and Jane gave me a new life I'm grateful for."

"We're happy to have you in our family," Jane said. "Plus, having your wedding here with the people that love you."

"Well, ladies. I'm going to bed. The next couple of days are going to be fun. Good night." Jim walked into the house.

<hr>

Jim walked out onto the deck, watching the sun rising and having a cup of coffee, when Jane walked out. "Good morning, my love."

"Good morning, you are in a super mood."

"Of course, you started my morning out with a bang." They both chuckled.

"Yes, it was a good way to start the day. Last night's dinner and the band were great. Everyone sure had a great time."

"Yes, Jim, it was. Oh, I see our helpers are getting the dock trimmed with flowers for the wedding today. This is a great idea: having the ceremony on the dock with roses along the dock edge and an archway at the end of the dock with white carnations. It looks so beautiful. Who did you say was going to do the ceremony?"

"Oh, Judge Anderson. We went to school together. Not only a good friend but a good judge. But he would shit his pants if he knew what I was involved with!"

"Well.... let's don't make him shit his pants." They both laughed.

"Looks like our caterer, Big Sky BBQ, got things going." Looking at his watch, Jim said, "The guys should be here in about an hour. It was funny last night watching Angelique betting Joker she would be a better water skier than him."

"Well, hon. I think those two have many challenges ahead of them."

"I think you're right, Jane. Joker is on a dangerous mission and may not return alive."

"Jim," Jane looked into his eyes, "I know exactly what that is."

"Honey, I would talk to you before I go on a mission. However, that is what Joker's job is. Reality is. I hope Joker retires from the team and he and Angelique have a wonderful life. Joker has made enough money; they could do that."

"I hope so," Jane replied. "Oh, I hear the limos coming. The team is here."

They got up and walked over to the parking area. "Hi, great to see you all walking. After last night, I wasn't sure how many would show up," Jim said.

"Well, Boss," Scorpio said, "this is an important date. We're here for Angelique and Joker."

"Angelique, I haven't seen you smile so big before!"

"Oh, thanks, Jim. I'm so happy. I love Joker so much, and having everyone I love here is the best."

"Boss, thank you for this," Joker said. "I didn't think having someone so special in my life would ever happen. I love Angelique with all my heart. But I also know my responsibilities."

Angelique looked into Joker's eyes. "I love you too. I have never been this happy. But I understand your responsibilities also. I will never interfere with that. That is your job."

They both looked at each other but didn't say anything.

"Well, let's get started with the events," Jim said. "The BBQ is about ready. The Judge is here. So, would you like to start the ceremony? Oh, Angelique, I understand you have a bet with Joker."

"Yup, but let us get married first. Jim, don't forget you are giving me away!"

"That's right!" Jim was smiling. "Okay, everyone, let's do this!"

Scorpio, the team, Senator T.J., the pilot and his family, the director of the CIA,

Captain Sixto, Mama Bear, Lizzy, Sister Karen, and others lined the dock.

Jim arranged music from the local high school glee club. The music started, and Jim walked Angelique down the dock to Joker. Joker was wearing a tux. You could see from his expression that it was a first. Angelique wore jungle fatigues, a 45 on her right hip, a bowie knife on her left hip, and Joker's green beret. They stopped in front of the judge. Joker stared at Angelique, not believing what he saw.

The judge said. "We are here today to join Angelique and Joker, their true love, to spend their lives in marriage. I understand each has vows they want to say. Angelique, you are first."

"Thank you, Judge Anderson. Joker, I love you more than life. The reason I'm wearing this is because I support what you do. I know you may not come home when you perform your duties. I accept that and hope our time together will also be special."

"Joker, your turn," the judge said.

"Thank you, Judge. Thank you, Boss. Angelique, I have never felt this way about anyone. I also love you more than I can express. I'm glad you support what I do. I promise I will soon retire, and we can spend our lives together."

"I'm unsure if I want to know what you do for a living, Joker, and I won't ask. You may kiss the bride."

Joker leaned over and kissed Angelique. "I pronounce you man and wife," Judge said.

Everyone congratulated Angelique and Joker. The judge walked over to Jim. "Well, Jim. This was nice. I feel this group of folks is special and does a special type of work. I don't want to know. But I wish you, Angelique, Joker, and your team the best."

"Thank you, Judge. You are welcome to stay and have BBQ and try waterskiing."

"Oh, thanks, Jim. Your team needs to have this time together. I wish you the best. Bye."

The BBQ and water sports everyone enjoyed. It was fun watching Mama Bear trying to waterski. Yes, Angelique did show everyone up as per her plan. The Senator, T.J., the Director of the CIA, and others had fun water skiing, ski jets, and fishing. When the sun went down, there was a big bonfire, roasting s'mores, hot dogs, and many drinks. The party went on for hours. Jim entered his office to get a book for T.J. when he saw an urgent message on his answering machine. He picked it up. Someone from the CIA was looking for T.J. Jim walked back to T.J.

"Hey, T.J., I have an urgent message for you on the phone in my office."

"Thanks, Boss," as he walked towards the office. He picked up the message on the phone. A few minutes later, he returned to the party and waved at the Senator. After talking to the Senator, she waved at Scorpio. A few minutes later, Scorpio walked up on the stage. "Can I have your attention, please? Okay, this has been the best thing we have been involved with. Angelique and Joker are getting married. We all had fun and a great time. However, we have a priority red alert, meaning we must return. But first, I want to thank our Boss and Jane for all they have done to make this event one to remember."

"What is the alert, Scorpio?" Jasper asked.

"I don't have the details. Most of that is classified, so we must wait and see what is in our secure e-mail box. I can only tell you that we're heading back to the Amazon River. We will get the rest of the details when we return to the base."

"Scorpio," Jim said. "It is getting late, and we all have had lots to drink. On the safe side, don't you all need a good night's sleep before leaving?"

"Jim is right," the Senator commented. "I only know a few details; this mission will be challenging. Need to sleep off the booze, get a good breakfast, and then head back to the base."

"I agree," the pilot said.

Everyone finished their drinks and headed back to the hotel.

"Good night, Boss. I'll keep you posted," Scorpio said.

Several days later, the team was busy reviewing several maps and documents on the new mission in the conference room.

Scorpio walked in. "Well, guys, what do you think about the mission?"

"Of all the missions we have been on, some have been hairy, to say the least. And we have lost a couple of guys. I think this mission is dangerous." Jasper continued, "We have three top politicians that went on a hunting trip in the Amazon and got tangled up with some bad guys. Their camp is well-fortified and has twenty-eight well-armed guys. They want five million bucks for these three idiots. Let them pay the five-mil. You know they will probably die anyway!"

"You may be right," Scorpio commented. "How about touching base with Mama Bear and see if she knows anything about these duds?"

"We did," Joker said. "She knows where their hideout is. She agrees it is well fortified. She also said these guys are the worst of the bad guys in the region. It won't be easy."

"Huh, see if you can get her on the horn. I have some questions." Scorpio paused, "Oh, what does the imagery show?"

"Looks like the only way we can get close is by river, as with most of the missions in the Amazon. We contacted Captain Sixto. He said he knew about this group. Even going by the river is still a long walk."

"Okay, Scorpio. I'll give Mama Bear a jingle. She said she'd be available for the next couple of days." Joker reached for the phone and dialed a number, pushing the speaker button. It rang four times.

"Hello," Mama Bear answered. "Who do I have on the line?"

"Hi, Mama Bear. It is Scorpio, and I have the team on the line."

"Oh, hi to all of you. I suppose this call is about the new mission?"

"Yup," Scorpio said. "Looks like river access is the only way to get in. Do you see it that way?"

"Pretty much right on. Even then, it still is about a 60-mile walk through the jungle."

"Well, Mama. How do these guys get in and out from their base?"

"That's easy. They have their helicopter. They come and go as they please. They have several buildings and a large helo-spot. There are no trails in the area. The jungle is heavy. I kind of know where they are. I was there once on an invite. But was told never to come back again."

"Thanks, Mama. Do you have any thoughts on how we get in and get out without getting blown away?"

"Nope! I recommend you forget about this mission."

"What about hijacking the helicopter and getting in that way?"

"Well, Scorpio, slim chance of that. Even if you did and got in, your chance of getting out alive is even slimmer. These guys are not worth getting your team shot to hell over."

"So, if I understand. If we have a plan, we can't count on you?"

"That's right, Scorpio. I'll back you up anytime except when it is a suicide mission. I'm sure I can speak for Captain Sixto. NO WAY!"

"Thanks for the info. Talk to you later."

Scorpio hung up the phone and redialed a number. It rang a couple of times. "Hello, Scorpio, you have a plan?"

"We sure do, Senator. The plan is no way in hell. It is a suicide mission. Your politicians have to kiss their ass goodbye."

"So, we just have to pay the ransom?"

"I wouldn't. You pay the ransom; they are still killed. Your best bet is to deal with the government. Maybe they can make a deal by not bothering them if they let those guys go. But for us to go in is not going to happen."

"How about if we double the fee?"

"Senator, how would we spend the fee if we were all dead?"

"I guess you have a good point, Scorpio. Okay, I'll get back to you later."

"Okay, Senator." Hanging up the phone. Scorpio looked at the team. "You sure there is no way we can pull this off?"

There was a long pause, finally. "Scorpio," Cosmo said, "I'm sure this would be a good-paying job. But I see no way we can do this without all or some of us dying!"

"You're probably right. Let's look at the data again and sleep on it. In the morning, we may have a bright idea.

It was a long night for some, thinking about the possible mission. Scorpio walked out on the deck with his coffee. In deep thought, he walked swiftly into the conference room to look at the data. "Yeah, maybe," he said to himself.

"Yeah, maybe what, Scorpio?" Cosmo said, walking into the room.

"I was just thinking. These guys get their supplies on Wednesday. They get back to the camp around 10:00 p.m. or 11:00 p.m. Is that right?"

"Yeah, and just the pilot and crew chief are the only ones on board," Cosmo responded. "What are you thinking?"

"Well, from the data, the area isn't that well-lighted, and only a few guards. Remember what Mama said: There are no trails in or out. They feel pretty safe, so the two guards probably aren't that alert. Probably only glance at the helicopter when it lands."

"Okay, Scorpio, so... you think we may have a chance?" Cosmo questioned.

"Let's work on this and pass it by the group when they get up."

They worked on evaluating the data and worked up some options. Three hours passed, and some team filed into the conference room.

"What's going on?" Bingo asked. "You are not working on that mission?"

"Okay, guys," Scorpio said. "Gather around the table."

They all formed a circle around the table, looking at the imagery and drawings of the base showing the positions of where the guards should be. Where the captives should be, and where all the others might be.

"This is my thinking. We know when they get the supplies. We know we can hijack the helicopter. We dump the supplies and load everyone up. We carry AR-15s with silencers, two fifty-round clips taped together for quick reload, a couple of bandoliers, and a couple of belts of grenades. From the drone photos and the thermal imagery from the classified satellite, I think their habits are they don't carry their weapons around in camp. They're so confident they are that safe from attacks. The map here," pointing to a couple of buildings. "This has to be the team house; it is the biggest and appears from the data they walk in and out all day."

"Right, Scorpio," Cosmo continued, "That means this building must be where they keep their weapons."

"That's right, Cosmo and I think they may be heavily armed when they go out to raise hell, but in camp, only a couple of guys carry weapons."

No one said anything. Bingo was going through the data, images from the drone, and thermal imagery.

After a couple of hours, Bingo said, "Looking at the imagery, the ones going in and out of what we call the team house don't look like they are carrying weapons, possibly only a sidearm."

"That's what I see also," Jasper said.

Everyone agreed with Jasper's comment.

"There are two guard posts. And looks like one guard in this small building. I'm betting that is where the captives are."

"Yeah, I think you're right, Scorpio," Joker said. "The data confirms the small building is where the captives are, like you said. Only because if you compare these four images, there is someone who looks like she has delivered what could be food and or water. Then leaves."

"So," Scorpio paused. "Let me run this thought by everyone. We take the helicopter when they get supplies. We fly into their camp from this direction." Pointing at the map. "We fly over the guard post and take them out just before we land. Once we hit the ground, everyone, and I mean everyone, had to be out and headed toward the two buildings. Bingo, you take out the guard at the small building. You won't have much time, only a few seconds before he realizes something is happening. The first group takes the team house. If no one comes out, get close and fill it with grenades. The second team secures the weapons building."

"Sounds too easy," a couple of guys said.

"I think we need to figure out if some of the guys in the team house have weapons," Joker stated.

"You may be right, Joker. Maybe we take a couple of M-79s and lob in a couple of rounds, then fill it with grenades," Barber and Zula said.

"We have been on this all day. I think we have a plan. We need to figure out where the group picks up their supplies and how we take over the helicopter when they land or do their pick-up. We need more data about the pick-up point." Scorpio said.

"I bet that is something Mama knows," Barber said.

"Let's call her." Scorpio picks up the phone and dials. After a couple of rings. "Hi, Mama."

"Hi, Scorpio. What are you up to?"

"Well, Mama, I think we almost have a plan regarding the mission. What is missing is data on where the helicopter picks up the supplies and how that is handled."

"Really?" There was a long pause.

"Yes, Mama. Really. Can you get us that information?"

"Yeah, I could have that this afternoon. I'll get back to you in a few hours," hanging up the phone.

<hr>

Jim was sitting on the end of the dock, having his coffee, watching the sun come up over the mountains. It was another beautiful day, he thought. He was wondering how the team was doing. Being retired maybe wasn't the best thing. He still was concerned about the team and wanted to be involved.

"Hon," Jane said, walking out on the dock. "I don't know why it has taken almost two months for the photographer to send us the wedding pictures." Handing them to Jim. "Oh, we have a letter from Angelique."

Jim was going through the pictures. "These are pretty cool—lots of pictures. The photographer did a great job. Oh, I like the waterskiing ones."

"Jim, Angelique is going to have a baby!" Jane was screaming. "She writes. Joker doesn't know yet, as I didn't want to tell him until he returned from the mission in Brazil. He needs to focus on the mission, not think of me and the baby."

"I can understand that," Jim replied. "I didn't think they were going to take that job on, that it was too dangerous."

"Yeah, I remember you telling me that. That is why she noted that in her letter."

"I think I'll give them a call later today. From what I knew about it, that mission was a suicide mission. I'm surprised they decided to do the job."

"I'll drop a note off to Angelique and send her the pictures. Some of them are genuinely funny. Look at this one. The Director was hanging on the tow rope, standing on the dock with water skis. Oh, this one of Joker flying through the air off the dock. The team will laugh at these."

"I'm concerned about keeping Joker in the dark about being a dad."

"I understand, hon. But what happens if he gets killed and never knew he was a dad?"

"Well, I just don't know. Jane, I would feel bad. I think Angelique would be sad if Joker died, not knowing he was going to be a dad. I know their business is abnormal, and the outcome can't be controlled. What happens will happen." Long pause. "I would just feel sad."

"Honey," long pause. Jane held Jim's hand. "But that is something they have to deal with."

Jim looked at Jane. "Yeah, I know you're right."

Phone ringing. Scorpio looked at the ID. He picked up the phone. "Hi Mama, what did you find out?"

"Well, they always go to the same place. The pilot lands next to the warehouse. You already have that information. While they load the helicopter, the pilot and crew chief go across the street to the local bar and have a couple of drinks, maybe a lady or two. A couple of hours later, they stumble back and climb in the helicopter. That would be the time to take them."

"Sounds like a plan. Thanks, Mama."

"I'm concerned, Scorpio. This is a dangerous mission."

"We thought so also, but after studying the data, we don't think it is as dangerous as we first thought. They are pretty relaxed at their base. We think we can do this job."

"Okay, Scorpio. I wish you guys the best. Will be praying for you." Click!

Scorpio walks into the conference room and to the bar. He fixed a drink and then sat down. "Okay, gentlemen, I think our plan will work. Jasper and Barber, you both are qualified to fly the helicopter?"

"Yes," Jasper said. "However, Barber has more time in the one we will fly. But it should be no problem."

"Okay then. You two will be in charge of the helicopter and fly it out, as it will be the only way we can leave the area."

"No problem, Scorpio. Both Jasper and I have it covered."

"Scorpio, we have a mock village set up, and Barber said he could have a similar helicopter here in the morning." Zulu paused, taking a drink of his beer. "That gives us a couple of days to practice the mission."

"Gentlemen," Scorpio sat down, putting his feet on the table. "After tomorrow's practice, we will decide if we're ready for this mission. If so, then we move forward and get it done. Any questions?"

No one said anything. Scorpio said, "Okay, see you all in the morning."

═══════════════════════════════════════

Scorpio was up earlier than usual, standing on the deck overlooking the desert. It had rained last night, and the desert flowers and cacti turned the desert into a garden. Taking a sip of coffee, he said, "I love this place. The beauty God set before us is amazing, makes life worth living."

"Good morning, Scorpio, you talking to yourself?" Jasper said in a hung-over sound. "But you are right, it is a beautiful day," looking to the south. "I see our mock village survived the storm last night."

"Yup. Jasper. This is what I live for. The desert brings God to our doorstep."

Jasper, a little confused, "Ah yeah, I guess so. Sure, it is pretty. We are looking forward to our training today. I think this mission will be okay. We will be ready for whatever we run into. Why? Because we are the best!"

"When was Barber going to be here with the helicopter?"

"Well, Sir," pointing to the East. "I think Barber is coming in with the helicopter now."

"Okay, let's get the rest of the crew up. We have a busy day ahead of us. I want us to come back alive; this mission could be a disaster if we don't execute it correctly."

A couple of hours later, the team stood in front of a helicopter similar to the terrorist type. Everyone was equipped as planned and eager to make it work.

"This is the best team in the world." Scorpio takes a sip of his Bloody Mary. "God, this stuff is good. Anyway, that being said, we have two days to practice this mission. If we don't get it right, we're going to have dead people, and some of those will be us. This job is going to net us close to five million dollars. Sure, be nice to be alive to spend it." He takes another sip of his Bloody Mary. "Any questions?"

No one commented for several minutes. "Guys, the chopper is warmed up; let's try a dry run and see what we need to fix," Jasper said.

The team did several practice exercises for the next six hours, and on the final one... "Okay, we have it. There is no reason we can't do this mission and come back. Any comments?"

"I think we're all on the same page, Scorpio." Jasper took a drink of water. "We are ready."

"Okay, according to our data, the terrorist will pick up their supplies the day after tomorrow. So, let us plan on that timeline. Let's do it."

"Let's get the Global and fly into Manaus. Be there in two days. According to Mama, Wednesday is their supply day. Let's get our shit together," Scorpio ordered.

It was a busy day. Scorpio was standing on the deck with a bullet bourbon, watching the Global make the final approach onto their runway. "Gentlemen, the Global is here. Get the gear ready."

The Global taxied up to the team house. The pilot waved at them as he opened the door, and the steps went down. "Great to see you. It looks like we will have a good flight. No weather to give us problems and have a little tailwind."

"Sounds great. Okay, get your gear on board. Let us get airborne," Scorpio ordered.

They loaded up. Angelique hugged Joker. "Honey, stay focused on the mission. Don't worry about me. I'll be here when you get home." They kissed.

"Don't worry, Angelique. Joker will make it," John said.

"I know John. But I should have told him he will be a daddy."

"Oh my god, you're going to have a baby?"

"Yes."

"Why didn't you tell Joker? He is the dad, right?

"Of course, he is!" She looked at John with an angry look.

"Oh, sorry, I didn't mean anything negative about the comment. But why didn't you tell him?"

"This is a dangerous mission, and I need him home. He must stay focused on the mission, not me and the baby."

"I understand, Angelique. Joker will be okay," John said.

It was about an eleven-hour flight to Manaus, Brazil. Scorpio could feel the Global slow down. He looked out the window and could see Manaus. The sun was coming up. The pilot came on the intercom. "Gentlemen, sorry to wake you, but we will land in about twenty minutes. Please make sure everything is strapped down. Thanks."

The Global touched down and taxied over to the corporate parking. A limo pulled up next to them. "Okay, get the gear, and let's go," Scorpio ordered.

"Scorpio, I'm Agent Smith. I work with T.J. He asked me to pick you up and deliver you to the warehouse."

"Thanks, but we're a little early."

"Oh, well, the helicopter you're supposed to meet is on the ground next to the warehouse."

"What? When did they get there?"

"Oh, I'd say about thirty minutes ago."

"Shit, let's get going. This is not a good way to start," Scorpio mumbled.

They pulled up behind the warehouse and got out. "Jasper, take a peek around the corner."

"Will do, Scorpio. The chopper is empty, and several boxes are next to it."

"I guess we just wait. Jasper, let us know when the crew comes back."

It was getting dark when Jasper whistled over to Scorpio.

Scorpio turned and looked over to Jasper. Jasper was holding two fingers up.

The pilot and crew chief were just about at the helicopter when the team came running out. The two guys went for their sidearms when Jasper took them out.

"Okay, get the two guys loaded along with the boxes," Scorpio instructed.

"What are we going to do with the extra cargo?" One of them asked.

"We can't leave the guys here or the supplies. Someone may get suspicious and call the camp, telling them their crew forgot the supplies. We can't afford for them to get any hints something is wrong. We will dispose of the cargo over the jungle somewhere."

"Okay, Scorpio." Bingo was nodding.

It wasn't long before Barber got the helicopter up to speed when the team loaded. Scorpio gave Barber the thumbs up, and the helicopter struggled to rise off the ground due to the weight. Thirty minutes later, Scorpio said, "Dump the cargo and bodies out."

Zula opened the door, got rid of the extra weight, then closed the door.

"Barber," Scorpio said. "It's dark out here; you think you can find the camp?"

"I'm on course according to our maps. We should see a light within the next hour. If not, then I'll say something stupid like Oops."

Scorpio just smiled, shaking his head, "I hope not."

Everyone was searching for a light when Zula said, "Off to your right, about ten degrees. There is a dim light."

"Yup, that's it," Bingo said. "I'll come in over the guard towers to the right to make it easier to remove the two guards. Then I'll swing to the left and slide on the helipad, making a clear shot at the guard by the building."

The guards were taken out as planned. So far, everything was working as intended, Scorpio was thinking. The helicopter touched down, and everyone piled out, running towards their assigned locations, when someone from the window of the team house started firing.

"Get some 79 rounds into that building," Scorpio said, pointing.

A few seconds later, it turned into a significant firefight. Several M79 rounds found their target, a large explosion. The plan lasted about fifteen minutes, and then it was quiet.

"Jasper, you and Joker check the building where we think the hostages are. Rest of you hit the team house."

"Scorpio," Jasper responded. "Joker and Star are down. It looks like Zula is down also."

Scorpio entered the team house. The 79s and grenades did their job. Scorpio ran over to where the guys were down and started medical attention. "Jasper, how are the captives?"

Jasper came running over to Scorpio, "The captives are okay. How are our guys?

Star caught one in the left arm and leg. Zule got one in the left leg. But Joker is pretty much shot up. Both legs are bad, one in the left shoulder and a head wound. He lost a lot of blood. I have a tourniquet on both legs. He totally lost the left leg below the knee. His right leg, I don't know if I can save it. Not sure if I can save Joker. Get someone to help you take the diesel fuel and dump it. I want to torch this place when we leave. Then we need to get everyone on board."

Several minutes later, everyone was on board, and Barber was raising the helicopter, and they were airborne. They were watching the camp in a blazing fire as they left.

"Barber, how far is Manaus from here?"

"I think about two hours Scorpio."

Scorpio grabbed the satellite phone and dialed a number. It rang two times.

"Hi, Scorpio. How is the mission going?"

"Hi T.J., not going to be good. We have all the captives, but I have several of my guys wounded. Do you have contacts in Manaus? We need medical help. We should be there in less than two hours."

"Yes, Scorpio. I'll get it set up and get back to you."

Jasper leaned over to Scorpio, "How is Joker doing?"

Scorpio shakes his head, "I don't know. I'm not sure if Joker is going to make it. He has lost a lot of blood, and his vitals are getting worse."

"You know he is going to be a daddy?"

"What? No, I didn't. Does Joker know?"

"No, Angelique didn't want to tell him until he returned. She didn't want anything to distract him from the mission."

The satellite phone rings.

"Hi T.J." Scorpio said.

"Scorpio, how are you guys getting back?"

"We stole the helicopter from the bad guys."

"Great, you want to land at the Hospital de Aeronautica de Manaus. It's located on the south end of Manaus between Highway 319 and the river. It should be on a map if you have one."

"Stand by," long pause. "Yes, Barber said he has the location."

"Who is wounded?"

"Star is, but have him stabilized. Zula got one, but he will be okay. However, Joker will lose both legs but may not live long enough to get him to the hospital."

"Sorry to hear that. I have an agent going to meet you. He has taken care of the arrangements. I'll let them know about the wounds so they can be prepared. Good luck. Talk to you later, Scorpio."

"I have been in contact with the hospital," Barber said. "They said to call this number," handing Scorpio a notepad. "They said that is where we will be landing. They have several questions we need to answer so they can be ready when we land. Oh, we should be landing in about fifteen minutes."

Scorpio made the call and talked with the doctor. "Okay, they are ready when we land."

Barber made a left turn, approached the hospital, and landed. The medical team was there, loaded Joker on the gurney, and rushed inside. Another team took Star and Zula.

"Scorpio?"

"Yes."

"I work for TJ. We set up things so the guys are shown as special ops. So, there should be no questions by the police."

"Okay, great. What about the helicopter?"

"No problem. I have a guy coming. We can always use another helicopter."

Scorpio grabbed a cup of coffee and sat down in the waiting room. He dialed a number on the satellite phone. It rang twice. "Boss, what are you doing at the base?"

"Angelique wanted Jane to come down and help her with... You know, lady things. Did the mission go okay?"

"Well, we got the captives and killed the bad guys. The bad news is Star and Zula were wounded in the arm and leg but should recover. But Joker got shot up pretty badly. If he lives, he will lose both legs."

"You said if he lives?"

"Yeah, Boss. He is in bad shape. He is in surgery now, but the outcome will be a while."

"You want me to tell Angelique?"

"No, Boss. That's my job."

"Understand. I'll put her on the phone."

A couple of minutes later. "Joker?"

"No, Angelique, it is Scorpio."

"Oh, god, no. Something happened to Joker?"

"Yes, we are at a hospital in Manaus right now. Joker was seriously wounded."

"How bad, Scorpio? I want to know the truth."

"It's bad. If Joker lives, he will lose both legs." Scorpio could hear Angelique crying and Jane talking to her.

"Scorpio, this is Jane. What are your thoughts on Joker?"

"I'm not a doctor, but he lost lots of blood. His vitals are not good. But he is in surgery now, and I will let you know as soon as I do."

"What are his odds?"

"Joker is tough, but I think the odds are against him. But God only knows that. We have to wait and see. Call you later."

It was getting late in the day. Joker had been in surgery for almost seven hours when the nurse entered the waiting room. "Sir, are you Mr. Scorpio?"

"Yes, ma'am."

"Mr. Joker, your friend? You guys have strange names."

"Yes, ma'am, we're special ops and use code names."

"Oh, I understand now. Anyway, Joker is out of surgery. If you follow me, the doctor will see you."

"Yes, ma'am. You lead the way."

They walked into a plush room. The doctor was sitting behind a highly polished oak desk. The doctor appeared to be in his 50s with a few gray hairs. The nurse said, "Sir, this is Scorpio."

"Thank you, nurse. Have a seat, Mr. Scorpio. You're part of a special ops team?"

"Yes, Sir."

"I probably get one or two special ops every month. You guys have a tough job. Anyway, your colleague Joker, you probably know, did lose both legs. His vitals are stable. However, he went through a tough surgery. If he lives the next 48 hours, I think he may have a chance to survive. But he will have other surgeries. Any questions?"

"He will survive. How long will he be here in this hospital?"

"Probably five, ten days. At least until we know there is no infection. I know you guys like getting your people back to your facility. I like that myself. Your special ops give me the creeps. You can probably talk to him late tomorrow."

"What about my other guys, Star and Zula?"

"They will be okay. Probably leave early next week."

"Okay, thank you, doctor. I appreciate your help. I will see you tomorrow."

Scorpio walked into the hotel bar and found the rest of the team having a drink. The agent was sitting there also. "Well, Star and Zula can go in a couple of days. Joker, I'm not sure yet if he will make it. Doc said the next 48 would tell a lot. If you all want to head back to the base, you can. I'll stick around until our guys can go home."

The following day, Scorpio had an update on Joker; he was stable but critical. Scorpio related that to Angelique.

"Okay, Scorpio. Thank you for the call." Angelique hung up the phone. She stood there looking at the phone. Jane put her arm around her. They walked over to the table where Jim was sitting.

"Scorpio said Star and Zula should be coming home tomorrow. The Global will pick them up. It's been five days, and Joker seems to improve a little daily." Angelique continued, "The doctor felt he was out of danger. He may be able to come home next week. There is a place in Las Vegas that Scorpio said he has been communicating with. It is a high-end rehab center for people who have lost their limbs. A lot of military veterans are learning how to walk again."

"That's great, Angelique," Jim said. "Probably can find a place near there for you to stay until he can come to the base."

It was a long three weeks. The team had been busy with training. Star and Zula were getting around with a cane part-time. Scorpio came out of the office. "Angelique, I have some news for you."

"Yes, I know. Joker is coming home in a couple of days."

"Ah, no." The sound of the Global flying over the team house could be heard. "That sound is Joker about to land."

"What, oh my god. My hair is a mess."

The Global taxied up to the team house. Everyone ran out. The stairs come down; Barber carries a wheelchair, and TJ carries Joker.

TJ got to the bottom of the stairs when Angelique grabbed Joker. "Oh god, it is great your home."

"It's good to be home, hon. Sorry, I'm going to be a pain," Joker said. "Not sure what is going to happen now. I don't have any legs."

"Don't worry about that. Scorpio made arrangements for you to get new legs. I should have told you before, but I didn't want you to worry. You're going to be a daddy."

<hr>

Cosmo walked into Scorpio's office. "Hey, you have a minute to come to look at this?"

"Sure, what do you have?" Scorpio asked, walking into the meeting room. "What's this, A CHRISTMAS TREE?"

"Scorpio, you passed the recognition test," Cosmo chuckles. "You know Christmas is a few days off, and we never had one before. Our guys don't have families to celebrate Christmas with, so we decided to do a tree this year."

"That is cool. Where did you get the decorations from?"

"Oh, they are just a bunch of do-dads we collected over the years. It makes it an unusual tree, wouldn't you say? The star on top of the tree, Angelique made."

"Yes, I would say that it is an unusual tree. I see dog tags and different things from our missions. What is this, a P-38? God, I haven't seen one of those in years. Where did you get that?"

"Oh, Bingo had it. I guess it belonged to his dad when he served in the Korean and Vietnam Wars. I guess it was in their 'C' rations."

"I see your garland is made of shell casings of various calibers. Neat idea," Scorpio commented.

The phone was ringing in Scorpio's office. He walked in and noticed it was the Senator calling.

"Hi, Senator."

"Hi, Scorpio. How are Star, Zula, and Joker doing?"

"Doing great. Star and Zule are back to normal, Joker is getting used to his new legs, and we're all excited for the new arrival."

"Oh, that's right, Angelique's baby is about due."

"Sure is, next month."

"Are the guys busy?"

"No, not really, just continued training and readiness. What's up?"

"We had another kidnapping. A well-known family was the target. That was several months ago. We just got word about it. The husband, the pregnant wife, and two boys, one four and the other nine years old, were being held near the town of Curillo, Colombia. That is according to the nine-year-old who escaped three weeks ago and finally made it to the U.S. Embassy in Bogota."

"What happened to the others?"

"The boy said they had an opportunity to escape their cabin and got a little way when the kidnappers started chasing them. The mom told the boy to keep running and not stop. So, he did. He doesn't know what happened to the others."

"What is it you want us to do?"

"We're not getting much help from the Colombian government. We did get a fax from the Embassy; the boy made a detailed map of the area. I pulled up an image of the site, and it looks like you may be able to jump into several open areas at night. I'll send you that info," Senator said. "We'd like your team to go after them. A ten-million-dollar ransom was paid some time ago. The dad is the son of the House Speaker."

"Okay, we will look at it. We will look at your information, and I'll get back to you," Scorpio said. "Cosmo, get me all our information on Curillo, Colombia. Senator is faxing some information regarding a kidnapping."

A couple of hours later, the team reviewed the information in the meeting room. "Looks like there were five guys involved from the boy's information. A small cabin is next to this field," Scorpio pointed to the image. "And a row of trees and another open field on the south side. Maybe take the Global to Panama City, pick up the Dash, and make a night jump into this field," again pointing to the image. "We'll devise a recovery plan once we are on the ground. Cosmo checked on helicopter pickup from the same outfit we used before. I think they also operate out of Bogota. After the mission and pick-up, we return to Panama City and catch the Global. Maybe the Embassy in Panama will take over the family. So, let's get busy and work out a timeline for when we can be airborne."

The team was getting the gear ready. Cosmo called the pilot for the Global and made arrangements for the Dasher. Bingo was checking on a helicopter pick-up arrangement, and others were working on the other details.

It was almost midnight when the team got back together again. Scorpio said, "I just got off the phone with TJ. The CIA has some hacker issues and needs Angelique ASAP. However, I don't think that will be possible with the baby about due. Bingo, you guys all set for the mission?"

"The Global will be here around 10:00 a.m. tomorrow, and we leave shortly after. The Dasher should be on the ground in Panama when we get there. The helicopter will be on standby in Bogota, and we need to call them when we need them. We should be over the target around midnight tomorrow."

"Jasper, where are we with the gear?" Scorpio asked.

"Everything has been checked out and ready."

Scorpio walked into his office and dialed a number on his phone. It rang twice. "Hello, Senator."

"Hi, Scorpio. You have a plan?"

"Yes, Senator, we leave here tomorrow morning, and we should be on the ground about midnight. Senator, none of us have a good feeling about this. The ransom was paid some time ago, and they weren't released. Our last image had a lot of noise and wasn't as clear as usual. But many people were lying on the ground. It was early in the morning, and they could have been asleep. The pattern, well… we think there are several dead people."

"You think so, Scorpio? I have to tell you the son told us there was another group in their camp several days before, and there was a lot of disagreement. However, he didn't know what it was about."

"That's good to know, Senator. I'll call you after we're on the ground or on our way home and give you a status." They both gave their goodbye.

Scorpio walked out on the patio. The deck was damp from a light sprinkle earlier that morning. Off in the distance, he could see an airplane descending. Scorpio thought it looked like the Global was coming in for a landing. He looked at his watch, and it was 8:52 a.m. he was early. That is good, he thought. He walked back into the team house, and everyone finished their coffee. "Okay, gentlemen, the Global will be on the ground in a few minutes. So, let's get an early start. Give us more time in Panama."

The team got their gear and headed towards the airstrip as the Global was taxiing in. The pilot opened the door and lowered the steps. "Hey, good to see you guys. You planned on working over Christmas, I see."

"Yeah, you know, take the jobs when they come. Christmas is just another day." We're ready to go as soon as we get the gear on board," Scorpio said.

"Hey, Joker. It looks like you are getting around okay with those new legs."

"Yeah, getting better all the time. I tried running several times but didn't feel the ground, so I wound up getting ahead of my legs and fell. But doing great and looking forward to getting back to work."

"Okay, let's do it," Bingo said. "We should be in Panama early evening. That would put the Dasher over the target before midnight."

"Sounds good. Let's get going," Scorpio responded.

It was a smooth flight. Scorpio looked at his watch, thinking they should be landing in another hour. He was looking out the port window and could see they were following the coastline and could see Panama City off in the distance. A few minutes later, Scorpio could feel the Global slow down and begin its descent into Panama. Forty-five minutes later, the Global was pulling up next to the Dasher. They made a quick exchange, down the stairs from the Global and up the stairs into the Dasher.

"Hi, Scorpio," the pilot said. "Good to see you again. Just let you know the weather over your LZ is overcast, but no rain is expected. You still want to be over your target around midnight?"

Scorpio looked at his watch, "If we left now, we'd be over the LZ at about 11?"

"That sounds about right. Also, I was in contact with your helicopter pilot. He was going to stand by in Bogota. That way, he is about an hour from your location." The pilot answered.

"Okay, let's go." On the way, Scorpio downloads a new image of the site. He was studying it. "Cosmo, take a look at this."

Cosmo walked over and took the printout of the image. "Is this a new one?" looking at Scorpio? Scorpio was nodding yes. "This looks just like the one we looked at before."

"Yes, I believe the people on the ground are dead. They haven't moved in the last 48 hours. I think we will change the LZ and land in the camp. I don't see any reason to believe there is anyone on the ground to give us any problems."

"Yeah, I agree," Cosmo said. "I'll change the coordinates on the laser to target the camp."

"Okay, guys, slight change. Our LZ will be at the camp. The latest satellite image shows everyone on the ground is dead. So, we will land in the camp," Scorpio said, taking a drink of water. "However, be ready on landing if I'm wrong."

The pilot came on the intercom. "Okay, gentlemen, we are about 30 minutes from the LZ."

"Okay, let us get our gear on and do an equipment check," Scorpio said. "Cosmo already changed the coordinates of the LZ to the camp."

Everyone was ready, gear on, and checked out. The door opened; the yellow light came on. A few seconds later, it started blinking. Then, the green light came on, and everyone was out the door. Then the door closed. The pilot made a 180-degree right turn and headed back to Panama City.

Scorpio was looking around, and everyone was close. The laser said they were on target and had another 4130 feet before the parachutes were deployed. A few seconds later, Scorpio felt the harness tighten up a few seconds later the parachute was opened. The night vision came on. Scorpio looked around; I was right, Scorpio was thinking. The landing went well. Scorpio pulled his sidearm out and looked around. It was quiet. No one was moving. He was right. They were all dead. "Everyone okay," Scorpio said in his mic.

Everyone answered okay. "This is eerie," Cosmo said.

"Yeah," Scorpio said. "Everyone goes check out the bodies and make a count."

A few minutes later. "Okay, what do we have?" Scorpio asked.

Cosmo said, "Well, all the kidnappers are accounted for. A few other bodies appear to be dressed like the pirates we saw before on the Amazon River."

Barber came walking out of the cabin. "The family is accounted for, and they are all dead. I thought the lady was reported to be pregnant?"

"Yes, that is right, Barber. Why are you asking?" Scorpio wondered.

"She doesn't look pregnant to me, but unquestionably dead. I also found one of the three bags that contained the ransom money."

"I think the pirates came in and raided the place. They knew about the ransom money. They killed everyone and lost a couple of their guys in the process. I'll call the Senator to see if we must bring back the family's bodies. We will bury the others when it gets light," Scorpio said.

Jasper said, "It is getting light. Look at the moon. I have never seen it like that before."

"It is not the moon, Jasper. It is a star," Scorpio said. "A beautiful star, like it is pointing towards us." He pauses for several minutes. "What is that noise?"

"I hear that too," Cosmo said. "It comes from over there and sounds like a baby crying."

Several of the team ran over to the location of the sound. They stopped and looked down. Cosmo, Jasper, and Scorpio stood there in disbelief. Barber squatted down, saying, "It is a baby. The grass around it looks like a manger." Barber looked up at them. "Interesting, it is Christmas, the star behind you, and you are the three wise men." Barber picked up the baby, "Hey, it is a boy."

"The lady must have had the baby and hidden him in the grass when the pirates attacked," Scorpio said. "What should we call him?"

Barber looked at them and said, "Well, for now, what about baby Jesus?"

The three looked at Barber and got misty-eyed. Scorpio said, "That will work for now." Wiping the tears off his cheek with his hand.

The other members of the team came running over. "What do you have there?" Zula asked.

"It's a baby," Scorpio said, "Baby Jesus." A tear ran down his cheek. Everyone stood there, thinking it was a miracle. Finally, Scorpio cleared his throat. "Barber, how about you clean up baby Jesus and find something nice to wrap him in? You guys," pointing to the others, "dig out the body bags. We will take his family home with us."

"What about the others?" Barber asked. "Still going to bury them?"

Scorpio looked around and paused for a minute. "No, leave them there. Let the animals take care of them."

Star said, "Just talked to the pilot. The helicopter will be here in about 40 minutes."

"Okay, thanks, Star." Scorpio pulled out his satellite phone and dialed a number that rang twice. "Hello, Senator."

"Hi, Scorpio. How did the mission go, and where are you?"

"Senator, we are still on site. The family members are all dead, and we will bring them back. The others we will leave. But," Scorpio paused, taking a drink of water, "we have a baby Jesus we will bring back."

"A BABY WHAT?" The Senator asked, thinking she may have not heard it right.

"Senator, the lady had a baby while in captivity. I'll give you all the details in my report. We gave the boy the temporary name of Jesus. It will be in my report. We will transfer everyone to Panama on the Global and head to Dallas. It would help to let me know how we will handle the bodies through customs before we get to Dallas. The baby is another issue."

"That's okay. Call me before you leave Panama, and I should have your answers. What a mission. I can't wait to read your report. Talk to you later." The Senator disconnected.

"Scorpio, the helicopter is about ten minutes out," Jasper said.

"Tell him to land in the camp," Scorpio pointed to a clearing. "Guys, let's move our people over to that clearing. Get your gear together. The chopper will be here shortly."

Before long, they were loading the bodies. The pilot said, "Scorpio, it looks like you had a battle by the looks of things."

"No, not really. They were all dead before we got here. Except for this little guy." Scorpio showed the pilot what he was holding.

"A baby!" Pilot exclaimed.

"Yup, we named him baby Jesus. I'll tell you why on the way to Panama," Scorpio said.

Everyone was in the helicopter, "I guess we are all ready, even baby Jesus," Star said.

The helicopter raised and hovered over the camp, then moved on for a four-hour flight to Panama City airport. No one said anything except for Scorpio telling the pilot the baby's story. Everyone took turns holding the baby on the way to Panama, and everyone enjoyed it, including the baby, who was always smiling. The time went by fast, and the helicopter set down next to the Global before the team knew it. The gear and body bag transfer went quickly without anyone paying any attention. The helicopter raised and moved over about 800 feet to the gas facility for refueling. A few minutes later, the jet engines on the Global begin to come alive.

Scorpio walked into the flight deck, "Hi, Captain, we're ready anytime you are."

"Okay, Scorpio, what the hell you got there?"

"It's a new member, a baby."

"My god, Scorpio, it looks like a newborn."

"Yeah, maybe a couple of weeks, cute little boy."

"The parents in the body bags?"

"Yeah, that's too bad. The baby has a brother who made it out alive a couple of months ago. We hope they will be united at some point."

"Okay, Scorpio, it should be a smooth flight. How do we handle the body bags at customs?"

"I don't know yet. I need to make a call. I'll get back to you." Scorpio walked back into the cabin and gave the baby to Jasper. Scorpio sat down, picked up his satellite phone, and dialed the Senator's number.

"Hello, Scorpio," the Senator said. "Are you on your way to Dallas?"

"Yes, Senator, you have any plans for dealing with things at customs?"

"Yes, the FBI will meet you there at customs. They will take custody of the body bags, and a nurse will take the baby. The baby and his brother will be put into the same foster home. We will let the brother name the baby for the record."

"Okay, Senator. This is one mission I know we will not ever forget. Please keep us posted on the kids. We want to set up an education fund for them."

"Okay, Scorpio, we will keep you in the loop." Senator hung up.

Scorpio walked into the flight deck, letting the pilot know the plan. Then he sat down, looking out the window, thinking about the past few days. He had tears running down his cheeks. Scorpio thought, why am I so emotional? This is a first for me. It's got to be baby Jesus. Why do people do stupid things? Do a little research on where you are going and take proper safety precautions. He thought he was getting too old for this stuff. He will be sixty-eight in a couple of months, and maybe retirement should be in his future—something to think about. He was in better shape than most thirty-year-olds, had several million in a bank account, and could retire comfortably. He had always dreamed of having a yacht in the South Pacific near some island—something he needed to put some real thought into. Maybe call the Boss and see how he is enjoying retirement. About then, the Pilot came on the intercom. "Gentlemen, we will be landing in thirty minutes."

The team got up, making sure everything was secured. The team made a last trip to the ice chest for a beer. They returned to their seats as the landing gear went down, and the Global turned right into the airport pattern for landing. A few minutes later, they were taxiing by customs. Scorpio saw several black vans and police cars parked near the customs building. The Global pulled up next to them, and engines shut down.

Scorpio opened the door and let the stairs down. A tall gentleman walked up the stairs and said, "I'm with the FBI. Are you Scorpio?"

"Yes, sir, you here to pick up our passengers?"

"Yes," he waved at the vans, and several guys came up the steps.

Scorpio said, "They are all the way back," pointing to the body bags.

After removing the bodies, a nurse said, "You have a package for me?"

"Yes," the team formed a line down the stairs. They handed the baby down the line, each member taking a moment to say goodbye. Scorpio was the last in line. He held the baby for a moment. He struggled to hold the tears back and said, "We wish you the best and will always remember you." He handed the baby to the nurse. "You take care of our baby Jesus."

"Yes, we will." She took the baby and walked over to the ambulance. She stopped and turned around, looking at Scorpio.

"You said baby Jesus?"

"Yes, ma'am. Baby Jesus."

The nurse looked at the baby, then back at Scorpio, and saw tears running down his cheeks. "Yes, Sir, baby Jesus, I will note that on his I.D. card."

The customs agent walked up the stairs, gave the pilot some papers, and said, "Thank you."

A few minutes later, the Global was off the ground, heading to the base. The three-hour flight will go quickly, Scorpio thought; he was relaxing with a shot of bourbon. He was about to doze off when he heard the landing gear going down. He looked out the window. He thought it was always good to get back home. The Global pulled up next to the team house. The engines idled as the team unloaded the gear. Everyone was tired and didn't have much to say.

The pilot said, "Good to serve you guys. See you next time. By the way, this was a good mission, regardless of the results. Let me know what happens to baby Jesus."

"I will, thanks."

The team walked into the team house. "Okay, guys, let's get the gear cleaned and ready. If you want some time off for R&R, let me know," Scorpio said, walking into the conference room and bar.

"How did your mission go?" Joker asked.

"Well, you won't believe this," Scorpio told them what happened. Bingo, Joker, and Angelique just sat there with their mouths open.

"What will happen to baby Jesus?" Angelique asked with tears in her eyes.

"I understand the baby will be in a foster home with his brother. I was told the brother would name the baby. We were going to provide an education fund for them. Not sure how that will be managed, but we have time to figure that out," Scorpio said.

"Joker, it's time," Angelique said.

"Time for what?"

"Speaking of babies, I think ours wants out."

"What do we do?" Joker wanted to know.

"Stay calm. We have a qualified nurse waiting," Scorpio said. "So, let's go have that baby."

Several weeks and then months went by. The newborn was doing great. There were missions, but no word about what was happening with baby Jesus and his brother. Scorpio thought they must be doing okay, and the Senator was busy with other things. He sat back with a bourbon. He and the team had just finished another mission with Mama Bear and Captain Sixto. Star and Cosmo both had minor wounds but were both doing okay. He looked at his watch. We should be landing in Dallas in a couple of hours. Scorpio got up and walked back to where Star and Cosmo were. "You guys, okay? Need another shot for pain?"

"No, I'm okay," Cosmo said.

"Same here," Star said. "How do we handle going through customs? They question wounded passengers?"

"Should be no problem. Look like you are asleep. We are never inspected—just a formality. The customs agent only comes on board, gives the pilot paperwork, and then goes. That's easy," Scorpio said. He took another sip of bourbon and thought more about retiring. This mission was difficult, and wound up with wounded guys. Someday, I may not be so lucky and lose several guys like several years ago, and I almost lost Joker a few months ago. He looked out the window and could see Dallas off in the distance. The satellite phone rang. Scorpio looked at the ID, and it was the Senator, "Hi, Senator, I was about to call you. We will be landing in Dallas shortly."

"Sounds good. I see from the news the general and top aides were taken out. Good job. Everyone okay?"

"No, Senator, Cosmo and Star were wounded but are doing okay. They will probably be out of commission for a couple of months. The mission got a little messy, and we had to take out a couple of different targets. But that happens sometimes. Something we don't like to do."

"I understand. It looks like the government lowered the boom on the remaining general staff and cleaned up the remaining troublemakers. It was another well-executed job; we accomplished the plan. You all get your rest and enjoy your time off. I don't have anything on the horizon that will change that. In a couple of days, give me a call. I have something we need to talk about." Senator hung up.

Scorpio heard the gear go down, and the Global started a deep descent into Dallas. He sat back and took a sip of his drink. This was an extended mission, and he was tired. Retirement was sounding better all the time. The wheels touched down, and a short taxi to the customs. It was a brief stop, and they were airborne again, heading to the base. Scorpio returned to Cosmo and Star, "Can I get you anything?'

"No," they said.

"How about you guys? Do you need anything?" Scorpio was looking at the rest of the team.

"No, we're okay," they answered.

"What's going on, Scorpio? You were acting like a mother hen. What's up?" Barber asked.

"I'm just getting tired of this business; you know I have been at this type of work almost 40 years. Will talk more about that later." Scorpio fixed another drink and sat down.

Everyone looked at each other and knew something was going on.

The rest of the flight was smooth, and so was the landing. After unloading the Global, they said their goodbyes to the pilot. The team walked into the team house.

"You all deserve an R&R," Scorpio said. "I think I will take one. See you all in the morning." Scorpio headed to his room.

Angelique got up and went over to Cosmo and Star. "Let me take a look at those wounds. These are infected. I will give you both a shot of antibiotics and let's monitor them."

The following day, there was a light rain, unusual for this time of the year. Later, Scorpio walked out on the deck. He looked at his watch. The Senator must be in her office by now. He dialed her number, and it rang once when she answered.

"Scorpio, we must be reading each other's minds. I was going to pick up the phone and call you."

"You said you needed to talk to me. I also need to run something by you, so what's on your mind?

"A couple of things. One of my colleagues will be taking over for me as the Chairman of the Intelligence Community. My term ends in a few months, and I will not be running for re-election due to health reasons. However, I have been feeling someone out about having a team like yours. I will brief them and have you there if they can do the job. Kind of an introduction, you might say."

"Thanks, interesting, Senator. I knew there had to be a day coming when the team would no longer exist, or major changes would be made. That brings me to my topic. I'm thinking of retiring myself. I haven't talked to the team yet but plan to talk to them in a few days."

"Scorpio, I guess I knew that was going to happen someday. I know the Baby Jesus mission was especially tough on you. Do you have someone to take over for you if we continue this work?"

"Yes, Senator, either Jasper or Cosmo, both have excellent management and supervision skills. But anyone could do the job, but those two would be my first pick."

"Okay, Scorpio. I'll let you know soon about the future of the team. I still think there is a place for your type of work. Good luck with your talk with the team. Oh, yeah, baby Jesus. His brother named him Richard Jesus Wilson. Richard was his dad's name, and

Wilson was their last name. The brother thought the middle name of Jesus was well earned."

Scorpio walked into the meeting room. Everyone was cleaning or working on the equipment, preparing it for other missions. "Just talked to the Senator. She said Baby Jesus was doing great; the brother named him Richard Jesus Wilson. And also, there is something I want to talk about." They all stopped and looked at Scorpio. "One day, soon, I will be retiring." There was silence. "I talked to the Senator. She said she is not running for re-election. The future of the team is unknown. That will be determined soon. I know we all have done quite well financially. We all probably could retire comfortably. I'll let that sink in, and we will meet this afternoon. I'd like to hear your thoughts." Scorpio walked out onto the deck.

The team just looked at each other, not saying anything for several minutes. Jasper said, "Wow, wonder what brought that on. Yeah, we all could probably retire. But I know I would be bored. I can only speak for myself. I enjoy this work. We take out a lot of bad guys. I'm for continuing if we still have the same arrangement with getting the job and being paid by the CIA. You guys?"

Cosmo stood up and walked over to the bar. Fixing a drink, he said, "I'm with you, Jasper. I think you would be our replacement for Scorpio. The big question is the jobs and source of funding. Yeah, I made lots of money and could easily retire."

Bingo joined Cosmo for a drink. "I'm for that also. I think we need to see what the Senator has to say."

The rest of the team agreed. Angelique walked in with Joker. She was carrying the baby. "I heard the conversation. You all saved my life, and you are my family. I'm with you as well. I could retire, but I am not as comfortable as you all. But I enjoy computer work and believe in what you all do. Probably most of the country wouldn't agree with this work. The fact is the team has saved a lot of people and given them a future. It sounds like the Senator holds the key to what we do."

Scorpio was standing by the door. "I guess we don't have to have a meeting. It sounds like you all are on the same page. We will wait, see what the Senator comes up with, and go from there." There was a long pause. "Oh, by the way, Angelique. How is the Little Boss?"

"He is doing great, Scorpio. He is going to be strong, just like his dad."

"Angelique, I think you and Joker naming him Jim after our Boss, and then the code name Little Boss fits just right."

"Thanks, Scorpio, we think so."

Several weeks went by. Everyone kept busy with continued training and equipment readiness. The phone rings, and Scorpio walks over to pick it up, glancing at the I.D. "Hey, it's the Boss calling. Hi Boss, long time no hear. How in the hell are you doing? Want to go back to work?"

"Hi, Scorpio. Yeah, it has been a while, and no, I'm not looking for work. However, I just got off the phone with the Senator. She told me about her plans and wanted to know what I thought. I told her I still felt the work you guys do should continue. She agreed and wondered if I would go back to coordinating the team now that you are retiring. You getting too old to do the work?"

"Boss, it is not about getting old. I'm still young enough and have the money to do things I have always dreamed of doing. Continuing this line of work doesn't fit in my plan."

The boss thought for a minute. "You have a hard mission?"

"Yeah, hard and long mission. I got two of my guys wounded, and Joker was almost killed. It got me thinking. I want to live long enough to enjoy a few things before becoming an old fart in a wheelchair or six feet under."

"Well, I can understand that. I told the Senator I thought Cosmo or Jasper could run the show."

"That's what I've also been thinking," Scorpio commented.

"The Senator approached one of her colleagues about a special ops team," Boss said.

"Did the Senator have a positive response?"

"Well, I understand this person was trying to form such a team but wasn't having any luck," Boss said. "The Senator told him about our present arrangement, and he was for it and told the Senator he would take it on."

"The team sure will like to know that," Scorpio said.

"The Senator will be calling to set up a meeting with her and the new guy, probably at the base. She also wants the team's know-how to be organized once you retire."

"Okay, Boss, you coming for the meeting?"

"Senator asked me to, but I will see."

"You know you are always welcome," Scorpio said. "Always love to have you at planning meetings. Talk to you later."

Several days went by before the phone rang. "Hello, Senator," Scorpio said. "Been expecting your call."

"Yes, I know about the meeting. However, I have Special Agent Merrow on the line. He is head of the Drug Lord Taskforce. He has a problem your team may be able to help with."

"Yes, thank you, Senator. Scorpio, we have spent several years tracking down a drug lord called Sebastian. He is guilty of several murders, kidnappings, and many other crimes. Two weeks ago, we found out where he had been hanging out. Presently, he is on an island off the coast of Venezuela. The island is well-guarded with patrol boats. According to our imagery, he stays in one of two small bungalows. Four to five guards patrolled the beach and two at one of the bungalows."

"Special Agent Merrow, what is it you want us to do? Take him out?"

"Not really. We want to capture him. He has a lot of information we can use for other cases, so we need him alive."

"Interesting problem. Please send me any information on this island, including imagery and background information. Senator has our secure e-mail information. Let us study it for a couple of days and see what we come up with." They said their goodbyes.

"Cosmo and Jasper, A Special Agent Merrow will send information on a possible mission. You two head up the planning on this one. Tomorrow afternoon, we will meet and see what you all come up with," Scorpio said.

They all adjourned to begin their research. Scorpio fixed another bourbon and headed out to the deck. He walked around, sipping his drink. This will be a good exercise for them to work on and test. He was thinking again about retirement, and he thought this would be an excellent last mission before calling it quits.

The next day, Scorpio was up, running down the runway and back several times, off to the showers, breakfast, and more coffee. He walked by the meeting room. Everyone was talking, looking at various imagery and documents. They had some equipment laid out on the floor, working on a configuration. It's good to see them working as a team. Maybe Cosmo is the team leader choice and Jasper the safety coordinator. Scorpio grabbed another cup of coffee and headed to his office.

It was getting toward 3:00 p.m. when Jasper walked into Scorpio's office. "We have a plan and are ready to review the details."

"Okay, let's see what you guys came up with," Scorpio said. He got up from his desk and walked into the meeting room. "Okay, let's hear it, Cosmo."

"We use the Global and fly into La Chinita International Airport servicing Maracaibo, Venezuela. There, we meet Captain Sixto and Mate." Cosmo stopped and took a sip of water. "We go to the nearby marina. Sixto has arranged that and goes through Venezuela's Golf towards the island. We plan to be off the island about a mile around midnight. I include Angelique in this mission because of her medical expertise. I don't expect to need that. However, these guys have potent weapons on their boats."

"They have different weapons onshore?" Scorpio interrupts.

"The guards onshore have sidearms and look like M-16s," Jasper said.

Cosmo continues, "We go ashore using our rebreathers and underwater scooters. We go to their dock," Cosmo pointed to the imagery. "We tie our dive gear off at the bottom of the first piling and swim to shore under the dock. Zula will maintain that position. Zula will keep us informed on the boats and guards' positions when we evacuate and remove anyone who will interrupt our escape once we are onshore and into the vegetation at this location," again pointing at the imagery. "Barber will take up a position here to support Zula if needed. Then the rest of us will go to the bungalows. I will take out the two guards. Star and Bingo will provide security, while Jasper, Scorpio, and I will go to the bungalow. Use a pin camera and evaluate our entry. The plan is to take out anyone in there except the target. Make sure you study the picture of him." Jasper passed out pictures. "We don't want to take out the wrong guy."

"Are these pictures recent?" Scorpio asked.

"They are about five months old, and I don't expect he has changed that much, except maybe a beard," Jasper said.

Cosmo continued, "This little guy is called a blow gun and shoots a knock-out-drug. Jasper and I have been trained on this, which is accurate up to 75 feet. We have been able to hit a dime at 75 feet consistently. It would feel like a mosquito bite to the target but will put him out within two seconds and will be out for up to two hours."

"Are we going to have to carry him? Hope he is a small guy!" Bingo said.

"Yes," Jasper said. "He is five, two, and weighs about 125 pounds."

"Okay, what do we do with him?" Scorpio asked.

"We have this outfit for him," Cosmo said. "It is a modified dry suit with a neck collar that this helmet attaches to. We put the helmet on once we were back at the dock. I have a hose on my rebreather that connects here, giving him air while we are underwater. We also attach a weight belt, giving him zero buoyancy to get him underwater. Once we returned to the boat and surfaced, we dropped his weight belt, removed the helmet, and disconnected my hose. Then we board the boat. That is about it except for things that develop."

"That sounds like a good plan. Be nice if it does go that way," Scorpio said. "Okay, what is your timeline? When do we go?"

"We leave here by 5:00 a.m. The pilot will be here for dinner and spend the night," Jasper said.

"Is Captain Sixto all set?" Scorpio asked.

"Yes, he left yesterday to make sure he would be at Maracaibo dock when we get there," Jasper said.

"So, when did you say the pilot would be here?" Scorpio asked.

"By dinner time." Jasper, looking at his watch, "in about two hours."

"Okay, let's ensure the gear is ready when the pilot arrives. We will load everything tonight. Good job, guys." Scorpio walked into his office to call the FBI Agent and tell him they were coming.

Scorpio was finishing some paperwork and heard the pilot buzzing the team house. "Cosmo, I figured out why the pilot decided to come tonight. It's seafood night."

"You got that right," Cosmo said.

Everyone enjoyed a fantastic seafood buffet and a few drinks. The team spent the evening reviewing the mission, and then they all turned in for an early morning flight.

The sun hadn't come up yet as the team boarded the Global. It was a relaxing flight, mostly reviewing the latest imagery of the target area. Most got additional shuteye. Scorpio looked out the window and noticed the Global was slightly descending. He looked at his watch. It was several hours before they got to their destination. Scorpio got up and walked to the flight deck. He noticed the pilot talking on the radio, so he sat down on the arm of the co-pilot seat. When the pilot finished his radio message, Scorpio said, "Are we descending for some reason?"

"Yes, I need to land in Panama for fuel. I found out there is a restriction on fuel for non-airline aircraft in Venezuela. I'm topping off the tanks in Panama to ensure we have plenty of fuel. We still will get to our destination in plenty of time."

Scorpio returned to his seat and told the guys they would stop in Panama for fuel and only be on the ground for a short time. Getting out of Panama didn't take much time, and they were on their way. The Global followed the coastline along Columbia, turning easterly over Cartagena and straight to Maracaibo, Colombia. The landing was smooth, and a short taxi to the corporate parking area. The pilot shut the engines down while Scorpio opened the door and lowered the stairs. He looked out the door and saw Mate driving in a van, waving, "Hi, Scorpio."

"Hi, Mate, Captain ready?"

"Yes, Sir, as soon as we get on board, we will head out," Mate said.

"Okay, guys, let's get our gear," Scorpio said. Then, they told the pilot they would return in a few days.

It was a short drive to the marina, and Mate pulled up alongside an excellent yacht. "Hi, Captain Sixto," Scorpio said.

"Hi to you, back. Good to see you again, and it sounds like an interesting mission. We have about an hour before leaving to stay on schedule."

"Okay, Captain, do you know the details of the mission?" Scorpio asked.

"Yes, Jasper gave me a briefing on the phone last night. I took a trip by the island coming here. They have three armed boats that circle the island. Anyone who gets within a half-mile is stopped or gets a shot across their bow. They are something you don't want to mess with," Captain said.

"Well, we don't want to mess with them."

"There is a channel marker, and if you get in the water at that point and go 178 degrees, you should be close to the dock." The captain said, taking a sip of water. "They only use the dock to refuel or change crews. I did find out from a guy who takes supplies to them that the other north bungalow houses the boat crews. Other than that, all the information Jasper gave me is correct."

Jasper looked at Scorpio. "Something we have to plan for. Maybe have one guy watch the crew bungalow. But we should be able to go as planned. I think we can get in and out with very little noise."

"Okay, Captain, let's head that way. That would put us where we need to be by midnight." Scorpio said.

"Actually, Scorpio, it will take us about three hours. We leave now. Would put us there about 11:30 p.m.," Captain said.

"That is good. Let's do it. Guys, get the gear out and ensure night vision and other gear are checked out. Be dark in a couple of hours," Scorpio said.

Captain Sixto was at the helm of a Fleming 78, 81 ½ foot, including the dive platform with a 21 ½ foot beam and equipped with the best radar. The yacht was modified with various defense equipment, meaning several M-79, .50, and .30 calibers, several M-16s, and a dozen shoulder-fired missiles.

Scorpio walked on the bridge. "Hi, Captain. How are we doing? Sure, it is dark out here."

"We're doing good. Once we lose the overcast, the moon should give you lots of light. In about twenty minutes, we will be at the channel marker and your jump-off point. Once you guys are in the water, I will head out further in the ocean, about five miles, and hang out. When I hear you are returning, I head in to pick you up at the same place."

"Okay," we'll get ready." Scorpio walked down to the dive deck. "Okay, let's get our gear on. We're in the water shortly."

Captain Sixto leaned out of the bridge a few minutes later and whispered down to Scorpio. "We will be alongside the marker in about five minutes."

"Okay, thanks. Guys, we need to get in the water when we come alongside the marker," Scorpio said.

Everyone was ready. Scorpio said, "Here is the marker; let's go." Everyone walked off the dive platform into the water while turning on their red pin light, allowing them to see each other underwater. "Okay, let's descend to twenty feet. Cosmo picks up the bearing on your laser, 178 degrees, and we will follow you," Scorpio said.

The water was clear, and visibility was ten–fifteen feet, even at night. About thirty minutes later, the ocean bottom began to appear. They were getting close. Traveling to the first piling should take a few more minutes. They reached a point when Scorpio said, "Stop, settle on the bottom. We should have made contact with the first piling. Stay in place; I'll check it out."

Scorpio slowly raised to the surface, eye level with the ocean. He looked right and then left and settled back to the bottom. "We are on target but about fifteen feet left of the piling. We make a right and a couple of swim strokes. We should see the piling."

Everyone gave a thumbs up. They swam a few feet, and the piling came into view. Scorpio slows to a stop and settles on the bottom next to the first piling. Everyone gathered around Scorpio.

"I can hear the slight sound of a slow-going boat with outboard motors," Scorpio said. "Jasper, go up along the side of the piling and take a look."

Jasper was at eye level with the water surface a short time later. He was looking around and along the shoreline. "A boat is heading away from us, about 400 yards out. I only see one guard walking along the shore, going the other direction." Jasper settled back down to the bottom.

"Okay, drop the scuba gear and anchor them to the piling, then surface and swim to the shore. Stay under the dock," Scorpio said.

The team did as ordered. Everyone gathered around Scorpio and pulled out their sidearm, attaching their silencer. "Okay, Zula, take a position here and update us on the activity. Rest of us, let's get up to the vegetation that will give us cover."

It didn't take long, and the remaining team knelt inside the cover. "Barber, take up a position here," Scorpio said. "Let's move slowly toward the bungalows." A couple of minutes later, they were in position. "Star and Bingo," Scorpio was pointing, "that would be a good place to give us cover from all directions." They crawled over to the location. Jasper, Cosmo, and Scorpio made their way to the first bungalow.

"I'll cover you," Scorpio said. "You two do your thing. Good luck."

Jasper and Cosmo made their way to the door. Jasper slid the pin camera underneath the door, and they both looked at the display. Jasper said, "Looks like one guy at the table is asleep. According to the picture, the guy sitting on the bed reading looks like the guy we want."

"Yeah, I think you're right," Cosmo said, pulling out the blowgun and loading it. "Okay, if you can open the door ½ inch, I'll get our guy, and then we'll remove the other one."

"Okay, sounds like a plan," Jasper said. He was opening the door slightly.

Cosmo slid the blowgun between the door and the doorjamb. He aimed and shot the dart, making only a muffling sound. The dart hit the target in the neck. The target laid back on the bed within seconds, making no sound. Jasper opened the door further and walked in, aiming his silencer at the guard and taking him out. Cosmo walked over to the guy lying on the bed. Took the picture out of a small sealed bag and compared the image with the guy on the bed. "Yes, confirms he is the one," Cosmo said.

"Okay," Jasper said. "Let's go," picking the guy up and throwing him over his right shoulder. "He's not heavy."

They walked out of the bungalow and met up with Scorpio. Scorpio said, "Star, Bingo, join us where Barber is. Zula, how are things looking?"

"We have one guard coming this way. He will be here about the same time you are. Let me take him out first before you get to the beach."

"Okay, we will hold up under cover until you take him out. Let us know when it is clear." Scorpio said.

A few minutes later, Zula said. "Guard is down. I'll drug him over under some vegetation. Okay, you can make it to the dock. I have the gear ready for our prize."

The team gathered under the dock. They got their guy suited up and ready for the underwater trip. Cosmo said, "I just talked to Captain Sixto. He will be at the channel marker when we get there."

"Let's float this guy to the dock's end, get some weight on him, and take him to the bottom," Jasper said.

The team got ready to go to the bottom and got their dive gear on when Bingo said, "We have a boat coming. It looks about 300 yards out, and two guys are coming to the dock."

"Okay, let's get down and out of sight," Scorpio said. "Let's not tangle with them unless we have to."

The team headed to the bottom. They put their gear on and were ready to head to the marker when the boat cruised over them.

"Let's go, guys," Scorpio said. "Jasper, you have our guy in tow?"

"Yeah, everything's okay," Jasper answered.

Fifteen minutes later, Cosmo said, "I think this is the chain that holds the marker in place." He hears a boat engine. "I'm sure that is Captain Sixto."

"Bingo, take a peek," Scorpio said.

Everyone hovered in place. Bingo slowly broke the surface and did a 360-quick look. "We're okay. Captain is arriving."

"Let's get to the surface," Scorpio said.

The team was almost all onboard the yacht when Star said, "We'll have visitors, a boat coming this way, and it is one of the bad guys based on the markings on the boat."

"Get the gear and the prize down below. Mate, grab an M-79 and hide under the tarp in the bow. If I say take them, put a round in their gas tank. The rest of you open up with your sidearms," Captain said.

Captain maintains heading and normal speed back to the marina. The other boat was gaining on them.

"Everyone grabs a beer and acts like we're having a party," Scorpio said. "Jasper, grab another M-79 and follow Mate's lead if we have to."

The other boat was coming alongside about 100 feet off the yacht's port side. Someone from the boat yelled. "You on the yacht! What are you doing here?"

"Just a private party and a moonlight cruise," Captain Sixto said.

"You are not supposed to be around here!"

"This is not restricted water."

"We're coming aboard and checking you out!"

"No, I don't think so. You do not continue," Captain Sixto said. He could see several heavily armed guys. Captain whispered to Scorpio, "If they raise their weapons, open up on them. Mate, do as planned. Get their gas tank. Jasper takes out the bridge."

It was a standoff. Captain increased speed. The intruders raised their weapons, and Scorpio and the team opened up. Mate planted an M-79 round just right; the tank exploded, and the boat's stern was in flames. Jasper took out the bridge. Before the boat exploded, they shot several rounds at Captain, Scorpio and the team. The whole attack took about 30 seconds. The intruder's boat was sinking. The captain was at full speed to avoid the fire from the other boat. He checked the radar to see where the second boat was. He noticed they were about 2 miles away and heading in the other direction.

"Angelique, I need your help. Both Star and Zula are down," Jasper said.

Angelique ran over to her medical bags, grabbed them, and headed toward Jasper's location. "How bad are they," she asked Jasper as she knelt by them.

"Star caught one in the leg," Jasper said, "and Zula got one in the left arm."

"Someone check Scorpio," Captain Sixto said. "I see he is down near the stern port side."

Bingo ran over to Scorpio, getting to him and kneeling. He turned pale. "Angelique, hurry. Scorpio is in bad shape."

"Jasper, keep the compress on Star and Zula. Control the bleeding. I'll be right back."

Angelique ran over to where Bingo was. "How bad?"

"You tell me, but I don't think it is good."

"I see one bullet hole in the left lower abdomen. It is through and through. There is lots of blood. Hold this compress on both sides. The other wound is in his upper right chest. You see the bubbles in the blood?"

"Yeah," Bingo said, "what's that?"

"This isn't a bullet hole; it looks like shrapnel, and it pierced the lung. When he breathes, he loses air from the wound, causing the bleeding to bubble. But good thing not much bleeding." Angelique reached for an 8x8 bandage. She peeled off the back and placed it over the wound. "This will seal it off." Angelique was checking Scorpio's vitals and for other injuries. "Looks like there are only two wounds. Hand me the O2 bottle." She attached the mask and placed it over Scorpio's mouth and nose. Then she turned the air on. "This should help his breathing."

Scorpio was regaining consciousness. "How bad is it, Angelique?"

"You have two wounds. One in the abdomen on your left side. It almost missed you. It is a through and through, so I'm not as concerned with that. However, your second wound looks like a shrapnel wound that pierced your lung. But you seem to breathe, okay?"

"Yes, it hurts to breathe."

"Yeah, I don't doubt that. When we return to the marina, we must get you to a hospital."

"I prefer not. We're not supposed to be here. Need to get back to the States."

"Well, I'll see when we get to shore; it depends on your vitals," Angelique answered. "I'll be back. Keep an eye on him, Bingo, and if any changes, call me."

Angelique walked back to Star and Zula to check their wounds. "Jasper, how are they doing?"

"Both are doing okay," Jasper said. "How is Scorpio?"

"He has two wounds, and one is serious. I want him to go to the hospital, but he doesn't want to."

"Hey, I checked on our prize. He said he would kill us if he gets loose," Cosmo said. "So, I gave him another shot to keep him quiet for a few hours."

"Guys, we're almost back to the marina, but we're going to pull into a large boat house so no one will notice the bullet holes and get the wounded off," Captain said.

"When we get tied up, I'll get our large bus. That way, Scorpio can travel better on a stretcher," Mate said.

"That's good," Cosmo said. He was reaching for the satellite phone. He dialed a number, and it rang a couple of times. "Hello, Senator, this is Cosmo. We have the prize and hope to be airborne soon."

"Glad to hear that. Any problems?"

"We ran into bad guys after returning to the boat and had a shootout. We have three wounded. Scorpio is in serious condition. He refuses to go to a hospital here, and I don't blame him. But he is stable. Angelique thinks we could return him to the States, but Scorpio will need medical attention."

"Okay, I will make arrangements in Dallas. I'll call TJ and let him know so we can develop a cover," Senator said.

"I'm not sure if I follow you, Senator?"

"Don't forget Cosmo. You guys are officially dead. Remember the trial and accident?"

"Oh yeah, that was several years ago. You think that will still be a problem?" Cosmo asked.

"We can't take a chance. I know TJ will come up with an idea. When you get a couple of hours out from Dallas, call me. We should have a plan."

"Okay, Senator, talk to you later." Cosmo replaced the receiver.

"Cosmo," Angelique said. "We need a medivac, now. Call the pilot and tell him we have wounded and need the medical unit set up for the flight back."

"Okay, I'll do that now," Cosmo called the pilot. "Hi, we should be there in about an hour. We have wounded, and Angelique wants you to set up the medical unit before we arrive."

"Okay, understand. I will have it ready. Who's wounded?"

"Star and Zula have minor wounds, but Scorpio is in serious condition."

"Okay, I will be ready, over and out." The pilot released the PTT on his walkie-talkie.

The next couple hours were spent unloading the yacht and getting the team and their prize loaded in the Global. The Captain and Mate were at the airport, ensuring they got on board okay.

Captain said, "Keep us informed on how Scorpio is doing. Also, I'll send you a bill for the repairs on the yacht. It didn't belong to me, so I must return it undamaged."

"No problem, Captain. We will take care of the damages." Cosmo waved goodbye as he closed the door to the Global.

Angelique checked on the wounded, ensuring they were comfortable and stable. The prize was livelier, so she gave him another shot to keep him quiet for the trip. She said, "We're ready, Cosmo," as she took her seat.

The trip seemed like it took forever, Cosmo thought. Maybe it was because he was concerned about Scorpio. He noticed that Angelique was back by Scorpio. Cosmo got up and walked back to join Angelique. "How is he doing?"

"His vitals are good, but he has trouble breathing," Angelique said.

"Yeah, and I hurt as if someone drove over me," Scorpio said.

"Good to see you awake. You need another shot to help you out some?" Angelique asked. "It may help you breathe better by reducing the pain."

"I'm okay, guys. I just wanted to complain. Thanks for taking care of me, Doc."

Angelique smiled. "I love you guys a lot. You gave me a new life. I will do my best so you will stick around a while longer."

Cosmo also smiled, "You get more rest. We should be in Dallas in about three hours, and then we will get you to a hospital."

"I don't want to go to a hospital; cause problems," Scorpio said.

"Don't worry about it. The Senator and TJ are working on it," Cosmo said. "That reminds me, I need to call the Senator."

"Okay, Scorpio," Angelique said, "you take it easy."

Cosmo returned to his seat, picked up the satellite phone, and dialed the Senator. She picked up on the first ring. "Hi, Senator."

"Hi, Cosmo. Here is the deal. The FBI will take your prize once you get to Dallas and go to customs. An ambulance will take Scorpio to the hospital, and TJ will accompany him. The story is that Scorpio is CIA Agent Smith, a top-secret agent. He will have a guard at his door 24/7. The doctor was told he had a wounded patient coming in during a classified mission. He was instructed not to talk about the patient to anyone. If an adversary knew he was alive and, in the hospital, it could mean problems for the hospital."

"Sounds like a good story. It seems we used that story before," Cosmo said. "I will let Scorpio know. He was concerned it would not work out. Thanks, Senator."

"That is okay. Talk to you when you get back to the base."

Cosmo grabbed a beer and walked over to Angelique and Scorpio. "It is arranged. Scorpio will be taken to the hospital when we land in Dallas. TJ will go with you. The cover story is that you are CIA Agent Smith and were wounded on a classified mission. The doctor was informed you were coming, and he was never to talk about you to anyone. A guard will be at your door 24/7. You okay with that?"

"How long will I be there?"

"Until you can travel to the base. Then we will come and get you," Cosmo said.

"That is a good deal, Scorpio. Oh, I mean CIA Agent Smith," said Angelique, chuckling.

Scorpio just smiled and closed his eyes, knowing he would be okay and in good hands.

Cosmo was sipping on another beer, looking out the window as the Global touched down in Dallas. It was good to be back in the States. This mission was challenging; he was thinking.

The Global taxied over to customs. Cosmo got up and opened the door, and the stairs went down. There was TJ and the FBI, and a couple of cops were standing by an ambulance.

"You have a present for the FBI?" TJ asked.

"Sure do. He is a little groggy and may need some help, but I'm happy to get rid of him."

The FBI came on board. Jasper unlocked the floor hooks' shackles and helped the guy up. "Enjoy your time here, you scum bag," Jasper said as he looked at their prize.

TJ and a couple of EMTs came on board. Cosmo told the EMT, "Take care of this guy. He is pretty special."

"We will, sir," they said.

"Cosmo, don't worry. We have everything covered," TJ said. "I'll be in contact. Are the other two, okay?"

"They will heal and be ready for missions in a few months," Cosmo said. A few minutes later, the stairs came up, and he closed the door. He stuck his head in the flight deck. "Okay, we're set. Let's go home."

The Global was airborne, turned to the left to a heading of 278 degrees for the first leg home. Approximately three hours later, they were touching down on the base runway. A short taxi to the team house and the pilot shut the engines down. Cosmo opened the door, and the stairs went down. Cosmo helped Star and Zula get off the plane, and Jasper and Barber carried them into the team house. Angelique and Joker helped with the gear.

The pilot walked down the stairs. "Cosmo, when Scorpio is released from the hospital, let me know, and I'll pick him up and bring him home."

"Thanks, I'll keep that in mind. Please have a good flight home, and thanks again for being there for us. Appreciate your service." They shook hands, and the pilot went up the stairs, closing the door. A few minutes later, the engine was revving to full power, and the Global was taxiing to the runway. Seconds later, it was off the ground and heading home.

The team was dragging, and they all headed to their rooms. Angelique said, "Star and Zula, ring my room if you have problems tonight. Also, in the morning, we must change dressings and check for infection. Good night, see you in the morning."

"Thanks, Doc." Both Star and Zula said.

Angelique just smiled.

The following day, the sun was rising over the desert. The light rain during the night gave the landscape brilliant colors. It looked like a painting, Cosmo thought to himself, standing on the deck sipping coffee.

"Good morning," Angelique said.

"Yes, it is," Cosmo replied. "I wish every day would start like this. Oh, how is Joker doing with his new legs?"

"He is doing great, thanks for asking. He is now running every day without falling. He thinks he wants to get back into the action."

"You think he can?"

"I'm sure one day, but, in my heart, I wish he wouldn't. There are a lot of things he can do to support the team."

"I understand both sides, but he is a good planner and can think out the details better than anyone except for the Boss."

"I agree, Cosmo."

"Something we can work on, Angelique."

"I'll call TJ in a couple of days and see how things are going with Scorpio. Be glad to have him back to the base."

"Yeah, doc," Cosmo smiled. He knew Angelique liked being called that.

Two weeks later, Scorpio sat at a chair looking out the window. He felt pretty good; the infection was under control, and his breathing was almost normal. He felt very well overall.

The doctor walked in. "Well, Agent Smith, I'd say if you keep improving the next couple of days, you should be able to go home. Do you have a doctor who can follow up with your wounds?"

"Yes, Sir. The same one that patched me up."

"Oh, you had a doctor on your mission?"

"Not during the mission but was at the rendezvous location. She was great and took care of the three of us."

"Oh, we have three Agents in the hospital?"

"No, Doc. The other two had minor wounds, and they went home. I'm sure she is taking care of them also."

"Take it easy," Doctor said. "I have ordered some x-rays and blood work. So, someone will be poking at you shortly."

"Thanks, Doc," Scorpio said, sitting back in the chair when TJ walked in.

"Okay, I hear they may kick your ass out of here in a day or two!"

"Yup, I'm ready now," Scorpio responded.

"I talked to Cosmo about arrangements for getting you back home. He said they would send you their plane when you are released. Must be nice to have such great service."

"TJ, we have the best of the best team," Scorpio said. "We will give our lives for each other, and we're trained at that level. The best way to know your back is always covered."

"Sounds like we could take some pointers on training techniques. Maybe I could come and train with you guys for a couple of weeks?"

"Love to, that would be fun. Get your thoughts afterward if we didn't kill you off first," Scorpio chuckled.

"I have heard your mission could include skydiving, scuba diving, crawling through mud, sleeping in mud holes, and perched in a tree for days," TJ said, believing they did.

"Yes, we have had a couple of those missions. Not fun, makes you appreciate luxury and great food," Scorpio said, smiling.

"Yes, I will always remember the seafood night, a buffet to kill for," TJ said. "Well, I'll be seeing you. Have a good trip back to the base." They shook hands.

Scorpio was sitting in the Global co-pilot seat three days later, looking out the window. He looked over at the pilot. "Everything looks so peaceful from this view. You ever think about retiring?"

"Scorpio, I'm always thinking about retiring. Then I figured I enjoy flying. I would be bored doing something else."

"Yeah, I see your point. It depends on what your work is, I guess."

"Are you thinking about retiring, Scorpio?"

"I was thinking about it. Well, I was actively planning on it. This mission tells me it is time to leave this line of work. Maybe I'll plan the missions. I don't know. Joker does a great job at that. I have been knocking scum bags off for more than forty years. There is no end to scum bags. But on this mission, I almost bought the farm."

"Well, Scorpio, in your case, it would be better to retire or do something less dangerous. Like maybe being a training coordinator or just planting a garden."

"Yeah, need to think about it. I see the runway. I wonder how many pilots have flown over our base, and though it is one hell of a runway with not much around to justify it."

"I think that every time I come here. It is one of the best runways, yet you have the worst road in the country." They both laughed. The pilot reached over, pulled a handle down, the gear went down, and the flaps came down ten degrees. The plane made a slight left bank and leveled out. The wheels touched down, another smooth landing. The pilot taxied to the team house. Scorpio got up, opened the door, and the stairs went down.

Scorpio looked at the pilot. "How about spending the night? I think this is BBQ night. Have a couple of drinks with us."

"You know, that sounds like a plan." They both walked down the stairs as the team came running out, cheering. "Maybe this is the start of retiring," the pilot said.

Everyone was happy to see Scorpio. A 'WELCOME HOME' sign was over the door. Scorpio said, "Thanks, guys, it is good to be alive and be home. I missed you all. BOSS, where did you come from?"

"I was talking to the Senator. She told me she would be leaving the Senate, that you were seriously wounded, and also talking about retirement. I thought I better come and see what the hell is happening!"

"Boss, walk with me." They both walked toward the runway. The team stood there on the deck watching them, and some had a tear in their eye.

"Boss, I almost bought the farm this trip. In the hospital, I was thinking about baby Jesus. It made me realize that our life is short and precious."

"What do you think, Angelique," Cosmo said as they walked towards the team house door.

Angelique stopped at the door and turned to watch Boss and Scorpio talking. "Well, I think this is the end. Scorpio is done." A tear ran down her cheek.